THE HAUNTING OF CAMP WINTER FALCON

Also by Jonathan Raab

The Secret Goatman Spookshow
and Other Psychological Warfare Operations

The Crypt of Blood: A Halloween TV Special

Camp Ghoul Mountain Part VI: The Official Novelization

The Lesser Swamp Gods of Little Dixie

THE HAUNTING OF CAMP WINTER FALCON

JONATHAN RAAB

For the ones who tried to help us
and for those who still try

My buddy's in a foxhole
a bullet in his head.
The medic says he's wounded
but I know that he's dead.

- "I Hear the Choppers"

THE FINAL FIELD REPORT OF OBSERVER/EXPERIENCER TEAM 4

"Pain is the important part," Sarge said, eyes pressed to binoculars, gaze sweeping across the barren fields and derelict buildings of Camp Winter Falcon. "Ghosts don't haunt places because they feel like it. Something drives them to it, binds them to fixed points in time and space." His voice was flat, matter-of-fact, like he was providing a bit of ancillary information during a pre-mission brief. Like he wasn't talking about the lingering spirits of the dead.

Observer/Experiencer Team 4 monitored the abandoned army post from a rooftop littered with radio antennae and frost-kissed satellite dishes. The mountain wind brought with it a deep, bone-chilling cold. A wall of grey clouds obscured the sun's slow descent across the yawning Colorado sky.

"I was wondering how long we'd make it before we got bored and started swapping ghost stories," Delta said. She only had a spotter's scope for this op, no rifle. That remained locked away in the armory trailer back at the Ranch. Being out in the field without her weapon produced a simmering, irrational anxiety, despite being on American soil. There were no insurgents here. Just ghosts, if the handlers running things back at the Ranch were to be believed. Ghosts didn't carry AK-47s or plant IEDs—as far as she knew, anyway.

"Dr. Polan provided his hypothesis as an appendix of the operations order for this mission," Sarge said, lowering his binoculars. "I try and read as much as I can."

"They pay me to sit out on observation points for days on end, but not enough to take this spooky stuff seriously," Charlie said from his perch on the north side of the roof. He hadn't said much all day, except to acknowledge the bi-hourly radio checks with O/E Mobile HQ set up near the camp's main entrance, and to excuse himself to piss off the roof when the energy drinks he'd been downing called for it. Wires and cables ran from his olive-drab backpack carrier to the portable satellite dish set on the raised edge of the roof, pointed up into the grey, oppressive sky.

"I should read the briefs a bit more closely," Delta admitted. "Learn anything useful from Doc Polan's X-Files, Sarge?"

The team leader observed the boarded-up windows of the nearest cluster of buildings for the hundredth time, hoping to see movement, hoping for any break to this monotony. Boredom was the ancient enemy of soldiers—and defense contractors—everywhere.

"A place is changed by human activity and suffering, like a body is marked by trauma," Sarge said. "Bones break and mend, skin scars, bad memories resurface and loop in the mind. A place absorbs the tragedy that people bring to it, just like a body absorbs injury."

"But not every place is haunted," Delta said. She pushed herself away from her spotting scope into a sitting position, then began to rub at a sore spot on her neck. "You figure, what, there's been billions of humans all over the earth throughout history? All living and screwing and killing and dying. Where are all those ghosts?"

"If there were any truth to that tragedy-causes-hauntings bullshit," Charlie said, "this whole country would be up to its eyeballs in the poltergeists of my ancestors, trying to fight the ghosts of my *other* ancestors."

Sarge lowered his binoculars.

"Maybe it is," he said. "But instead of poltergeists,

it's negative psychic energy. Mass shootings, crime, global pandemic, endless wars, terrorism, social alienation, rising inequality. You feel like things are going well in America, lately?"

Charlie grunted in response.

"Dr. Polan writes about something he calls *factors obscura*," Sarge continued. "The as-of-yet undefined characteristics of a place that capture energy produced by human suffering. Mineral composition in the soil, electro-magnetic waves, cosmic radiation. Ley lines. He hypothesizes that the human mind can interface and integrate with *factors obscura* through precise rituals and spiritual practices to direct that energy."

"Rituals," Delta said. "Devil worshippers doing black magic. Heavy metal music and *Dungeons & Dragons*."

Sarge shrugged.

"Every religious and cultural group has its own method for conjuring spiritual energy," he said. "You two were in the Army. Formations, parades, cadence, institutional history, call-and-response catchphrases. Martial energy, real power, summoned via ritual, to prepare the mind and spirit before battle."

"So does the suffering make the place haunted, or does the haunted place cause the suffering?" Delta asked, to no one in particular. No one answered, save for the low moaning of the cold, mountain wind.

"You two sound pretty up on this occult stuff," Charlie said, fishing through his assault pack for another energy drink. "You didn't strike me as the believer types."

"Twenty years in uniform, you find yourself with some downtime," Sarge said. "Books don't need a battery, except for maybe your headlamp. You see death enough times, you start to hope that maybe there's something more to it than just blood and screaming."

Delta popped her neck, then returned to peering through her scope. Charlie found a lukewarm can of liquid sugar and popped it, gasses escaping with a hiss.

"I've been with the Observer/Experiencer program long enough to know that there's something to all this," Sarge said. "If you spend enough time at the Ranch, you'll see a few things to put the fear of God into you. How long have you two been O/Es?"

"Just shy of a year," Delta said. "And I've spent enough nights up on the back forty of the Ranch to know better than to make fun of any of this, even if it's boring most of the time."

"How many UFOs have you seen?" Sarge asked.

"Depends on what you mean by that," Delta said. "I've seen some lights up there I can't explain two or three times and some ghostly figures moving through the brush. Nothing too close. Could have been anything, really."

"Six months," Charlie said, sitting upright against the low lip of the roof. "I haven't seen any spooks or specters, and when I hear you old-timers talk about that kind of stuff, I'm pretty sure you're just putting me on. But this ain't a bad gig. Beats IED roulette down range. Beats living on post."

"I've been with the program for two years next month," Sarge said. "I've never participated in a resonance ritual, but I heard some of the science staff talk about it. The more time I'm with the program, the more I'm sure they aren't exaggerating."

"Contact," Delta said, shifting her tripod-mounted scope a few degrees to the south. "Between the two far buildings dead ahead. The ones with the sloped roofs."

Sarge pulled up his binoculars.

"Lot of buildings with that description on that side of camp," he said.

"Lot of buildings, not a lot of glowing green clouds."

"Oh."

Charlie crawled up next to Delta and produced his own small pair of binoculars. He perched on his elbows, peering over the bricks. "Looks like a strobe light," he said. "Blue, maybe green."

"What you got, Delta?" Sarge asked.

"Definitely not a vehicle or dismounts with flashlights," she said, dialing in to focus. "I'd say three hundred, three-twenty-five meters from our position. Smoke or fog, localized around that cluster of buildings. Lights, yeah. Maybe a ground-level weather event."

"Do you see anyone nearby?" Sarge asked. "Maybe Observer/Experiencer Team 2?"

"No, just mist," she said. Delta pulled away from her spotting scope to stare wide-eyed at her team leader. "Is that what they got us out here looking for, Sarge?" He opened his mouth to answer, but struggled to find the right words.

The swirling bank of glowing, ethereal vapor churned with impossibilities. Forms emerged from whirling tendrils of psychospheric fog, materializing into the visual spectrum. Glowing stalks of half-light formed collections of malformed sinew and bone, legs leading to transparent torsos, arms composed of matter and energy vibrating at dead frequencies. Misshapen heads and sunken faces aglow with shimmering slices of light that left afterburns in retinas.

"I think that's it," Sarge said, throat dry.

Adrenaline ticked into Delta's bloodstream. She tried to blink out the burning after-images of the horrors forming in the mist, to interrupt the troublesome questions that were already popping into her mind. A part of her wanted to look again, wanted to see what was emerging from that maelstrom of light and effluvium.

Another part wanted to run for her goddamned life.

"Charlie, radio HQ and let them know we have contact," Sarge said. "Class 4, maybe a Class 5. Delta, give me your best try at a coherent description. I can't really make sense of it through the binos."

"Roger," Delta said, obeying orders on reflex, overriding her own fear. She settled back in behind her scope, ignoring the sharp needles of anxiety working their way down her spine.

Through the scope, she saw light. Impossible, reflective, inverted. She saw herself—or a twisted, funhouse version of herself—perched within the fog, staring back at them, back at *her*, eyes locked on one another through the distance and the swirling mist. A dreadful, leering smile crawled over the face of her doppelganger.

Hands emerged from the pulsing, glowing mist. They reached for her twin, whose leer split the sides of her face, revealing secondary and tertiary rows of serrated teeth stretching back into a limitless black maw of mouth and throat. Those grey hands pulled the not-Delta apart, burrowing into her skin, pulling away handfuls of pale flesh that dissipated into roiling vapor.

"Greenfield, what's wrong?" Sarge said, breaking protocol by using a real name in the field. To know a name was to have a certain kind of power. That was in the briefing, too.

Delta—Greenfield—offered a low, droning moan.

"I can't—"

Her vision went blurry with tears, her dominant eye pressed to the scope to bear witness to the tableau of horrors. Her ghostly twin and those terrible hands were gone. There was only the slow drift of mist, rolling toward their position in a patient advance.

"It's coming this way," she said, forcing out the

words, doing her job, like she had been trained for all these many years. "We should break cover and exfil. Like, yesterday."

"I agree with that recommendation," Sarge said. "Charlie, tell HQ we're breaking the hide and moving back to Gate One. I'm not waiting for permission." Sarge set to work collecting his gear. "Charlie, you read me?"

When the radio operator didn't respond, Sarge gave him a light slap across the back of his shoulder. Charlie looked back at him, cheeks wet, mouth struggling to form words.

"*Get on the goddamn radio,*" Sarge said through gritted teeth, wanting to sound surer than he did.

"Yes, Sarge," Charlie mumbled.

"What's the matter with you?"

"In the mist, I saw—I saw myself, and—"

Sarge reached down and grabbed Charlie by the collar of his camo jacket.

"I need you to do your job," Sarge said, voice even, words slow. Experience had taught him that, despite what happened in war movies, yelling didn't do a whole lot of good in these types of situations. "Tell them Team 4 confirms presence of anomalous activity. Tell them they're welcome to send follow-up teams for whatever-the-fuck it is that they want to do out here. We'll be at Gate One in ten mikes."

"What does it mean?" Delta said, wanting to know if the mass of fog and light was closer, but refusing to look through her scope again. "I saw myself, too."

"Don't talk about it," Sarge said, picking up his camo backpack. "Grab your gear and prepare for extraction. You have thirty seconds. Get moving."

Delta forced herself to retrieve the scope and set it back in its carrying case. She kept her focus directly in front of her, refusing to look beyond the edge of the roof. She rolled up the thin blanket she had been lying on for most of the day, then secured it through the straps in her assault pack.

As Charlie stammered out a radio message to HQ, Sarge did a final visual sweep of the roof for his gear. Satisfied it was all safely stored in the assault pack slung across his right shoulder, he risked another glance at the anomaly. In the handful of adrenaline-slowed moments since he had given the order to exfil, the bank of shimmering fog and light had closed almost half the distance to their position.

"Break down the SATCOM," Sarge said. "Now."

"I'm waiting on confirmation from higher," Charlie said. "They're generating a new code—"

Sarge stomped over to the portable console and began to pull cords. He collapsed the foldable satellite dish into its preset bundle configuration, then shoved it into the carrying case.

Delta was already climbing down over the edge of the roof. The tips of her boots found the stepladder, then she scrambled down to the barren earth. Charlie went next, the SATCOM system case and his assault pack slung across his back. Sarge followed him down, pausing at the top of the ladder to look back toward the anomaly one final time.

The fog now covered dozens of meters of flat, open terrain directly ahead of their position. Glowing arcs of light crackled beneath its expanding, encroaching mass. At the heart of the anomaly was an ovoid of clustered mist, heavy and dark. Brilliant light leaked out from fissures in the oblong shape. Fingers emerged from within, sloughing off layers of fleshy shell, prying them open, tearing through. Glowing eyes set in hideous faces emerged, illuminated in the nauseating radiation of dying stars. Skin stretched taught over misshapen skulls, warped and shimmering.

Delta screamed for Sarge, begging him to get down so they could run, so they could *get away*, damn the project and the field reports. Sarge willed his body to move, to push himself down the ladder. One of those proto-faces began to change, to shift, to assume the familiar contours of skull, of brow, of jaw. Dreadful warpings of bone and flesh. Maddening recognition.

The mist covered everything. The whole world was electric. The air was pure ozone.

Sarge's mind spat up a single thought, one final bulwark against the madness that even now began to overtake him.

Pain is the important part.

EVOLUTION ONE

DAY ZERO

A sputtering Department of Veterans Affairs bus laden with passengers passed through the front gates of Camp Winter Falcon, waved on by bored soldiers on guard duty. Tires passed over lines of salt, poured out in formations of power and protection. The spirits watched and understood, in patience, that the time for communion was nearly at hand. Soon, the rituals would begin.

Ray felt the camp's eagerness for him and his fellow passengers. The bus's heat was on full blast, but the moment the gate closed behind them, a chill fell over him all the same. He had made the right choice in coming here. He was here for a reason. To get better. To get well. To shed the pain and mistakes of an old way of life, and to become something new.

The bus followed a crumbling road past squat, wood-paneled buildings with A-frame roofs built sometime around the Second World War. Their initial utility expired long ago, during the golden age of the empire, before the decades of its steady and painful decline. Most of the camp's buildings were boarded up, their windows covered and wrapped in plastic flapping softly in the icy wind, their doors sealed with crookedly applied planks of wood or yellow warning tape. Light fixtures sprayed sickly yellow light on men and women in digital pattern camouflage uniforms or white lab coats as they watched the bus roll by. They smoked cigarettes or sipped steaming liquid from foam cups.

The bus made several lurching turns down gravel streets with no signposts or names. In the quickening dark, Ray had tried to keep his bearings—an old infantryman's habit—but the sudden turns and the overwhelming gloom made that impossible. Within the limits of the camp's barbed-wire-topped fences, he had only the nearby mountains to keep himself oriented.

The exhausted transport squealed to a halt beneath a yellow island of illumination cast by a cluster of overhanging street lights. Beyond a stretch of persistent shadows stood a solitary chapel, its chipped white paint exterior leading up to a sloped, triangular roof and thin, angular frontispiece belltower. Twin front doors facing the street stood open, home to dark figures lingering on the precipice, shadows framed against the meager light within.

The bus doors pushed open with a hiss of air.

"Everybody out," the driver said as the overhead lights flickered on.

Ray stood up with the others, a sense of unease boiling within his core. Flashbacks to Basic Training: arriving at the Fort Benning 30th Adjutant General Battalion in the dead of night as a fresh-faced 19-year-old soon-to-be-college-dropout on summer break between freshman and sophomore years, well over a decade ago. Time was flattening out and looping back in on itself.

Ray and the rest of the patients filed off the bus, carrying suitcases or military-issue duffel bags of competing eras of camo and service branch colors. Ray carried his old-school olive drab duffel in his right hand and slung his assault pack over his shoulders. The pack's early generation blue-and-green digital-squares-style pattern was worn and faded under countless hours of field operations. Its visible wear and tear had once been a point of pride for him. A long time ago, anyway.

"Fall in, falcons," bellowed a short man in an immaculate Army uniform. He stood directly centered between the two open doors of the chapel, the weak light framing him in a soft, sad halo. Ray squinted at his chest, spotting a dark mass of lines and insignia. Probably a senior non-commissioned officer.

"Two ranks, centered on me," the man said in a voice with the volume of a shout but the tone of a conversation. "Don't worry about who's squad leader. Just fall in for now."

The new arrivals slowly arranged themselves in two uneven rows before the NCO.

"Been a while since you've been to formation, huh?" the man said. "Don't worry, I got you. Flashback to my drill sergeant days." He proceeded to gently move the arrivals as they lined up, whispering instructions to adjust individuals until the formation looked halfway professional. He resumed his post at the head of the formation, then stood ramrod straight, arms at his sides and fists pressed tight to his legs and hips.

"Fall in!"

Ray's body reflexively stood at attention, years of muscle memory resurfacing like embarrassing memories. Behind the NCO, shadows moved toward the formation. White medical coats barely visible in the dark. Glasses reflecting dim light from the moon. A couple of others in Army uniforms, too dark to see their names or rank.

Ray felt an instinctual dislike for this situation, suddenly not so sure he had made the right choice in signing up for the program. A trickle of adrenaline worked its way through his nervous system as cold sweat dripped down his back. The air was sharp and iron-tinged, the smell of blood, like a skinned buck hanging in the garage.

"Roll call," the NCO said, accepting a clipboard from one of the shadows. "Sound off when your name is called. Since we are all professionals, you will follow your 'here' with 'Sergeant Major.' Most of you don't hold rank anymore, but I do." He reached up to his forehead and clicked on a headlamp, which spilled painful light over his papers.

"Adams!"

"Here, Sergeant Major."

"Boskins."

"Here, Sergeant Major."

"Bozell."

"*Here,* Sergeant Major!"

"Calhurst."

"Roger, Sergeant Major."

"Dodonna."

"Here, Sergeant Major."

"Eckart."

"Sergeant Major!"

"Faris. Faris?" The sergeant major looked up from his clipboard.

"Yeah," a man said.

"How about a 'Sergeant Major' to keep things professional?"

"Nah."

"What was that?"

The man snickered and whispered something. A few muffled curses and a caustic tone of voice.

Jesus. This really is like Basic, complete with the assholes who decide the rules don't apply to them, Ray thought. He was trying to decide if he found the parallels funny or dread-inducing.

The sergeant major wasted no time. He suddenly appeared in front of Faris, who stood in the front row near the end of the line.

"You're not in the military any more—and thank God for that—but you will abide basic respect and good-faith participation, if not formal customs and courtesies, while you remain a member of Class Zero-

Zero-One within this program. Now, let's try this again, *Mister* Faris. Sound off."

"Oh my *god*," Faris said, shifting in formation. He turned his face upwards. He was a good deal taller than the sergeant major, and wiry. Ray thought he spoke with the inflection and accent of someone in an east coast rapper's entourage, but even in the dark, he could see the kid was whiter than the moon. Ray smirked, remembering his own first forays into hip hop and adopting some of those affectations in early high school, before accepting his fate as just another normal-ass white boy who happened to like Busta Rhymes and DMX.

"I ain't taking orders from these motherfuckers," Faris mumbled.

"Listen to me, falcon," the sergeant major said, his voice going low, but with the hard edge of a man preparing to commit to violence. "This is your first and only informal counseling on your behavior. Profanity, disrespect, refusal to acknowledge the orders of Camp Winter Falcon staff and cadre, and conduct unbecoming a member of this program is unacceptable and will not continue, at risk of penalty of summary expulsion from the program. You can shape up and acknowledge what is being asked of you, or you can get back on that bus, which will return you to the bus station in Colorado Springs and let you find your own way home."

The sergeant major took a moment to catch his breath. He leaned in close, his headlamp shining up, directly into Faris' pale face.

"Now, what's it going to be?"

Faris snickered.

"I'm only here because the judge said so," he said. "I ain't got no choice in the matter."

"There's always a choice," the sergeant major

said, his tone softening. "Believe me. There's always a choice."

"How 'bout you *choose* to suck my dick, then?" Faris said.

The formation of incoming patients was already silent, but, if it was even possible, they became *more* silent, all holding their breath, wide eyes going wider, willing their heartbeats to slow down so as not to miss what came next.

The old NCO stood up straight, but his voice was calm and clear.

"You are dismissed from this program," the sergeant major said, making a notation on his clipboard. "You are to leave this formation and board the bus, immediately. It will be leaving shortly. Fall out."

"Whoa, don't do me like that, little man. I'm gonna go to fuckin' jail if I don't do this shit."

"Then maybe you should have listened to me, son."

"Man, I'm not your son. Fuck this program and fuck *you*." Faris threw his lanky arms up, shoving the sergeant major back a few feet. The NCO stumbled but kept his balance, then lowered his head as his breath quickened.

"You have made this very easy for me."

The clipboard fell from his hands. Papers fluttered. The sergeant major sped forward in a blaze of speed, arms flying up to strike Faris across the jaw, legs slipping between Faris' to knock him off balance, sending them both to the ground. The other patients broke formation to back away, cursing and shouting.

The sergeant major had Faris pinned down from above, legs pressed tight against the sides of Faris' torso. Fists pounded down like pistons against the younger man's face, again and again, until he stopped struggling. Ray found himself drawn closer, crowding in with the others, eager to see the violence, like one of the fights that would break out in formation in an embittered unit after resentment and insults had simmered long enough. The other camp staff made no move to stop what was happening. They stood impassive, content to let things play out.

Faris coughed a spattering of blood as the sergeant major stood back up, releasing him. He rubbed at his forehead, which had broken out in a quick sweat in the cold autumn air. A smear of blood remained in a slash across his forehead. A marker of violence and power.

"Get back on that bus, right now, and we won't mention that you assaulted a member of the military to the police," the sergeant major said through heavy breaths. "I'm sure your parole officer would be interested in hearing that you laid hands on a member of this program's cadre, but I'm willing to let that slide if you walk away without saying another goddamn word."

Faris offered a moan of pain. He rolled himself over to lean his forehead against the cool earth. He mumbled something through a mouthful of blood.

"Get on the bus, kid," Sergeant Major Haaster said.

A man and a woman in Army uniforms came forward, roughly pulling Faris back to his feet. Two of the other patients grabbed his bags and followed as the soldiers helped him limp back to the open door of the bus. Inside, the driver leaned against the steering wheel, a smirk visible in the running lights of the cab, a lit cigarette between his lips.

"Looks like we've had our first washout of the program, and we're only on Day Zero," the sergeant major said, plucking his clipboard from the ground and retaking his position at the head of the formation. "Form it back up. If anyone else would like to join Mr.

Faris on the bus back to the Springs, now's the time, with or without a broken nose. Garcia!"

"Here, Sergeant Major!"

"Halloway!"

"Yes, Sergeant Major!"

"Kairns."

"Yes, Sergeant Major."

"Morales?"

"Right here, Sergeant Major!" a woman said, just a few spots down from Ray.

"Nowinski."

"Roger that, Sergeant Major!"

"Parnell!"

"Here, Sergeant Major," Ray said.

"And Robertson."

"Hoo-ah, Sergeant Major!"

"Hoo-ah, falcon. Alright, that's everyone." He set the clipboard behind him and clicked off his headlamp. "Let me be the first to officially welcome you to the Camp Winter Falcon Veteran Reintegration Program. I am Sergeant Major Haaster, non-commissioned officer in charge of patients—that's you—whom we lovingly call *falcons*. As you've already seen, this program is a privilege. We're not here to give you anything. Your success and reintegration as veterans will succeed or fail based on your willingness to get well. Lack of motivation is a dismissible offence. This isn't some chewed-up reserve unit where we're desperate for bodies. This is your last chance to get some help from the system, before the system gives up on you."

Haaster began to pace in front of the formation. He spoke with the practiced cadence of a drill and ceremony instructor, voice echoing back to the group from all corners of the dark camp.

"What we're offering at Camp Winter Falcon is

opportunity. My cadre and the medical staff are not your babysitters. We're not your family members that you can beat up and push around. We're not your dipshit friends who are going to enable your bad behavior. What we are is your last chance.

"You're here because you screwed up somewhere along the way, more than once, probably for most of your life. Screwing up here means we kick your ass to the curb. Screwing up here means the rest of your short and miserable life is spent alone and without the support of the VA. You're here because that system—or your military unit, or your doctor, or the few loved ones and friends you've not yet managed to push away—they don't know what the hell to do with you. The usual stuff isn't working.

"You're here because you're about one or two bad decisions away from life on the streets or in prison, an early death due to suicide, a drug overdose, or an incident with a cop with an itchy trigger finger. You're here because someone decided that despite whatever shitty behavior you've engaged in since you came back from the sandbox, there's still a chance you might make something out of your life. Camp Winter Falcon is your *last-fucking-chance.* Do not blow it. You read me?"

A smattering of responses from the formation.

"Good. It's still Day Zero, which means you got a few hours to load into the barracks, unpack, fill out intake paperwork, take a shower, get some rest. Lights out at 2200, sharp. First formation is right here, this very spot, at 0500, with PT at 0515. Formations and PT are mandatory. Meals are at 0600, noon, and 1700 hours at the dining facility—DFAC—two buildings over, down that way." He pointed to a darkened, single-story building in the near distance. "You'll receive a schedule for the next day's events at final formation, which is to be held at 1900 here at the chapel or near the barracks. Being late or AWOL results in counseling. Receive a second counseling and you will be considered for termination. Am I clear?"

"*Yes, Sergeant Major!*" the patients shouted, almost in unison.

"For some of you, leaving here without graduating means your court-ordered rehab will be incomplete, you won't get that discharge status upgrade from dishonorable to general or honorable, you won't be able to re-join your reserve or National Guard unit. You need to be here to develop the skills necessary to cope, to navigate the civilian world, to get back into conventional mental health counseling and support.

"My advice to you, this group of strangers before me—strangers who at one time had the good sense and privilege to wear the uniform of one of the hallowed branches of the United States military—is to take this opportunity. Or, you can act like that jackass on the bus and earn yourself a one-way ticket to a short life on the streets and an early grave. It's up to you."

He turned and nodded toward one of the figures in a white medical coat, who promptly stepped forward. Her glasses reflected errant moonlight and the pallid glow of the nearby streetlamps. She stood a good half-foot taller than Sergeant Major Haaster, confident and imposing.

"Good evening, falcons," she said. "I am Dr. Glasse, chief of medicine and research for Camp Winter Falcon. I am responsible for the physical, therapeutic, pharmacological, and spiritual regimen of the program, specifically tailored to your individual and group needs. As members of Class Zero-Zero-One, you represent the first wave in a revolutionary pilot program that holds the potential to improve how we treat our military and war veterans."

Glasse paused, letting her words hang on the air. She looked from face to face, making eye contact with whomever would meet her gaze. There was a practiced warmth in those eyes, a welcoming glimmer borne out of years of professional work with troubled patients. Her height and posture communicated a sense of confidence and ease, of being in control of the situation.

"Over the next three weeks, you will be challenged. You will be healed. You will be changed. But only if you trust Sergeant Major Haaster and his cadre. If you trust my medical staff. If you trust one another. If you trust me." Her eyes settled on Ray's. She gave him a soft, confident smile. "Our cadre will escort you to the barracks so you can settle in. Get a good night's sleep, and I will see you all in the morning. Welcome to Camp Winter Falcon, Class Zero-Zero-One. Welcome to your last chance."

The bus rumbled to life behind them and the door shut with a squeal. It moved down the gravel street, then took a turn toward the mountains, disappearing into the rows of isolated and darkened buildings. At no point did it circle back around toward the main gate.

Ray watched until its pale headlights were gone, absorbed into the deep shadow of the mountains. Snow began to fall in heavy, slow flakes, blown in from over the great wall of the Rockies.

He kept his eyes on those haunted mountains that so defined the horizon of Colorado, but all he could see was Afghanistan.

PT

The nightmare knocked Ray out of an uneasy sleep. He found himself with his feet pressed to the ice-cold, cracked linoleum floor, sucking in frigid air with an aftertaste of cleaning chemicals. He steadied his breathing and pressed his toes against the floor, grounding himself. Breath drifted from his lips, heavy and visible, before disappearing into the dark.

Nightmares aside, the misshapen mattress and the creeping, icy air precluded a good night's sleep—not to mention his crawling anxiety about being back on a military post. Ray kept expecting the lights to burst on at any moment, with NCOs or officers shouting to *get the fuck up*, soldiers scrambling for their body armor and weapons as explosions thudded in the distance, getting closer.

When he had managed to drift off, he dreamed of faceless men in uniforms wandering the grounds of Camp Winter Falcon. They were all flickering light and shadow, warped images from a film projector illuminating the walls of ancient concrete tunnels buried deep beneath the earth. The soldiers were looking for something. Looking for him, maybe.

If it wasn't nightmares that kept him awake, it was usually one of the late-night anxiety greatest hits, his thoughts dwelling on a Humvee rollover, an argument with an old girlfriend, or just the lingering, ever present feeling of being close to death. Close to *oblivion*. Feeling so foolish that he might once have believed that the world held magic, that life and self could endure beyond the physical, material death of the body and brain, a death sure to come very, very soon.

Where was he before he was born? Was that what death was like? All void and suffocating time? Would

God and his friends and family be waiting for him, ready for an eternity of idyllic summer afternoons and hoodie-weather autumn evenings? Or, more likely, was it Hell instead, suffering in death not unlike the suffering of life—because why should it be any different? Would his soul be shunted into the abyss by an uncaring, blind, mechanistic process, or by a selfish God angry at him for picking the wrong religion, or no religion at all?

The cold grounded him. Layers of present, conscious thought rose out of sleep to paper over those animal anxieties. His heartbeat slowed; his breathing steadied. He just hoped he hadn't shouted or screamed in his sleep.

Ray slipped into his black-stencil ARMY sweatpants and a camo hoodie his parents had gifted him a few Christmases ago, before they stopped talking to him, or he stopped talking to them. The details were a bit fuzzy. He had enough savings to get a new pair of running shoes before the program started, but hadn't had time to break them in, as he was too busy taking extra shifts at work. The Queen Supers grocery store front-end manager promised his job would be waiting for him when he returned. But Ray had seen just how secure the jobs were for reservists and National Guard soldiers. *Support the troops* to the fullest extent as required by law, and then find a way to fire or replace them anyway.

Years spent in an infantry rifle company had taught Ray the value of getting up early to get a toilet or a sink to himself, so he gave up on the possibility of more sleep and slipped on his headlamp and headed out into the dark to find the latrine. Outside, the air was still. His breath was a stream of ghosts passing through the headlamp beam. Something about the glowing vapor reminded him of his nightmare.

With the sun still hiding far beyond the eastern horizon, Sergeant Major Haaster led Class 001 in a light run around Camp Winter Falcon. Ray was out of shape, his flabby gut a testament to his lack of discipline since leaving the National Guard. But he found himself wanting to push harder, to run faster, to reactivate those neural pathways that allowed him to not only tolerate but enjoy difficult exercise. There was a soldier encased within the flesh of the bitter veteran. He just needed to be carved out.

"Keep it moving, falcons, keep it moving!" Haaster shouted, clearly not at all winded despite being in his late 40s, his face aged beyond those years by countless days spent in the sun—not to mention drinking and smoking habits common to career soldiers. One doesn't make sergeant major without a few coping mechanisms. "Feels good to get back into it, don't it? Feels good to PT!"

They followed the main road to the center of camp, then cut east down the gravel street that led to the gate and the guardhouse beyond. Haaster then took them north along a footpath that ran adjacent to the fence itself. Somewhere, in the distant dark beyond the fence line, a road led to a highway that connected to Everywhere Else. Camp Winter Falcon's remoteness was a physical sensation, a heavy, cold blanket draped around Ray's shoulders.

The trail they followed broke away from the perimeter, back toward the mountains and empty buildings of newer and hardier construction: squat, brick annexes, atop which sat aging antennae arrays, radio towers, defunct satellite dishes and metal outgrowths that glistened with frost in the early light.

"Spooky, huh?" a woman asked.

Ray turned to see her jogging next to him, long hair put up, loose strands bouncing against her shoulders. He tried not to shine his headlamp beam directly in her face. "What kind of post was this, you think?"

"Don't know," Ray said as they passed another building whose roof was home to a tall, groaning tower of crisscrossing metal, wire, and satellite dishes that stretched deep into the dark sky. "By the look of the comms gear, this was probably connected to the Cheyenne Mountain Complex. NORAD."

The woman looked up at the antenna structure as they passed beneath and nodded, her eyes going distant and her mouth twisting like she had something else to say, but then thought better of it.

Sergeant Major Haaster, jogging at the head of their ragged formation, turned back to face the patients, most of whom were struggling to keep up.

"Alright falcons, good energy so far!" he said. "Anybody tired yet?"

A scattering of "No, sergeant major!" and ironic "hooahs" went up from the group.

"We'll jog back across camp, just another quarter mile. Once we reach the barracks, you'll have one hour for personal hygiene, showers, and breakfast chow. Then it's formation at the chapel. Do not be late. Now, let's finish strong!"

Haaster turned around and quickened his pace, challenging the others to keep up with him. The woman next to Ray increased her stride and sprinted up to the front of the pack. Ray wanted to follow and run alongside her, but a cramp in his side held him back.

The spirit was willing, and all that.

WELCOME BRIEF

Bad coffee is still coffee, especially when it's hot.

Ray kept this maxim in mind as he dumped a pair of creamers into his foam cup of steaming black liquid, then chased them with a sugar packet, just to be safe. The elements swirled together, twisting, changing, becoming something new in a swirling vortex of light and dark.

"We're going to begin shortly," a woman said in a familiar voice, her words spoken with the cadence and authority of someone used to being obeyed. "Please take your seats."

Ray tossed out the stirring stick and made his way to the open circle of metal folding chairs arrayed in the center of the room where the other patients gathered. The bare floorboards of the old wooden building groaned and snapped. The air was cold and tasted of sawdust. The furnace struggled to pump heat up through rusted vents.

As he took his seat, Ray got a good look at his fellow patients under the light of struggling bulbs and grey morning sunlight streaming in through thin, fragile windows. The youngest veteran among them was probably a few years shy of 30, while no one could have been older than 45. Playing soldier was a young person's game.

A woman sat next to him. The same one from the run earlier that morning. Her long hair, black and vibrant, was tied up in a bun. She smiled back at him and held out her hand. Her eyes were brown but bright, complementing her light olive skin.

"Morales," she said, offering her hand for a firm shake. "Terra."

"Parnell," Ray said. "Ray."

"Your mother call you 'Raymond?'"

"How'd you know?"

"Catholic mothers be like that sometimes," she said.

"How'd you know I was Catholic?"

"I'm guessing you *were* Catholic, with a name like 'Raymond Parnell.'"

"Fair. You?"

"Lapsed," she said, bright eyes focusing on her coffee. She slipped a hand in her pocket and pulled it out again, revealing the black beads of a rosary. "Lapsed, but still looking back."

"Is there any other kind?"

Terra smiled, then turned to a younger woman who sat down on her other side, offering her hand and making introductions.

"Coffee any good?" A man sat in the other metal folding chair next to Ray, a long finger pointing at Ray's foam cup. "How bad is it? Give it to me straight."

"Bad coffee's still coffee," Ray said, hating the banality of it, but slipping into that style of communication effortlessly. A soldier's life was banality. A veteran's, even more so.

The man smiled wide and easy. "Dodonna," he said, offering his hand. "Friends call me Mike."

"Parnell," Ray said, gripping his hand. "Ray. I'm new at camp, too. Wanna be friends?"

"You got it, partner. Who were you with?"

"Army," Ray said. "National Guard."

"Nasty Girl!" Mike said. "Weekend warrior."

"Couple year-long weekends in the desert," Ray said.

"Ha, year-long weekends!" Mike laughed again. Ray found himself laughing, too. "I was Army. Active. Cav scout."

"Infantry."

"Tell me something, Ray Parnell. Many brothers in your National Guard unit?"

Ray's face went red and he laughed involuntarily.

"We were based out of a rural part of the state, so—"

Mike held up one his big hands. A thick silver ring glittered on one of his fingers.

"Say no more. I won't hold it against you."

"Academy brat?"

"Oh, this?" Mike said, pulling his hand close to rub at the ring. "No, I didn't go to West Point." Pride flashed across his face. "I was a mustang. I attended Officer Candidate School later in my career. Ended up at captain before retiring. A bunch of us got rings when we graduated OCS." He went silent for a moment. His gregarious smile fled his face. "Lot of good soldiers in that class. Lot of *good* soldiers, good men and women. Damn."

Ray waited a beat, sparing a moment of silence for the dead.

"I thought you had to be well-adjusted to be an officer," Ray said, leaning closer to Mike as if in conspiracy. "I mean, I heard they give you a frontal lobotomy when they give you your captain's bars, but... What's a guy like you doing here?"

Mike shrugged.

"Probably same as you, or anyone else, I guess. You know the story. I went over a couple of times. When I came home, I was still over there. Know what I mean?"

"I know what you mean," Ray said.

"What about you? If you—if you're okay with talking about it."

"I guess I wouldn't be here if I wasn't," Ray said. "I came off the factory line a little defective. Army didn't help."

"No, I don't suppose it would."

Mike smiled warmly, genuine, and Ray found himself liking the guy. Mike had an innate charisma that would have served him well as an officer.

Dr. Glasse stepped into the center of the chair formation, clearing her throat and speaking up in the same authoritative tone that had brought the patients together. She was probably in her late 40s, with large brown eyes under wire-frame glasses flanked by her long brown hair, highlighted with subtle streaks of silver. The seats filled up. The murmurs died own.

"Good morning, Class Zero-Zero-One," she said, sweeping her gaze across the room. "I am Dr. Kara Glasse, chief of medicine and research." She paused a moment, her eyes meeting Ray's, locking him in place, before releasing their hold and moving on to the next patient. "As one of the foremost clinical research psychologists for the U.S. Department of Veterans Affairs and the Department of Defense, I am well-educated, highly trained, and draw on a vast repertoire of professional medical, academic, and research experiences. I am—and please do not think me a braggart—quite simply one of the most qualified medical professionals working in the veteran mental health field today. My experience with veteran clinical psychology extends back to 2004, when I began my work with wounded veterans and enemy combatant detainees on-site just west of Baghdad. Yes. I have been *down range*. I have been to the sandbox. I have spent time in rocket shelters and I know what it is like to fear for my life in a combat zone."

Glasse paused, letting those statements hang.

"My medical staff likewise boasts a broad range of clinical and research experiences involving the servicemember and veteran mind. The competence of my team is not in question. Your success here at Camp

Winter Falcon is wholly dependent on your own effort and participation. Am I clear?"

No one spoke. The furnace kicked on again, all metal groans, dull thumps, and tepid, lukewarm air coughed up through the vents.

"If you are experiencing difficulty with an activity or in crisis, inform the staff or cadre. We are here to support you, even and especially as things become difficult or painful. Because they will."

A hand went up across the room. A man with a dark black goatee wearing a faded Cypress Hill sweater silently tapped his combat boot as he waited for the doctor to acknowledge him.

"Yes? State your name for the group, please."

"Uh, thank you, ma'am, I'm Adams. Thomas Adams. Third Marines. Formerly." He looked around the room as a few others nodded and held up their fists.

"Welcome, Adams. We're proud to have the Marines represented here at our program."

"Thank you. Uh, is there any way to check in with our families? My cell phone doesn't get any signal here."

Dr. Glasse nodded.

"Thank you for asking, Mr. Adams. I would, however, like to specify that any logistical questions should be directed to Sergeant Major Haaster, as he and his military cadre are in charge of your care and feeding, to put it bluntly. They are also responsible for the security of this facility, which, while technically decommissioned, is still home to mothballed communication arrays and military equipment of some value that is under guard. It is that equipment—and our remote location—that is likely contributing to your inability to get a proper cell phone signal."

"Ok," Adams said. "Is there a landline we can access then, ma'am?"

Glasse smiled.

"In the information packet you received upon your acceptance into the Camp Winter Falcon program, you'll find mention of a 'total reset.' When you signed the consent form, you agreed to participate in that reset—to include no outside contact with friends or family for the duration."

"I don't remember that, ma'am."

"Did you read the packet, Mr. Adams?"

"Marines don't always read good, ma'am."

That drew a few laughs from the group and a smirk from Glasse.

"We do have a landline on post, yes, but access is restricted to medical staff and cadre for official business only, including emergencies. The point of contact you added to your intake paperwork has that number and can reach us at any time. We do not pass along messages unless it is an emergency situation."

Dr. Glasse let the silence linger. The creaking floorboards, sputtering furnace, and icy wind outside held the floor for a brief moment.

"This is a veteran rehabilitation and reintegration program, designed for those with substance abuse problems, post-traumatic stress, mental health challenges, and employment and reintegration issues. This program runs three weeks—twenty days and a wake-up—here in colorful Colorado. As a patient here, you will receive a modest stipend equivalent to a servicemember at the rank of E-5. Not bad, right?"

Several people nodded. Ray suspected that was more money than many of them were used to making. It certainly was more money than he could scrape together since he took off the uniform.

"In short, we're offering you your lives back," Dr. Glasse said. "We recognize the unique challenges you are facing, but you should be made to understand that there are rules here. No sexual fraternization, no drugs or alcohol, no disrespecting the staff, no harassing or insulting your fellow patients, no trying to leave the camp, no going beyond the approved boundaries of the main post area. Don't be late for formations or training events. Don't display a lack of motivation during PT, counseling, group activities, or any other official programming."

A door opened on the far side of the room. A pair of uniformed soldiers wheeled out a large whiteboard. Neat, condensed handwriting in black marker covered its surface, split into three columns of varying detail and density. Headers at the top of each column read "EVOLUTION I," "EVOLUTION II," and "EVOLUTION III." The column beneath EVOLUTION III was blank.

The cadre set the board at the edge of the circle of patients, then returned to the other room, closing the creaking door behind them.

"Three evolutions," Glasse said, pointing at the white board, "broken down into week-long segments. Today marks your first day in Evolution One. Light PT to ease you back into regular physical activity. Psychological and physical evaluations, initial briefings, acclimation to the altitude, team-building introductory activities, et cetera. We'll also begin our individual and group counseling sessions as well as skills training across this first week. Busy days ahead."

She pointed to the second column.

"Evolution Two is where our medical and psychological health staff customize their care and attention to your individual needs as patients," she said. "We also introduce intensive individual and group therapy sessions focused on depression, post-traumatic stress, hypervigilance disorder, and pathologies indicated by your profiles."

She pointed at the final, blank column.

"Finally, we have Evolution Three." Her voice dropped low, almost to a whisper. "Evolution Three is very, very special. It builds off of our work in the previous two phases. It is the key to our program."

The far door opened. A soldier poked his head into the room.

"The computers are set up for our patients, Dr. Glasse."

She clapped her hands together.

"Perfect." She stepped back and turned to address the whole group. "Let's file into the computer room, nice and orderly. Take any seat inside. Please let our staff know if you have any issues. And remember to be honest."

"About what, Doc?" Ray asked, as the others stood up and made their way to the open door.

"Everything," Glasse said.

PSYCH EVAL

The patients filed into the expansive, windowless room, far warmer and more well-lit than the meeting area. Cramped, segmented booths had been set up in neat rows. White paint hung in heavy layers and curling flakes on the walls. The ceiling was open, the bare rafters home to cobwebs that danced in gusts of heat spat out through rusted vents. The hum of computer fans was a constant underlying sound, broken up by the creaking of floorboards as the patients took their seats.

Ray followed Terra into the room. She took a seat on the far side of the room; he spotted an open booth to the right at the end of the row. The booths were composed of thin, flat layers of polished wood that held whorls of black and brown along the surface like dark galaxies held in amber. They served to hide the faces of the computer screens from anyone not sitting directly in front of them.

The monitor before Ray was perfectly square, a style that had fallen out of favor at least a decade ago as widescreen devices became more commonplace. The glass of the screen itself had an odd curvature, a subtle bulging and warping that captured his reflection and gave it a slight but unpleasant distortion. The computer tower must have been hidden beneath the booth's paneling, as he felt a shallow vibration and hum coming up through the floor.

The black keyboard and mouse were held on a flat plane of polished wood. The keyboard held slightly oversized, square grey keys for the alphabet, numbers, and arrow and command keys. Placing his wrists against its curvature, his hands were stretched up at too odd an angle to type comfortably. The mouse, likewise, was misshapen and odd, with a single, large grey button.

The screen remained black and blank, reflecting only that dim, warped outline of his head. He stared at that shadow version of himself as the staff directed the patients to the open booths.

"You're here because somewhere along the way, the system failed you," Dr. Glasse said, suddenly in the center of the room, between the rows of computers and booths. "But a system never acts in isolation. It is influenced and shaped by its inputs. A person is marked and changed by the systems through which they pass. Therefore, the failure of the system is not merely *someone else's* fault. You had a role to play in the shape of your life.

"You may have contributed to the failure of medical and psychological professionals to properly assess and treat your case," Glasse said. "You may have not always told the truth when you should have, especially when it came to your mental health. As children, we learn that lying is wrong. And yet, as adults, we often see the opposite. We see lying, sociopathy, and selfishness rewarded, again and again." Glasse paused, content to let the patients of Class 001 wait for her next pronouncement. "Without raising your hands, how many of you had leadership or peers who warned you against being honest with the doctors? How many of you were afraid of being 'sick call rangers,' or of opening up about your true feelings of hurt and pain, fear and terror?"

Glasse let the question hang on the air.

"How many times in your personal relationships have you answered 'I'm fine,' when you were anything but? How many times did you power through an illness or injury while in uniform, or at work, or for school, because the trouble it would cause would cost you something? How many times did you neglect to answer a psychological evaluation truthfully because you didn't want to be labeled as crazy or weak? How many times have you thought to yourself, 'what I went through wasn't that bad,' and then proceeded to bury your own pain under a mountain of self-deception, drugs, alcohol, sex, or other risky activities?"

Ray stared at the muddled shape that was his own reflection in the screen, focusing on it. He didn't like what he saw.

"Your pain will come out here," Dr. Glasse said, her voice almost a whisper. "That's the important part."

The medical staff exited the room through its only door. Glasse followed them through, closing it softly behind her.

The lightbulbs above began to dim as her footsteps led away. Soft green light splashed against the faces of the patients as their computer screens flickered to life. The floor vibrated with an electronic hum. Ray's screen crackled with a wave of static, then sputtered out lines of bright green text. Bootup code and status displays. Gibberish that called to mind his father's MS-DOS 486 PC from decades past, afternoons and nights spent playing *Wolfenstein 3D* or shareware games of questionable quality.

"He's wasting his life away," his father would say. His father only used the computer for... what? Why did they have the computer, if not to play games? Why did Ray feel so guilty, now, here, decades later, for playing video games as a child?

"He needs to be outside," his father's voice said, echoing through his mind. Those words were always followed by footsteps leading out of the house, out the door, leading somewhere else. Leading away from him. Never *to* Ray, to take him somewhere, to show him things, to teach him things. No, that was too difficult.

It was easier to berate, to yell, to—

Christ, I'm a fucking sad-sack, he thought. One thing at a time.

Ray leaned toward the screen, closing his eyes and pinching the bridge of his nose. This was just like him. When he was supposed to be focusing, to be paying attention, his mind conjured some pitiful, *woe-is-me* conflation of events and feelings. He hated himself, then, like he often did. He hated himself for being sucked into a memory, triggered by some secondhand association. He hated himself for feeling bad about a situation that *wasn't that bad.*

He put those feelings in a small, wooden box, which he visualized closing and pushing into the shadows under his bed.

Appearing in the center of the screen was a vector-graphic rendering of a logo in retro-futuristic typeface, followed by green text on a black screen:

```
  MALTHUS AEROSPACE AND DEFENSE
            APPLICATIONS
                 AND
  THE U.S. DEPARTMENT OF VETERANS
               AFFAIRS


          WELCOMES YOU TO THE
        OCCLUDED RE-INTEGRATION AND
       REHABILITATION PROGRAM BETA


     CAMP WINTER FALCON, COLORADO
              CLASS 001


         [PRESS ANY KEY TO CONTINUE]
```

The spacebar depressed with a satisfying, chunky

plastic sound, echoed by others around the room. A brief "LOADING..." line appeared, followed by a request for his first and last name. He tapped away on the keyboard's out-of-proportion keys.

```
WELCOME $FIRSTNAME $LASTNAME...
WELCOME RAYMOND PARNELL


THIS PSYCHOLOGICAL EVALUATION
WILL PROVIDE MUCH OF THE DATA
NECESSARY TO FACILITATE YOUR
TREATMENT AND REHABILIATION
DURING YOUR TIME AT CAMP WINTER
FALCON. PLEASE BE TRUTHFUL AND
TRANSPARENT, EVEN AND ESPECIALLY
IF IT IS PAINFUL FOR YOU.


PLEASE PUT ON YOUR HEADPHONES
AND KEEP THEM ON FOR THE
REMAINDER OF THE EVALUATION. DO
NOT SPEAK OR GET UP FROM YOUR
STATION UNTIL THE PROCESS IS
COMPLETE.


ANY INTERRUPTIONS OR BREAKS
TAKEN WILL NULLIFY THIS
EVALUATION AND REQUIRE ANOTHER
ATTEMPT AT A LATER DATE. FAILURE
TO COMPLETE THIS EVALUATION IN
A LIMITED TIMEFRAME MAY RESULT
IN YOUR DISMISSAL FROM THIS
PROGRAM.


PLEASE DON THE HEADPHONES BEFORE
PROCEEDING.
```

[PRESS ANY KEY TO CONTINUE]

The headphones were pure black, made from a gleaming, hard-plastic material that absorbed the hazy light from above and caught and refracted the green text shining from the screen. They fit snuggly over his ears, drowning out most of the ambient noise of the room.

The headphones produced the faintest overtures of some distant music—droning, synthetic notes held too long, punctuated by footfalls on underbrush and a swirling, whooshing sound that implied the passage of cosmic bodies overhead. Radio interference, some signal coming in over the mountains, refracted through the sensitive metals and mechanisms of the communications arrays.

CHOOSE THE NUMBER THAT BEST
REPRESENTS YOUR SYMPTOMS
DESCRIBED IN THE PROMPTS.

A RESPONSE OF "1" INDICATES
TOTAL DISAGREEMENT WITH
THE PROMPT AND/OR A "NOT-
APPLICABLE," ANSWER.

A "5" INDICATES TOTAL AGREEMENT
WITH THE PROMPT AND/OR
"INTENSE," "OVERWHELMING," AND
"HIGHLY FREQUENT."

NUMBERS "2-4" INDICATE VARYING
DEGREES BETWEEN THE TWO
EXTREMES.

Ray found himself drifting back a few years, back when he was still in uniform, stuck at some post that was a vector of crime and despair. He filled out endless questionnaires in front of a computer screen, thinking about what the NCOs and officers had told them all before going inside. They said that should you come forward with any sort of mental health condition, it meant weeks of sick call, of talking to doctors who had the authority to send you home but wouldn't. It meant being subject to the Big Green Weenie's whims for another six months or more, while everyone else got to go home and take off the uniform to be with their friends and families.

Is all that hassle worth it, really?

Ray snapped back to the present. He closed his eyes, concentrated on his breathing.

No. That's not where I am anymore. That's not what this is.

He was ready to try something new.

[PRESS ANY KEY TO CONTINUE]

Ray slapped the spacebar.

YOU OFTEN FEEL ALONE AND ISOLATED, BUT FIND EXCUSES NOT TO LEAVE YOUR HOME OR ENGAGE IN SOCIAL ACTIVITIES.

[4]

The question caught him off guard—but so too did the rush of relief he felt by answering it truthfully.

The green text faded out, the contours of its script

becoming blurry ghost-trails, only to be replaced by the next prompt.

YOU ARE OFTEN ANGRY AT OTHERS,
BUT YOU ARE MOST OFTEN ANGRY AT
YOURSELF.

[5]

The strange, droning music piped through his headphones grew in volume, becoming harder to ignore. It wasn't quite music as he might understand it. Despite its sinister tones and irregular rhythm, he found it almost relaxing, like the rumblings of a distant thunderstorm, or the creaking and groaning of an old house in the deep night.

YOU FIND IT HARD TO CONCENTRATE
ON TRAINING OR WORK TASKS AND
YOU ARE OFTEN FORGETFUL, DESPITE
YOUR BEST EFFORTS.

[4]

YOUR THOUGHTS ARE OFTEN
INTRUSIVE AND UPSETTING.

[4]

YOU SEE THINGS IN YOUR MIND THAT
YOU WOULD RATHER NOT, REAL OR
IMAGINED.

[5]

YOU BLAME OTHERS FOR YOUR
FAILURES.

[3]

YOU BLAME YOURSELF FOR YOUR
FAILURES.

[4]

YOU HAVE THOUGHT ABOUT ENDING
YOUR OWN LIFE.

[3]

YOU DRINK TOO MUCH.

[5]

YOU CONSUME OTHER ILLEGAL OR
NON-PRESCRIPTION NARCOTICS TOO
MUCH.

[2]

YOUR DRINKING AND/OR DRUG USE
HAS NEGATIVELY IMPACTED YOUR
RELATIONSHIPS WITH OTHERS.

[5]

YOU DRINK AND/OR USE DRUGS TO
COPE.

[5]

YOU DRINK AND/OR USE DRUGS TO
DEAL WITH PAINFUL MEMORIES.

[4]

YOU DRINK AND/OR USE DRUGS TO
DEAL WITH SPECIFIC PAINFUL
MEMORIES.

[4]

YOU DRINK AND/OR USE DRUGS TO
DEAL WITH SPECIFIC PAINFUL
MEMORIES RELATED TO CHILDHOOD
EVENTS.

[3]

YOU DRINK AND/OR USE DRUGS TO
DEAL WITH SPECIFIC PAINFUL
MEMORIES RELATED TO CHILDHOOD
EVENTS INVOLVING MISSING TIME,
ODD LIGHT FORMATIONS, AND THE
PRESENCE OF STRANGE, NON-HUMAN
ENTITIES OR INTELLIGENCES.

Ray paused, his finger hovering over the keyboard. He re-read the prompt several times, trying to understand what it meant. Confused, he went to press [1], but something stayed his hand. Additional text faded in, slow and smooth, beneath the initial prompt:

TRUST YOUR INSTINCTS, EVEN IF
YOU DO NOT FULLY UNDERSTAND THE

IMPLICATIONS OF THE QUESTION.

YOU DRINK AND/OR USE DRUGS TO
DEAL WITH SPECIFIC PAINFUL
MEMORIES RELATED TO CHILDHOOD
EVENTS INVOLVING MISSING TIME,
ODD LIGHT FORMATIONS, AND THE
PRESENCE OF STRANGE, NON-HUMAN
ENTITIES OR INTELLIGENCES.

Ray pressed [3]. That felt right. He couldn't explain why—or even wrap his head around the prompt. But it felt right all the same.

LOADING...

THERE WAS AN ABOVE-AVERAGE DELAY
AS YOU CONSIDERED AND PROVIDED
AN ANSWER TO THE PREVIOUS
QUESTION. PLEASE EXPLAIN.

A blinking green cursor appeared beneath the text. He wasn't sure how to respond to that either, but he tried: ["I didn't understand the question. It seemed weird."]

The computer accepted his response with a hum and a series of clicks audible even through his headphones. The strange, quiet music took on the texture of synthesized elements of human voices, odd and electronic, forming incomplete syllables or nonsense words.

The wood panels of his booth hid him from the other patients. He wanted to stand up to ask someone else what they were hearing. Maybe there was some sort of technical problem with his headphones.

What if I'm the only one listening to this weird music?

The screen before him flashed, drawing his attention back to the evaluation.

HAVE YOU EXPERIENCED MISSING TIME?

The cursor blinked for a moment, then new lines of text sputtered out beneath the question, one character at a time, in a staccato sequence:

"MISSING TIME" IS A PHENOMENON WHEREIN EXPERIENCERS FAIL TO RECALL SIGNIFICANT PERIODS OF TIME, WHETHER MINUTES, HOURS, OR EVEN DAYS. THEY ARE UNABLE TO ACCOUNT FOR THEIR WHEREABOUTS OR ACTIONS. THESE EVENTS CANNOT BE ATTRIBUTEABLE TO DRUG OR ALCOHOL ABUSE OR AS THE RESULT OF A NORMATIVE MEDICAL EVENT.

EXPERIENCERS OFTEN CITE "SCREEN MEMORIES" THAT OCCLUDE SUCH PERIODS. THESE MEMORIES ARE USUALLY OUTLIERS OF ILLOGICAL WEIRDNESS, CURIOUS IN THEIR COMPOSITION AND TOO BRIEF TO ACCOUNT FOR THE DURATIONS IN QUESTION.

IF YOU HAVE NEVER EXPERIENCED THIS PHENOMENON, SELECT 1. IF

YOU HAVE EXPERIENCED IT ONCE OR TWICE, SELECT 2. IF YOU HAVE EXPERIENCED IT SEVERAL TIMES, SELECT 3-5, WITH 3 REPRESENTING A LOW FREQUENCY OF OCCURRENCE AND 5 REPRESENTING A HIGH FREQUENCY OF OCCURRENCE.

Ray read the description twice. The room was getting too warm, probably due to the many computer fans blowing out hot air from enclosed wooden spaces within the booths. A thin veil of sweat accumulated on his forehead. He wiped it away quickly, feeling a flush of anxiety creep over him, the kind he sometimes felt when he had to go out in public and get something done and his brain chemistry decided to get all screwy and go on high-alert. The beginnings of a panic attack, maybe.

He wanted a drink.

He pressed [2].

There's something buried back there, he thought, picturing himself standing at the foot of his bed, the sweat on his chest cool against the night air of his childhood bedroom. He faced the window, the one overlooking the expansive back yard. The blinds were drawn, but light spilled through the cracks and around the edges. Blue light that fluttered and flickered, softly rising in intensity and sharply contracting back to darkness before repeating the cycle. Fog wrapped around his ankles. He thought: *that's strange, the fog never comes this far up from the swamp*, and then something drew his attention back to the window...

The screen flickered and brought up the next question.

YOU HAVE WITNESSED STRANGE

LIGHTS IN THE SKY OR AT GROUND LEVEL, INCLUDING UNIDENTIFIED AERIAL PHENOMENA, ANOMALOUS ATMOSPHERIC EFFECTS, "FLASH BULB" BURSTS, "BALL LIGHTNING," OR UNACCOUNTABLE GLIMMERS THAT CATCH YOU OFF GUARD OR APPEAR IN THE PERIPHERY OF YOUR VISION.

Something wasn't right here. These questions were ridiculous. They had nothing to do with his mental health.

Unless, of course, they were trying to figure out if he was crazy.

He pressed [1].

RAY, IT'S IMPORTANT THAT YOU'RE HONEST WITH US.

IT'S IMPORTANT THAT YOU'RE HONEST WITH YOURSELF.

THINK HARD ABOUT YOUR ANSWER.

TRY AGAIN.

He leaned back in his seat, taking his headphones off and setting them down. He looked around the room, expecting to see the medical staff looking at him, expecting to see someone over his shoulder, someone stepping forward to tell him he had screwed up somehow, or that this was all a prank.

Ray. The system had called him *Ray.* Is that the name he had entered when he signed in? He didn't think so, but he couldn't be sure.

Around him, none of the other patients seemed distressed. Most of them continued on with the questions, keyboard clicks and shuffling feet and coughs, mostly hidden behind their own booth's privacy panels.

The prompt appeared on screen once more, this time with an addendum:

THE SUCCESS OF YOUR TREATMENT HERE DEPENDS ON YOUR HONESTY AND ACCURACY IN RESPONDING TO QUESTIONS OR PROMPTS. TRUST YOUR INSTINCTS.

Ray slipped the headphones back on and closed his eyes, the semi-musical electronic droning filling his mind, helping to pull him back and down to that sliver of memory, of a hot summer night during his childhood, his feet on the cool wooden floorboards of the old farmhouse. He saw himself reaching out to those window blinds. They were new—something his mom bought and his dad had made a big deal out of installing, only to berate Ray later at dinner for not helping him, or of not *wanting* to help him do tedious work, of *playing those goddamn videogames and staying in your room all goddamn day*, until Ray was looking at his dinner plate and wishing he could just be invisible, more invisible than he already was. He wanted to disappear into those open stretches of fog-covered swamp beyond the fields. He wouldn't have to hear about how much of a disappointment he was, how the things he liked weren't what a man should like at all.

The cursor blinked on the screen.

He remembered now. That cyclical glow beyond the

blinds became like the reflection off of a car windshield, rising up, passing over the house. That's what got him to press his fingers between those blinds and peer outside, that strip of illumination splashing across his eyes.

Something looked back.

He pressed [3].

The system accepted his answer without further protest.

WERE YOU EVER ACCUSED OF RUNNING AWAY FROM HOME, WHEN YOU WERE SURE THAT YOU HAD NOT? DID YOUR PARENTS OR GUARDIANS COMPLAIN ABOUT YOUR EXTENDED ABSENCES, FOR WHICH YOU COULD PROVIDE NO ACCOUNT?

[3]

HAVE YOU EVER AWAKENED IN A STRANGE PLACE, WITH NO MEMORY OF HOW YOU GOT THERE (DRUGS AND ALCOHOL WERE NOT INVOLVED)?

[3]

DOES THIS IMAGE FRIGHTEN YOU?

The text disappeared, only to be replaced with a pixelated image that emerged in gradually revealed layers: three tall, slightly stooped figures wrapped in robes or long, flowing sheets, their heads bulbous and warped, home to eyes that were gaping black holes. Their mouths were twisted open in rictus howls. They stood in front of a garage or outbuilding revealed by the dim illumination of a distant floodlight mounted on an isolated telephone pole. A patch of sky was visible above the reaching hands of twisted, naked trees, where half a dozen glowing points of light glowed brightly against the dark.

Ray blinked hard and the image was gone. There wasn't even an opportunity to enter a number for his response.

HAVE YOU EVER ENCOUNTERED "STRANGE BEINGS," OR BEEN TOLD THAT, AS A CHILD, YOU HAD IMAGINARY FRIENDS?

Eyes staring back at him through the blinds of his childhood bedroom on the second floor.

[4]

HAVE YOU EVER ENCOUNTERED STRANGE MEN OR WOMEN WITH SHIFTING FACES?

[2]

DO YOU HAVE A FASCINATION WITH FAIRY TALE LORE AND MYTHOLOGY?

[2]

HAVE YOU EVER THOUGHT OF A MUNDANE OCCURRENCE OR ENCOUNTER AS AN "OMEN" OR PROPHETIC WARNING FROM SOME UNSEEN

SPIRITUAL FORCE?

[3]

DO YOU BELIEVE IN THE PARANORMAL
AND/OR THE OCCULT?

[3]

IF SOMEONE WERE TO SAY THE WORD
"SASQUATCH," ON THE SCALE OF
1-5, 1 BEING PHYSICAL, 5 BEING
SPIRITUAL, WHAT WOULD BE YOUR
ASSOCIATION WITH THE WORD?

[5]

DO YOUR RELIGIOUS VIEWS OR
LACK THEREOF PRECLUDE YOU
FROM PARTAKING IN SPIRITUAL
CEREMONIES RELATED TO THE
SUMMONING OF ENERGIES, SPIRITS,
ENTITIES, ALIENS, FEY, OR PAST
OR FUTURE VERSIONS OF YOURSELF?
(Y/N)

[N]

The program accepted his answer and then went
dark for a moment, before displaying the end state text:

THANK YOU FOR COMPLETING THIS
EVALUATION. YOUR HONESTY AND
WILLINGNESS TO PARTICIPATE HAS
BEEN NOTED AND APPRECIATED.

PLEASE REMOVE YOUR HEADPHONES
AND EXIT THE ROOM. DO NOT
DISTURB YOUR FELLOW PATIENTS
AS THEY COMPLETE THEIR OWN
EVALUATIONS.

YOU ARE ENCOURAGED TO DISCUSS
THESE SUBJECTS WITH THE STAFF
AND PATIENTS WHO HAVE COMPLETED
THE EVALUATION SUCCESSFULLY.

YOU ARE ENCOURAGED TO RECALL
TRAUMATIC EVENTS FROM YOUR
CHILDHOOD.

YOU ARE ENCOURAGED TO RECALL
TRAUMATIC EVENTS FROM CHILDHOOD
INVOLVING STRANGE LIGHTS,
MISSING TIME, AND NON-HUMAN
INTELLIGENCES, CREATURES AND/OR
OBJECTS.

GOOD LUCK AS YOU CONTINUE
EVOLUTION ONE.

THANK YOU FOR YOUR SERVICE.

SMOKE POINT

Ray didn't smoke—not anymore—but he topped off a foam cup with steaming coffee and stepped outside with the others seeking a rush of nicotine. The Army taught him that smoke points were where connections were forged, where the best gossip could be heard, where even the most hard-assed officers and NCOs might let their guard down and act like real people, if only for a moment.

The others stood around a gnarled tree in a flat stretch of scrub grass and dirt. Terra was already there, talking with another woman: rail thin, dyed blonde hair cropped short to her scalp, an oversized blue Navy jacket hanging off her shoulders. She looked like she belonged at a local punk show, not on a military post.

"Hey," Ray said. "That was something, right?"

"Smoke?" Terra asked, holding up a pack.

"No thanks," Ray said, raising up his coffee in salute. "I'm Ray." He held out his hand for the woman he hadn't met. "Parnell."

"Stacey," she said. "Bozell. Are we using first names or last names here?"

"Ray's fine for me," he said.

"First name for you it is," she said, smiling. "You can call me Stacey." Her large brown eyes were bright and friendly, but there was a weariness in her smile. The shadows and wrinkles beneath her eyes were premature on her young face.

"Did you guys...?" Ray started, unsure of how to begin. The cold air was refreshing, helping to ground him to the present moment—but his mind was muddled. "The questions on that test were, uh..."

"Yeah, holy shit," Terra said. "Weird as hell."

"Did they ask you about missing time and weird

lights, all that stuff?" Stacey asked, taking another drag on her cigarette.

"Yeah," Ray said, nodding. "The weird thing was, I tried to tell them 'no,' like I selected a 'one,' and the system was like, 'are you *sure*?' And to be honest, I wasn't."

"Right," Stacey said, smiling a sort of nervous smile, a shield she could throw up to look pretty and pleasant instead of confused and scared. She blew out a pillar of smoke, which drifted into the grey sky. "Me too."

"I have these memories," Ray said, not sure why he was opening up. Maybe he was serious about changing after all. "It's late at night, and there's something outside the window that I feel like I have to see..."

He trailed off when he realized he held Terra and Stacey's full attention. There was no judgment on their faces, but he felt embarrassed all the same.

"Nevermind. It was just real odd, that's all," he said, taking a long sip of coffee, which had already begun to cool in the open air.

"I told it 'one' or whatever a couple of times," Terra said, "but it wouldn't let me progress until I gave it at least a 'two.' And the thing is, I think they're right. I *do* recall missing some time, here and there. Not when I was drinking, either. Real buried deep stuff, from when I was a kid. And then at least once on deployment."

"I thought it was some kind of coping mechanism," Stacey said. "Caused by service-related trauma or something. But the questions about the lights and then that image they showed us." She shook her head. "Jesus. Kind of spooked me out."

"That's gotta be it, right?" Terra said. "We got post-traumatic stress, and that's a common thing—to have holes in your memory, to be afraid of things, to create false memories."

"I don't know," Ray said. "The image they showed me didn't seem to have anything to do with combat. It was just three gangly looking weirdos and some stars behind them. A copy of a copy of a Polaroid."

Terra frowned.

"That's not what they showed me."

"Me neither," Stacey said. "Mine was an owl or a bird with big eyes, but it was too big, and the trees..."

A voice called over to them:

"If you've completed the eval, you've got working party duty!"

The three patients looked up to see Sergeant Major Haaster leaning out the building's front door. "Wrap up your smokes and rally on me. We move out in five!"

Terra groaned.

"I thought police call and trash duty ended when I got out," she said.

"Hey, at least he didn't call us 'dumb pieces of shit,'" Stacey said, putting her cigarette out in the metal barrel half-buried near the tree. "That's a step up from what I'm used to."

The equipment shed's stark yellow siding and white trim marked it as a newer addition to the camp. Haaster pulled the doors open, hinges groaning in want of oil. Ray and Terra followed him inside, with Stacey and two other patients close behind. The shed smelled of gasoline and oil-on-metal, heavy but not unpleasant on the air. For Ray, it trigged vague recollections of being in his grandfather's garage, of watching him work on the lawnmower or tinker at the bench, his coffee steaming in a metal tumbler.

Haaster flicked on his headlight, casting a strong, shimmering beam of white into the dark. It revealed a pair of push lawnmowers, two weed trimmers, a couple plastic containers of fuel, and bottles full of additives and oil. Gloves and gardening tools, all of them surprisingly new.

Hanging at the back of the shed—suspended by brackets in the wall, like a shotgun over a fireplace—hung the chainsaw. Unlike most of the other tools and equipment, it had character, a history of use. The yellow paint on the protective case housing was chipped to reveal the rough metal beneath. The chain looked fresh, its teeth glistening in the headlamp's sharp glow.

"Hand these out," Haaster said, giving Ray a stack of working gloves. "Take a couple of garbage bags each, too." Ray stared at the chainsaw. Haaster shook his head, smiling. "We'll let you play with the big toys eventually," he said. "Gotta work your way up to the fun stuff."

SKELETON CREW

They conducted the police call—a fancy term for *soldiers picking up trash*—in an uneven, staggered line, covering a few hundred meters from the shed back toward the barracks and chapel. Ray quickly realized that this was a time-waster, an example of the *troops should be doing something all of the time, even and especially if it is pointless* policy of armies everywhere. But there was trash to pick up, oddly enough, most of it blown in from distant county roadways over the many long years of the camp's isolation.

Haaster led the group, calling for them to straighten out the line or to keep pace, but never quite slipping into the angry NCO voice that directed exhausted troops the world over since time immemorial.

"Just when I thought I was out," Stacey said, effecting a poor Al Pacino as she dropped a bent cigarette butt in her bag, "they pull me back in!"

Ray smirked. Complaining about the tedious bullshit they were forced to do was about as military as it got.

"Sergeant Major, if there's just us here, why is there so much goddamn trash?" Terra said.

Haaster took a moment to pick up the shredded remains of a plastic grocery bag.

"Army camps, like all military bases, attract garbage," he said. "It's a law of physics."

"I guess that explains how we ended up here," Terra said.

Haaster barked out a quick laugh.

"Whoa, a sergeant major with a sense of humor," Terra said, "and he picks up trash. Now I've seen everything."

"I'm out to pasture, same as you," Haaster said. "This'll probably be my last duty station before retirement. You headed back to the Big Green Machine when this program's wrapped up, Morales?"

"Sergeant Major, I'm not sure even you and Dr. Glasse can put all my pieces back together again."

"We'll do our best," he said.

"I meant to ask you," Terra said, pausing a moment to stand up straight and stretch her lower back. "Are we really the only ones out here? No other units?"

"I command about a dozen cadre for security and operations support for Dr. Glasse and her staff," Haaster said. "There's seven or eight of those medical types: doctors, nurses, an admin or two."

"Skeleton crew," Ray said.

Haaster tossed a rusted-out Coke can into his trash bag.

"Prototype project," Haaster said. "You're the guinea pigs." Haaster paused, his eyes going distant. A frown spread across his face. "I'm sorry, I shouldn't have said that. I think what you're doing here is a good thing, and brave. I mean it. I shouldn't joke like that."

"We appreciate what you're doing too, Sergeant Major," Terra said. "Not a lot of senior NCOs would put much faith in rehabilitation and therapy."

"I hope that will change," he said. "I came in right before 9/11. Different Army back then. Different *world* back then. The old timers—maybe some of them saw action in the Gulf War, maybe Somalia, Kosovo, Bosnia. That wasn't anything like Iraq or Afghanistan. Wasn't like twenty years of goddamn war, watching your guys get blown up or come home to eat a gun, or drink themselves to death." He cleared his throat, feigned a cough.

"Completely decommissioned otherwise, then?" Terra said. "Nobody else on-post but our happy few?"

"Far as I know," Haaster said. "Mostly my troops

just man the gate, run errands for Dr. Glasse's folks, chase coyotes away. Quietest assignment I've ever had. A few of my guys are fresh from the sandbox. We've earned some quiet time, I think."

Terra took a moment to consider how to broach what was on her mind.

"I saw... It looked like a few men in uniform the first night," she said. "It was dark, but I think they had flashlights or headlamps, because I could see their faces lit up. Were they your troops?"

Haaster shrugged.

"Might've just been a couple of my guys walking the perimeter," he said. "Not much to do here when off duty, except play videogames in the cadre barracks and PT. No drinking allowed here, out of deference to the patients. So, yeah. Probably bored Joes."

"Probably," Terra said, not sounding convinced.

"Could also be tweakers, vagrants," Haaster said. "It'd be easy to disappear and stay hidden in a facility like this. She's bigger than she looks. There's a decommissioned hospital around the south bend of the mountains, there." He pointed toward the mountain wall to the southwest. "I wouldn't be surprised if we opened up a building and found a meth lab or encampment inside." He shook his head. "Country ain't what it used to be."

Their group went quiet for a while, content to shiver against the gusts of plains-bound wind. Gradually they wandered toward a cluster of buildings that sat on old stone foundations, flimsy wooden doors nailed shut with water-damaged planks. Their sloped roofs shed shingles like tears. Wind whistled through cracks in the thin glass of shattered windows. The smell of old, wet wood hung heavy on the air. The buildings were set in a perpendicular "T" formation, their main doors pointing toward a stone fire pit set directly between them.

"You didn't tell us we had a barbecue pit," Terra said, trying to spin a joke out of the awkward silence.

"I didn't know this was here," Haaster said, his voice quiet, his eyes on the grey stones wrapped in barbed branches. Ray approached the oval pit. The structure came up to his thighs, its walls made of heavy, smooth grey stones held together by dark mortar. Inside the pit was a dune sea of grey ash. The wind blew waves across its surface.

Ray bent down and reached his gloved hand in toward a shape just beneath the surface of the ash, its off-white curvature charred by a dead flame. His fingers found the contour and brushed away ash.

"Bone," he said. "There's bones in here."

"Let's head back toward the work shed," Haaster said suddenly. "One last sweep. We'll double-time it. Grab what you see. Don't want to be late for lunch chow."

Terra came up next to Ray, her arm brushing against his, her eyes on the shape.

"What kind of bone?" she asked.

The wind began to shift more ash away, revealing what was buried beneath.

NIGHT TERRORS

On Ray's first full day down range in Afghanistan, the non-commissioned officer in charge of the outpost decided the best way to break in the new guys was by screaming at the top of his lungs well before first call.

Ray and the rest of his team scrambled out of their racks, throwing on their body armor over their PT shirts and pants, grabbing their weapons and donning their helmets.

The NCO—Ray had forgotten the asshole's name—shouted, telling them to *get the fuck up, fall in you stupid fucks!*

Ray's team leader was just as confused as the rest of them.

"Sergeant, what is the situation?" the team leader asked, eyes wide, confused.

"The lights are *out*," the NCOIC said. "You notice that, *Sergeant*?"

Ray's team leader looked at him, then up at the light fixtures in the small building that they would call home for the next nine months. It couldn't have been any later than 0400. This same NCO had told them wakeup would be 0530, with a pre-mission briefing an hour later.

"Yes, Sergeant," Ray's team leader said, in that passive way all soldiers agreed with their leadership when they had no idea what the fuck was going on or why they were in trouble.

"It's *your* goddamn responsibility!" the senior NCO shouted, voice going shrill, eyes bulging along his pale face. "I showed you the goddamn generator yesterday!"

"Sergeant, I don't know how to operate the—"

"Why the *fuck not?*" the NCO shouted, his voice going liquid-gurgle with rage.

"I'm an infantryman, I've literally never operated a diesel generator in my life."

"You better goddamn *learn!* Get your ass out to the generator right *fucking now!*"

"To do what, Sergeant? What are you asking us to do?"

To do, to do, to do...

Ray snapped awake, sure his team leader was getting chewed out by that crusty old fuck back at the outpost, sure that he was back on the first real day of his deployment, one in a long string of days of pointless fear and petty harassment and rockets and blood.

Christ, I gotta let that shit go.

The wires and metal of the top bunk's empty frame hung suspended above him, gathering rust. Someone had been shouting, and not just in his dreams, either. He stood up, placing his feet on the floor, the cold of the tile flooding up through his nerves. He slipped on his shower sandals and grabbed his headlamp from its hiding place in his right sneaker.

The barracks went blood-red as he flipped on the headlamp. The crimson wash swept over empty bunks and half-covered mattresses, the sleeping figures of his fellow patients, lockers, shoes and tan combat boots, laundry bags, water bottles, and paperback books.

Maybe the voice crying out had been his brain misfiring—an auditory hallucination dredged up from the edge of unconsciousness. He'd experienced that plenty of times. Being ready to drift off, to lose that sense of self and just be still in the night, truly asleep, only to be drawn back, suddenly and with a great rush of anxiety, by a strange sound: a voice, a handclap, a siren; a presence lingering over his bed, whispering secrets. Whispering his name.

He passed bunk after bunk, finally reaching the end

of the building. He found a form covered in blankets just one bunk shy of the exit. Limbs thrashed about, swift but blind, torso tossing from side to side, big hands balled into fists. The red light revealed eyes held shut and a mouth wound tight in anger or pain. *Captain Dodonna.*

"Mike," Ray said, leaning forward to place a hand on his shoulder. "Hey, Mike. Wake up."

The former officer twisted toward the sound of Ray's voice, his distressed face revealed in a crimson wash.

Ray gave him a shake. Eyes snapped open, the whites wide and bright in the dark.

"Huh," Mike said.

"It's me, Ray. You're having a nightmare, man."

"Ray. Weekend warrior."

"Yeah. The weekend warrior."

"Shit." Mike closed his eyes and rubbed at his face. Sweat had broken out along his wide forehead, despite the chill of the barracks air. "Where am I?"

"Camp Winter Falcon," Ray said. "Best post in the Army, right here in colorful Colorado."

"Coffee's still coffee," Mike said. He breathed slow and heavy. Ray averted the light from his face. "Why did you wake me up?"

"You woke me up, sir," Ray said. "Maybe these other rocks can sleep through your shouting, but I can't."

"Sorry," Mike said. "What was I saying?"

"Dunno," Ray said. "You okay?"

"Yeah." He propped himself up on his elbows, then stared toward the far wall. "Happens sometimes. Since..." He nodded. "I'll try to be quiet."

"No problem, Captain."

Mike smiled and lay back down, closing his eyes.

"How many men were assigned to this barracks?" Ray asked.

"Mmm. Seven. Seven at first."

"At first?" Ray said.

"Yeah. Nowinski's gear was gone by the end of the day."

"AWOL?"

"Couldn't say," Mike said. "Didn't really talk to the guy, just remember not seeing him before lights out. Just gone, now."

"That seem weird to you?"

Mike opened his eyes, staring into the springs of the top bunk.

"This whole place seems weird to me," he said. "But to be honest, this is the first time I've been dry for a couple of weeks. Everything seems weird when you're used to being half-lit most of the day."

Ray nodded, then tapped the top bunk.

"Get some sleep," he said.

"Ray."

"Yeah?"

"Thanks for pulling me out of that. It was one of the bad ones."

Mike's breathing settled back into a soft rhythm. Ray admired the ability of other people to fall asleep in moments, as opposed to their brains tossing a parade of embarrassing and upsetting imagery at them for an hour or more. Stress response, he supposed. Stress from being a broke-brain dipshit. No combat experience required.

Movement, seen from the corner of his eye, drew his attention. A light reflecting off the glass of a spider web-cracked window. Shifting, pulsing.

I'm already up. Might as well check it out.

Outside, the cold air clawed at Ray, piercing the long grey sleeves of his Army PT shirt. The light again. Bobbing in the dark, near the female barracks a few dozen yards away. Small, amber. Someone smoking, the cold air making the exhalations visible, revealing phantoms.

Terra's eyes caught his, even in the dark. Ray crossed the distance, the struggling grass reaching up over the edges of his shower sandals to nip at his toes.

"Careful," Terra said, breathing out a cloud of smoke, "female barracks are off-limits."

Ray put up his hands.

"I wouldn't dare." He flipped off his headlamp and Terra went from red light to black shadow. "Can't sleep?" he asked.

"Looking for my ghosts," Terra said. "You?"

Ray shrugged.

"One of the guys was having a dream. Woke me up."

"Dreams don't wake other people up," she said. "Nightmares do."

"Yeah." Ray looked off toward the west, beyond rows of empty, dark buildings to the impenetrable shadows of the mountains. "Wish I could have a drink."

Terra pointed at him with the hand holding her cigarette.

"You're an alcoholic." A statement of fact, not a question.

Ray shook his head, about to protest. He stopped himself. Might as well save everyone the time and effort.

"Yeah, probably."

"Takes one to know one," Terra said. Her voice changed into a flat, deep tone: "'Has your drinking ever interfered with your relationships or responsibilities? Do you ever drink in the morning? How often do you drink by yourself?' Etc. etc." She shook her head, laughing at herself. "You want a smoke?"

"I don't smoke. Haven't since I've been in."

"Not what I asked."

"Okay."

She withdrew a white cylinder from her soft pack. He took the cigarette and placed it between his lips. She found the tip with the flame from her lighter, their faces bright and warm against the dark.

"From Colorado?" Ray asked, trying not to cough. The smoke was like sharp nails against the back of his throat. His eyes watered.

"Back east, originally," she said. "Western New York, but been in Colorado Springs for about ten years. Lots of family here. And before you ask, no, I'm not from New York City. Been once, wasn't really my speed. You?"

"Born and raised in the Centennial State," Ray said. "I'd say I'm a 'native' like all those bumper stickers but I try not to be too insufferable. Only real natives here are Ute or Arapahoe or whatever."

"Fucking white people," Terra said.

"Fucking white people." Ray grinned.

Terra gestured at the sky.

"Living in the Springs, I forget how pretty the sky is at night, away from all the light pollution. Back home, me and my friends would just stare at it for hours, drinking beers or smoking pot or whatever. But being out under it was always their idea, not mine. Made me too nervous."

"Like you were going to see something you shouldn't," Ray said. Terra nodded.

"Like something was going to spill out of the stars and reach down and get me. Just being outside at night felt dangerous. Like I was being watched." She took a long drag on her cigarette, then held it out in front of her, inspecting the diminishing length. "I guess I was crazy before I joined up."

"Me too, I think," Ray said.

Terra finished off her cigarette. Ray made to put his out.

"It's fine," she said. "I'll wait with you."

Ray smoked. Terra held herself against the cold.

"What did you mean by 'ghosts,' earlier?" Ray asked.

"If we hadn't just had that weird psych eval test earlier today, I wouldn't bring it up. You remember me asking Sergeant Major Haaster about those soldiers I saw? The ones walking around with their faces lit up?"

Ray shrugged.

"Well, I'm not buying that it was guys with headlamps. Looked way spookier than that. And their uniforms were olive-drab. Not the newer OCPs, not ACUs, or the Marines' MCUs."

"Ghosts, then?"

"Yeah, I think so," Terra said, nodding. She looked at him sideways, defensive. "Got a superstitious bone in your body, Ray Parnell?"

"I'm sort of Catholic, remember?"

"Catholicism is the spookiest of all Christian religions," Terra said. "My grandmother used to be into that Day of the Dead stuff. I just viewed it as bonus early Halloween time. I wish I had learned more about it before she died."

Ray finished his cigarette. He flicked the butt off into the dark.

"Why don't they keep more lights on?" she said. "There's, what, thirty, forty buildings spread across a hundred acres? And it's mostly dark. It's like there's no one here at all."

"Well, not *no one*," Ray said. "There's someone over there. Maybe one of your ghosts."

Ray pointed east, beyond the rows of longhouse buildings on the main streets. Somewhere between them and the darkness that swallowed the world, figures moved along the edge of the veil of night. Green luminescence, emerging from the earth itself to set low-hanging fog aglow, revealing their forms in the dark. Three or four people wandering between the distant buildings, aimless and slow, arms slack and heads bobbing, as if sleepwalking.

"That's what I saw," Terra whispered. "Holy shit, dude. That's what I saw."

They stood in silence for another long, cold moment, watching the light shift and pulse. The figures disappeared into the distance.

"Could be anything," Ray said. "Could be headlights reflecting off the clouds, could be the guards making the rounds. Fireflies."

"Could be ghosts," Terra said.

A noise startled them—fluttering wind or the flapping of wings of some great bird nearby, one or two buildings over. Something large and heavy moving in the dark, unfolding itself from unseen shadows. Moving with a purpose. Then the night air went still and silent.

"I think we should get back inside," Ray said, his voice much louder than he intended.

"Yeah," Terra said, retreating to the relative safety of the door to the female barracks. She opened it slowly, the hinges squeaking like a small animal in distress.

Something bellowed in the near distance. A heavy and sonorous cry.

"Ray," Terra hissed. "Get back to the barracks. Those lights are coming closer."

"No, they can't be, that was just—"

Terra slammed the door shut. Metal on wood sound. A lock slipping into place.

Ray was already running back toward the male barracks, his legs taking great strides, all thoughts of cold and discomfort forgotten. He risked a glance behind him when that great flapping sound emerged again, closer. Fog rose up out of the earth to receive him, suffused with a terrible glow.

GROUP SESSION

"Why are you here?"

The voice was Dr. Glasse's, but the words came out of the mouth of an imposing first sergeant, leaning over the chow hall table and staring straight at Specialist Parnell.

"First Sergeant?"

"Stand at parade rest when talking to an NCO, you dumb piece of shit," the first sergeant said, Glasse's smooth voice giving way to the gravel bark of a lifetime smoker.

"Is there a problem, First Sergeant?" asked Parnell's team leader. If one thing pissed him off—besides a soldier failing a PT test—it was other people fucking with his Joes.

"No one is speaking to you, little girl," the first sergeant said, eyes locked on Parnell. "Mind your own fucking business."

The team leader stood up and went to parade rest.

"First Sergeant—"

"Why are you here, troop?" the first sergeant said, to Parnell and Parnell, only.

Specialist Parnell dropped his fork and stood up, a burn in his lower back, his eyes weary from the before-dawn wakeup, the skin on his face red from the two-hour drive north in the turret through sub-zero temperatures and winds. This was the last goddamn thing he needed.

"Eating breakfast, First Sergeant."

"You're not with a unit on this post."

"No, First Sergeant. We're from one of the outposts to the south."

"Your uniform is dirty."

"Yes, First Sergeant. It was a two-hour drive north.

I was in the turret, we haven't eaten yet today—"

"You young soldiers have no respect for the uniform!" the senior NCO snapped. "Being in a combat zone is no excuse for a dirty uniform! Bring an extra uniform with you to change into before coming to my chowhall! If I catch any of you in this DFAC with a fucked-up uniform, with unclean weapons, with dirt on your goddamn boots, *I'll string you motherfuckers up. Shall-I-go-on?*"

"No, First Sergeant!"

"*Ray*," the First Sergeant said, in someone else's voice.

"Ray?"

"Hmm."

"Why are you here, Ray?"

Ray blinked, and he wasn't standing in some chow hall in the Green Zone, getting dressed down for having the gall to get breakfast after coming off mission, having traveled down a road on which Americans were routinely killed or dismembered. No. He was in the chapel with a few others: Adams, the guy from Third Marines; Stacey Bozell from the smoke break and police call yesterday; and Garret Calhurst, the tall Army vet with a heavy beard and soft voice who had spent some time as a cavalry scout sniper.

They sat on metal folding chairs set up ahead of the front pews in the space before the stage and altar of the post chapel. Lights hung from the steepled ceiling overhead, dim and weak. Dr. Glasse had chosen to light candles on the altar. They didn't help much with the struggling light, but they had a pleasant, familiar smell.

"Are you okay?" Dr. Glasse asked, leaning back in her seat, pen moving over her clipboard like automatic writing.

"Yeah. Sorry."

"Where did you go just now?"

"It's nothing."

"It's never nothing," she said.

Ray held out his hands, trying to grasp the right words.

"I get pulled back into things. Memories. Sometimes the traumatic ones, sometimes just embarrassing ones. Things that most people would just forget."

"Was this one traumatic or embarrassing? Or maybe both?"

"Embarrassing, mostly. I was just—we had just come off a long trip north to Kabul. I was exhausted. We were getting chow at the DFAC and some NCO came over and fucked with us because our uniforms were dirty. But they were dirty because we just came off mission, and it's fucked up that we got fucked up for it. But that's the Army for you."

"Amen," Calhurst said.

"Marines were like that too, at the bigger bases," Adams said. "Best to stay away from those rear-echelon motherfuckers."

Stacey laughed. Her fingers tapped against her leg, ready for another smoke.

"I don't know why shit like that bothered me so much," Ray said. "I know that's just how the military is. People fuck with you. It's part of discipline, or so they say. If you can't take an ass-chewing, you're in the wrong business. Well, I guess after a while, after I saw what the war was really like, I realized I *was* in the wrong business." Glasse's pen stopped moving over her clipboard.

"It really isn't about discipline in most cases. I think it's about damaged people using their rank to damage other people. Making someone eat shit because you can. That first sergeant had no business fucking with us. We weren't doing anything wrong. He could have had a conversation with us. Maybe he could have asked us some questions, pointed us to the rec center or showers or whatever. Instead, it was just, like, *fuck you*. The next thing I could have done that day was get back on that road and get turned to bloody mist because a Taliban trigger man got lucky. Do you know what that's like, just getting shit on all the time by the institution that's supposed to take care of you?"

Glasse's expression was blank.

"I hated the Army more than I ever hated the Taliban," Ray said. "Not the guys to my left and right. The job was hard enough. I don't understand why so many others who didn't have to face all that danger felt like they had to make things worse for those who did."

He went quiet.

Dr. Glasse pushed her tongue against the inside of her left cheek, her brow furrowed.

"What you're feeling is legitimate," she said. "I've found that it is sometimes the small things—the small slights, the comments in passing, the routine degradation, the toxic environment—these are the things that stay with us the most, that serve as triggers for episodes of anger, or negative feelings towards oneself, or others. It's actually easier for the mind to dwell on these episodes than it is to dwell on those involving explicit, violent trauma. You shouldn't linger on your negative feelings, but you should acknowledge them. Chances are you're not really upset about some first sergeant in a chow hall ten years ago. You may be upset about what that interaction represents for you."

Ray nodded.

Calhurst laid a heavy paw on Ray's shoulder.

"Look man, I got tired of that shit too," he said. "We all did. We all got out for various reasons. Yeah, you can say 'the Army is the Army,' but the truth is, it's a fucked-up organization, and it's stressful, especially downrange. It's alright to be angry, man. Can't speak for the Marines or Navy, but I'm willing to bet they don't exactly screen out shitheads from leadership. Am I right?"

"That's right," Adams said. "I think being a shithead is a requirement for some ranks."

Stacey nodded, too.

"Look at what they do to Navy captains who go public when their ships and crews don't get the support or help they need, whether it's a COVID outbreak, unhealthy living conditions, or whatever," Stacey said. "They don't reward you for taking care of your sailors, but if you cover up something, you get promoted."

"Was it the question I asked you?" Dr. Glasse asked Ray. "'Why are you here?' Was that the trigger?"

"I know why I'm here," Ray said. "I'm a fuck-up and can't-get-right, not since I got out. I need some help managing how shitty I feel all the time. I probably need to quit drinking. I probably need professional help, and any chance I can get at getting some sort of decent job after all this, I'll take. I can get angry about how the Army treated us, but in reality, I'm the one holding myself back right now. That what you want to hear? Because I think that sums it up for me."

Glasse nodded.

"I understand being here—especially in this place, this Army camp—I understand that it may trigger some uncomfortable feelings and questions for you," she said. "That's by design. Dealing with the pain and the insecurity is important. I appreciate your honesty, even and especially in your anger."

VIDEO #1

Late in the day, the patients of Class 001 gathered together in the front pews in the post chapel. The door leading to the back room opened and two of Haaster's uniformed cadre emerged, rolling out a grey old-style television set on a black stand. It was a bulky, pre-HD TV, complete with a built-in VCR beneath the screen. Something from Ray's high school days, when the teacher was hung over and just wanted to put on a science video or something.

The soldiers rolled the stand up to the lip of the chapel stage, then carefully lifted it down the six or so inches to the main floor.

"Some of you may find our methods unorthodox," Dr. Glasse said, walking between the rows of pews toward the altar and transept. "We're going to ask you to participate in activities that may not make sense to you, at least at first. We're going to ask you questions that might seem confusing or strange. You've trusted us with your care these first couple days. Please continue to trust us in the training events and evolutions ahead."

The cadre connected an extension cord to the outlet on the far wall, then gave Glasse a thumbs up before leaving. The furnace below clicked off and the chapel fell into cold and quiet.

"We're going to watch some videos," Glasse said. "I want you to take notes on what you see. I want you to record how you feel, and how your memories might reflect the activity on screen. Some of what you see may seem frightening. Fear is a normal response. Pain is the road we take to success."

Dr. Glasse turned on the TV/VCR. The screen lit up with a field of grey static. The lights in the chapel went down. A few of the patients giggled, their faces suddenly cast in the pallor of the screen's glow. Dr. Glasse turned up the volume, the harsh noise of non-signal grating against their ears.

The static disappeared and the screen went blue, the word PLAY displayed in the upper left-hand corner in heavy white letters. The room went silent again, save for the whirring of the tape deck and the low hum of the curved screen.

The patients sat in reverent silence. Black and white images emerged from the ether as analog memories. Ghosts appearing at the far end of a hallway in a haunted house.

A young man is strapped to a medical examination chair in the center of a cramped room. White-painted concrete walls, harsh lighting from above. Low-resolution images coated in a thick layer of visual grain and distortion. His face is young but weary, a juxtaposition shared by many of the veterans in the chapel. This is a CRT TV displaying an analog video recording on magnetic tape, so the picture's relative lack of clarity obscures some of the finer features of the subject's face—except for the scar. The scar along his right cheek is clear.

The screen flickers. A band of vibrating white distortion descends the screen. Perhaps this is a copy of a copy recorded off some static-ridden, pirate broadcast late at night, when the transmissions get weird and wild, and anything can happen during those desperate witching hours.

The only sound coming from the speakers is muted,

warbling music. But then that soft, droning melody is subsumed by the grating metal-on-metal sound of a heavy door opening on dry hinges.

Enter two figures wearing stark-white hazmat suits, tall and imposing, whose footsteps land in the small room with reverb-laden echoes. They are explorers entering a subterranean tomb. Their faces are hidden behind rectangular glass viewports on their hoods, revealing nothing but dark reflections.

Panic spikes across the young man's face. The hazmat weirdos shuffle to either side, laying hands on his arms. He's screaming now, shouting out indecipherable terror-gibberish. Semi-melodic synthesizer notes of the warped soundtrack hold on several beats too long, like the tape's been warped by heat or cosmic radiation. This gives way to the subtle rhythm of a military drumline and horns playing at something like Taps, but likewise distorted and melancholy.

A third figure in a white hazmat suit approaches from the edge of the frame, wielding a heavy gauge syringe, light glimmering from the silver-grey liquid dripping from its point and sloshing within its clear glass barrel housing.

The young man in the chair screams and struggles, but the others hold him down. The syringe punctures the skin on the patient's left arm, sending a jet of blood to spatter across those otherwise pristine white protective suits. The patient's face falls from fearful rage to a flat, neutral look; his eyes grow heavy and his breathing becomes shallow.

He then offers a smile—deadened by some sort of narcotic rush—and his tears flow freely as his muscles relax. Those in the hazmat suits turn to follow the patient's dead gaze up to the camera perched overhead. Three darkened face shields and one stupefied face acknowledging the audience, finally. They all offer *thumbs-up*, even the patient, although his wrist is held in place by one of the unyielding straps. A happy ending after all.

They hold their pose in eerie tableau, creating the illusion that the video is lingering on a freeze-frame, but the slight wavering of their limbs and the patient's occasional blinks indicate otherwise. The moment stretches on and on, and the audience of such a video might be left wondering just what, exactly, this is all about.

How does this make you feel? Dr. Glasse asks, speaking over an intercom from another room, voice projected from speakers hidden somewhere high in the rafters of the chapel. *Do you believe that that patient represents you, as military veterans? Do you feel a special kinship with him? What about the people in the encounter suits? Do they strike you as medical staff, or might they be something else entirely? Perhaps you want to be the one driving needles into open veins. Perhaps you are satisfied with simply being the one watching the video, safely removed from the events unfolding on screen.*

There is confusion in the audience, of course, but some are scribbling down thoughts in their notebooks, being good sports about this whole thing, or maybe just scrawling a series of question marks then underlining or circling them.

The image on screen drops to darkness in waves of retreating light. This is no editing trick—the lights in the room on screen have gone out. But illumination returns, gradually, like a dimmer switch slowly being turned back up, casting the room and the figures in a dull glow that in any other context may have been calming or pleasant. Blue. Blue light, coming from a video that was, until just moments ago, in black and white. Wasn't it?

The light is coming from the patient. The audience can see him clearly now, despite the dark, because that blue glow suffuses his skeletal structure, revealing the revenant within the folds of his muscles and flesh, his skull grinning through. Those bones are straining against the restraints again, but this time, the people in the hazmat suits are helping them break free, loosening straps of leather and releasing metal clips, guided by the ever-growing blue light emanating from beneath strata of pulsing, living tissue.

The light reflects across the hazmat suits' face shields, creating mirror images of the glowing skull. Several faces of grim, radioactive death. He rises, glowing bones going airborne, limbs stretching outwards like the branches of a plant reaching for sunlight, torso pulled toward the top of the frame. The handlers back away, heads bowed low in supplication, hands coming together and apart again like the ritualistic motions of prayer.

The glowing-skeleton-within hovers in the center of the frame, arms and legs in a great X, da Vinci's Vitruvian Man writ in irradiated marrow and transparent flesh.

VIDEO #2

The screen went black. The lights came up in the chapel. Short bursts of tepid air flowed through grime-encrusted ducts.

Ray rubbed at his temples. Dizziness washed over him. He was glad he was sitting down, because the room and his body felt distant, his mind sluggish, his vision blurry.

The uniformed cadre were in front of the TV/VCR set now, swapping out tapes. Ray looked over at Mike, who returned his glance with a *what the fuck* expression.

Dr. Glasse spoke through hidden speakers once again, her voice tinged with static. "Record your thoughts, feelings, and questions in your notebooks. Let us save discussion for the end."

Ray started to jot a few things down:

Patient in cell – VETERAN???

PRISON or research center?

Hazmat suits or "encounter suits" – encounter what?

Feels like waking up from a dream too fast.

"We have one more video to watch for today's session," Glasse said. "Please be sure to start a new section of notes for this viewing. Your responses will help inform your course of treatment."

The VCR whirred and struggled, unseen mechanisms clicking and winding tape. The cassette had given it indigestion. The screen cycled from blue to grey static, then to a hazy, pitch-black wash as the tape started to roll.

The lights clicked off. Ray wanted to run, to put this place and the images that were to come far behind him, before whatever information was stored on that tape copied itself onto the physical structures of his brain.

The first images emerged from the analog past, laden with distortion and static.

The camera is set above the front door of an old house, elevated to capture the front porch, the stairs leading up to it, and the street beyond. More houses stand nearby, all crooked siding and chipped paint, built along the sloping contours of a great hill, the neighborhood's sidewalks and streets laid at odd angles. Trees sway with a smattering of leaves clinging to branches tossed by wind that barely registers on the audio track. From somewhere behind the camera, the porch light flickers on, spilling a pale, yellow glow to hold back the encroaching night. There is a mild hum of static on the audio track, punctuated by soft, distant *pops*. A quick succession of grainy, black and white shots follow:

An attic, cloaked in heavy darkness. A lone, circular glass window lets in the last few moments of failing light to reveal cylindrical shapes arrayed in a rough circle along the floor. Candles.

A hallway leading to what is presumably the front door, likewise falling to shadow.

A living room, home to a disused fireplace and old, fraying furniture, framed by a curved staircase on the far wall that leads upstairs.

A basement, home to the laundry machine and dryer, set against concrete blocks riddled with cobwebs.

An exterior shot of the narrow side yard, which leads up to a set of uneven, thin red oak trees that have shed most of their crimson leaves and dead branches.

The backyard, where the camera is set over wooden stairs leading down into the overgrown grass. A metal fire pit stands flanked by folding lawn chairs in disordered formation. More trees beyond, blanketed by shadows that twist and move. Maybe the wind flowing through the weeds and branches, maybe analog distortion in the deep black. Maybe something else.

Back inside the house: a kitchen, the camera set across from the sink and the dark window above. Dirty dishes sit on the counter and are piled high in one of the sink basins. The refrigerator stands on the left side of the frame, humming. A man stands up from behind its open door then steps back, beer in hand. Rubber-plastic crunch of the fridge door closing, the shuffling of feet along the linoleum floor, the hiss of release as he twists off the bottle cap. His ear is pressed into a rectangular cell phone perched on his shoulder.

"I'm just about to check that. All set up. Yeah." He turns to face the camera, eyes drifting across the lens, breaking the unspoken contract made between viewer and subject in works of fiction. But maybe there is no fourth wall here. Maybe this isn't staged.

The man is of average height, his build a little on the heavy side. The gut sticking out indicates that he's had quite a few of those beers lately. Face unshaven, hair in the early stages of a pathetic beard. Black hair along his head is matted or sticking up at odd angles, like he just woke up from a nap. This is a man who has not been taking care of himself.

He raises his bottle toward the camera in mock salute, then turns away and walks out of the kitchen, only to appear in the shot of the darkened hallway, walking toward the front door, his footsteps accompanied by the creaking of floorboards.

"Did you read that pamphlet I sent you? Yeah.

'Night Trains.' Keeps me up at night. Real black budget operations. Moving nuclear waste through exurban and rural communities. Downed UFO parts and exotic metals ferried to underground mountain labs for study, like Bob Lazar. No, I haven't tried to phase through the walls yet, I'm working my way up to it. But what I was thinking about recently is how the entities can materialize in closets or dark corners. Do you think that's where the 'monster under the bed' thing comes from? Kids know that, instinctually, the creatures can only appear in the dark places. The recesses of the human world. It's like our brains map our living spaces and categorize them into *light* and *dark*, and if it's in the *dark* space, the n-zone, the entities can manifest there. They just need to get the tip of one of their claws in, then they can pull themselves into our world. The human brain's perception of reality has something to do with it. Yes, I'll hold."

He stands by the front door, his form a shadow, his head bobbing in the light streaming in from the glass window panes. For long, awkward stretches of tape and time he says nothing, occasionally shuffling his feet to get a different angle to see what lies beyond the front porch. The audio track picks up the settling and creaking of the old house, encouraged by a patient, soft wind that underpins these images, low moans almost lost to the hum of interference and static generated by the camera and its mysterious energies.

Cut to the camera set above the front door: the porch, the street, the houses nearby, lights in their windows—lights flickering out, one by one. A tree's branches shimmer and dance. No cars. No people. The buzzing porchlight struggles against the vigorous dark, dimming, failing, going low and weak.

Back in the living room. The walls and thin windows

rattle. A plume of dust emerges from the fireplace.

From the front hall, the man's voice:

"Yeah, I'm still here. You're just in time. It's starting to happen, I think. Getting dark, fast. Lights are acting weird. Vibes are bad. If I were to take some cannabis, I bet my mind would be receiving the signals, loud and clear."

Footsteps on groaning floorboards. The wind, growing impatient, sends finger-like tree branches to *rap* against the windows.

The man walks through the frame, left to right. The sound of a door opening, unoiled hinges squealing. The flipping of a light switch.

Cut to the basement camera, the area now illuminated by bulbs hanging from the open ceiling. Coronas of light. Halos. The man descends halfway down the rickety staircase and pauses at the window to look out into the dark.

"Hold on."

The audio track pops and hisses. Indistinct, swirling faces appear in the texture of the image, then are gone again, just as quickly. Maybe this tape has been recorded over several times, its ghosts trapped in eternal recurrence, desperate to be seen.

He turns away from the window.

"I just think the city should do something about it. Well, you keep taking my calls, yeah? I mean they *can* send out a cruiser, but I don't think the cops are going to do anything about this. Last time they were here they gave me a ticket for expired car registration." He turns to look back out the window.

"Okay." His voice shakes. "I think they're here, now."

He scrambles back up the stairs, flips the switch to send the basement back into darkness, and shuts the door. His voice is barely audible through the layers of floor above. Footfalls *thump-thump-thumping* above the camera. Twin red glimmers appear in the window, just bright enough to be seen before the shot ends and we shift to the camera set in the side yard.

A floodlight sizzles to life, revealing overgrown grass and the withered trees beyond. There's movement among those crooked sentinels, but it's probably just branches moving in the wind, or rabbits or squirrels scampering in the dark. Probably.

Cut to the backyard: floodlight clicking on, audibly, coughing up yellow light. There are footfalls on the audio track, and a muffled voice coming from beneath and behind the camera. The thin, white back door opens. The man pokes his head outside and takes a furtive step onto the wooden stairs.

Action in the upper portion of the screen draws the eye away, beyond the fire pit, to the dark of the trees beyond. Movement. Not of the wind-shook trees and overgrown weeds, but of long, pale limbs retracting suddenly into the cover of branches and bush.

"Jesus Christ!" the man says, stepping back, disappearing from the frame.

The wind picks up and lines of distortion arc along the screen. A flashlight beam sweeps across the yard, illuminating the firepit, reflecting off of the metal of the scattered lawn chairs. The beam crawls over to the trees in the dark, its strength dissipating over the distance. The beam reaches the tree line, revealing twin red glimmers. Eyes in the dark, reflecting, watching.

The flashlight beam clicks off. The man curses and slams the door shut. Locks slide and click into place. He's shouting into the phone now, stomping away from the door.

The floodlight flickers, then dies. There's just

enough ambient light to discern movement as grey forms emerge to shamble toward the house.

The kitchen. The man runs through the house, somewhere close by, his voice assuming a mantle of panic.

"...at least three or four of them out there. I need you to start the resonance ritual. I'm going to—will you listen to me? I'm going to start it on this end, hopefully we're not too late."

Just before the shot cuts to the hallway, there's a flash of movement seen through the window over the kitchen sink: a flapping of heavy, grey wings, a flash of red eyes, and a trailing afterglow.

In the hallway. The man reaches the front door just in time to see the porch light die. The house groans and creaks as if its old wooden skeleton is trapped in the long stretches of a cold winter night. He dashes into the living room, where the camera reveals the overhead lights are failing here, too. He clambers up the staircase, failing to notice the displaced ash piled up around the edge of the fireplace and the odd footprints within.

Cut to the attic, with its low A-frame ceiling. Errant illumination from the flashlight dances around the room, accompanied by heavy, labored breathing.

The man emerges in the frame from the right side, walking with his head bowed to avoid the exposed support beams and cobwebs of the low ceiling. He holds his cell phone high to reveal a stark-white pentagram drawn in white powder across the floor. The outer circle's diameter is several feet across, large enough within its circumference to hold the angular lines of a crooked star, a candle set at each of its five points. The man is cautious as he steps over the salt lines that compose the symbol, careful not to disturb or break them.

He sets the cell phone down, its screen casting blue light from below to illuminate his face, and he picks up a book of matches. He proceeds to light the thick, fleshy candles, one after another, the striking of matches and the rush of fire hypnotic in its rhythm. The flames are rail-thin and stand several inches high, offering a view of the limits of the room in flickering inconsistency. Wavering shadows, disturbed dust, old wood.

Sometimes, there are faces.

The attic window goes dark, the early evening moonlight suddenly occluded by shadow. He doesn't seem to notice. He grabs a blue container of salt and kneels down, carefully reinforcing the pentagram formation, repairing breaks, strengthening lines, securing intersections. It's important that he gets this *right*.

Lines of distortion and electronic interference crawl up the screen, accompanied by strange noises emerging over the low-static hum of the audio track: voices, almost, whispering at the edges of distortion, speaking in clipped sentences in an unnatural, arrhythmic cadence:

...dead stars collect the psychic detritus of the endless mausoleum of history...

...always wanting for the heart of God, content instead to consume the souls of men...

...Goblin boys and gargoyle discourse...

...all of us lost in endless woods with knives for welcome...

The man finishes reinforcing the pentagram. The flames of the candles are taller than ever, revealing more and more of the room's limits, which are beginning to give way to the crawl of molecular chaos, the wood of the sloped roof and walls fading and becoming immaterial. Beyond the limits of the dissipating veneer of material reality is a field of dreadful stars, points of light that are caustic and nauseating, sunspots of decay like burning afterimages. The voices on the audio track grow even more distorted, their nuggets of transgressive wisdom unintelligible. Synthesized words ground into a cataclysm of sputtering cosmic despair.

The attic—the whole house—begins to shake.

He steps into the center of the pentagram, fearful that the formation isn't perfect, that it isn't exactly the correct dimensions required to channel the protective energies necessary. But time is short. He tosses the cylinder of salt over his right shoulder, where it disappears into the blue-black vortex of deep space appearing behind him, swallowed up by limitless darkness, punctured by the serrated light of diseased stars.

The shaking of the house jars the camera loose, dropping it down an inch and changing its angle by several degrees. A beam of light pierces the dark, fixing him in place. He closes his eyes. The light blinks out. The camera's autofocus feature struggles to recapture a clear image.

The man floats above the pentagram, suspended some small distance in the air, his toes stretching out to touch the floor but separated by impossible inches. His face is stark-white and flat, illuminated from below by the candlelight, the flames tall and menacing. Static and distortion crash in around this uncanny, flickering image, the camera damaged or the recorded data corrupted.

A handful of frames emerge from this degradation:

The man floating above the pentagram, his face twisting into a mask of morose terror, his hands grasping at his own throat.

Arms reach for him from the portal, from the ceiling,

from behind the camera, from all sides of the frame.

Another burst of brilliant white light, chasing away all darkness in a singular moment, revealing a floating blue-light skeleton hologram, jaw hanging open in a silent scream, grasped and groped by arms that dissipate into tendrils of pulsing white smoke.

The winding, near-silence of lo-fi background static.

The creaking and settling of an old house.

The wind, soft and calm.

Cycling through each shot, revealing an empty house, empty basement, empty yards, and empty attic, save for a ring of candles set around a smeared salt pentagram and extinguished candles.

The final shot: an empty porch set above a sloped street. Dark houses in the near distance, lights flickering back to life.

THE SLAUGHTERHOUSE HALLWAY

"Thank you for joining me here," Dr. Glasse said, smiling as she leaned back in an office chair behind her wide, expansive desk. Ray, Mike, and Terra sat across from her. "I am meeting with small groups to get a direct, personal sense of your progress."

She tapped the end of her pen against the old wood of her desk. The room's only window stretched tall along the outer wall, almost to the limit of the high ceiling, but the office remained dim and harried by shadows, save for the soft light emanating from a pair of standing lamps set on either side of her desk, like ceremonial torches flanking an altar.

"How long have you been in this office, Doc?" Ray asked. "Looks like a real nice place, not like the barns they've got us bedding down in."

"I consider this a long-term assignment. I took the liberty of moving most of my professional library here." She gestured at the tomes arrayed on the old wooden shelves behind her. "I'm not looking to run back off to the academy any time soon. Besides, I enjoy the outdoor life this deep in the mountains. Fewer people crowding the hiking trails, smaller crowds." She paused, then pointed to Mike and Terra, who sat to either side of Ray. "You three are friendly with one another, right? Fast friends, or just tolerable acquaintances under unusual circumstances?"

"We've only known each other for a few days," Ray said. "But we get along. Mike's alright. For an officer."

"Offense noted and taken without further comment," Mike said. He pointed a long finger at Ray. "This one's a smart-ass, but I've had worse company over Army coffee, post-PT. And Terra is a good troop. I know we're supposed to be miscreants and fuck-ups and we've only been together shy of a week, but I've enjoyed getting to know the others here. It's been a while since I was around this many vets, not counting the awkwardness of a VA waiting room."

"That's why I selected you for this small-group session," Glasse said. She turned her attention to Terra.

"Ms. Morales?"

"Yes, sorry, Doc."

"Sorry for what?"

"I'm just used to reflexively apologizing for anything. Habit from the military."

"Even when something isn't your fault?"

"Everything is your fault in the Army," Terra said, "or so I was told, anyway."

"I understand," Glasse said. "Maintaining your focus in a stressful environment can be difficult. What drew your attention?"

Terra shuffled her feet for a moment. Her hands gripped her notebook.

"What kind of psych books are those?" She nodded toward the shelf over Glasse's right shoulder. Nestled among the dust jackets and bare spines of academic journals, reference texts, and a handful of university press-run books with Glasse's name on the spine, were three books of uneven size, color, and material.

"*A Grimoire of Dark Magic as Revealed by the Lesser Swamp Gods of Little Dixie*," Glasse said, pointing at the oversized black book nearest her, "*Malthus Para-Astrophysics and Temporal Studies Research Center Annual, July 2009*," she said, pointing at the baby blue volume in the middle, "and the prize of my collection: a rare first edition of *The Crypt of Blood* by Countess Blair Oscar Wilflame, printed in Dublin in the 19th century."

"Strange books for a psychologist," Terra said.

"Not so strange for an industrial-organization psychologist," Dr. Glasse said. She leaned forward, folding her hands together on her desk. "As much as I'd like to talk rare books, our time together today is limited. Captain Dodonna, I'd like to start with you."

"Yes, Doctor."

"I understand you've been having trouble sleeping since you arrived."

"You do? I haven't told anyone."

"Haven't you?" she said.

Mike shook his head, then gave Ray a quick, puzzled look. Ray shook his head, *no, wasn't me.*

"But you are experiencing sleeping issues, correct? Would you mind talking about it?"

"Sometimes I have trouble sleeping, yeah. Having kids helps, because I'm so damn tired all the time. That, and I'm older than I used to be. Funny how that works. Been taking CBD chocolate. They got the taste right now, you know? Not like it was back at the start of legalization, when everything tasted like lawnmower trimmings. Never thought I'd be into weed. But it helps me sleep most of the time."

"Never thought things would turn out how they did in a lot of ways, huh?" Terra said.

Mike nodded.

"If you're tired—and, let's say, *mature*, not *old*—why can't you sleep sometimes?" Glasse said, getting him back on track.

"I just get to thinking," Mike said, hands floating in front of his face, palms facing one another, fingers outstretched but not quite touching. "Like, I'm going to die soon. And no, I don't feel like I'm in danger, and no, my personal firearms are not a threat to myself or my family. I mean, I get this sense of doom. The oblivion of non-existence. Rushing towards me. Like a flood. Whether it's next week or next decade. A part of me, deep within, just starts *howling*. Because death is coming. I'm about to tumble over the brink. Into the abyss. I'm going to close my eyes, and open them, and I'm old or sick with lung cancer from the burn pits, holed up in a VA hospital somewhere, years from now. Something like that. It's always with me lately. A lingering presence of death."

Ray and Terra shuffled their feet. Glasse tapped her pen against the desk, keeping time.

"I see," she said, finally, moving the pen back to a yellow legal pad to scribble some notes. "I want to hear from Terra and Ray on this subject. Do either of you ever experience anything like this 'lingering presence of death?'"

Terra nodded. Ray stared at those strange books on the shelf, seeing them, but not really seeing them. They lodged themselves into his brain, into what would become his memories and impressions of this moment.

"Yeah, I do," Terra said. "More when I wake up in the middle of the night, though. It's like my brain just goes into overdrive at the last minute when I'm trying to sleep, and it won't let up."

Ray nodded. Mike snapped his fingers.

"Exactly," Mike said. "So, if I do fall asleep, and sometimes that's hard because my brain just conjures all this bullshit that stresses me out, but when I do fall asleep, it's like my brain just flips a switch and all that anxiety about death comes flooding back in."

"I want to point out that both Ray and Terra indicated they can relate to these experiences," Glasse said. "Mike, you're not on your own here. Did anything traumatic happen to you while you were overseas? Or, of equal importance, has anything traumatic happened to you while you were stateside, either before or after your wartime service? Trauma is trauma, not limited by the context of deployment. We treat the whole person here."

Mike leaned back and pressed his fingers together, forming a steeple in front of his lips.

"I was company XO on my second tour. We lost one soldier, and three others had to be MEDEVAC'd out of the country. I was on one of the patrols, but not near the MRAP vehicle that got flipped and torched. Saw some blood, nothing serious. But I had to help file the paperwork. I knew the men and women injured. Knew the man who got killed. Ours was a good unit, lot of cohesion, personal connections. Can't say the same for all the units I served in. But this one was solid."

"Being exposed to death and dismemberment is traumatic, even if it is secondhand," Glasse said. "I've been working with the military long enough to know that servicemembers attempt to project themselves as impervious to pain, to sadness, to fear. But the fact is that one thing, one incident, can stick with you. One thing—or a dozen things, big or small—become something you carry. Dead weight in your memory, dragging you down."

"That's the thing," Mike said. "Normally I don't even really think about those times. But at night, when my brain shakes me out of a dead sleep... I have an image, a scene in my head. I'm seeing myself from behind. I'm walking down a metal hallway—big sheet metal walls bolted into place. Rust at the edges. Smells like metal and blood. The hallway is uneven, like it was slapped together. I start to lose my sense of balance, because I can't get a grasp of the geometry of the space, and maybe because the hallway is *moving*, like, shaking me loose, so I'll tumble toward the other end. There's a big metal door there, which I don't want to reach, but there's no other choice. Gravity is pulling me towards it. I'm trying to keep my balance but I keep falling over, sliding against the floor, against the walls.

"The door slides back, and it's bright in there, like heat lamps in a chicken coop, amber-red light. And I can see metal. Buzzsaws, starting to spin, to spit up blood and sparks. I'm going to tumble head-first into them. And there's nothing I can do about it. I think that outside those metal walls, far away, there are people that I care about. Places I've been. Places I want to go. But that world is closed off to me. It's over. I've wasted what little time I had left. There's only the fall. Only the door sliding back. Only death waiting for me at the end of that hallway. That's what I see. That's what I think about."

The wind whispered along the edges of the great window, seeking entry through unyielding glass and brick. Voices murmured through the walls, emanating from elsewhere in the building.

"Christ, that's spooky," Terra said suddenly.

"Yeah, no shit," Ray said.

"Sorry," Mike said.

"No, it's good to hear I'm not the only one who is fucked up," Terra said.

"Yeah, man," Ray said. "Keep going."

"It's entirely reasonable to be afraid of death," Glasse said. "Our species is unique in that we're aware of our own mortality. Sometimes that spurs us to action, to live life to the fullest. Sometimes it cripples us with anxiety and makes the time that we do have less pleasant, or perhaps even unbearable to the point of generating self-destructive behaviors, even a death drive. But I can assure you, Mike—assure all of you— that we are safe, here. We're far from the dangers and distractions of your lives beyond Camp Winter Falcon, or of the wars. We're in a place where our number one priority is the safety and treatment of our patients. As we explore these difficult topics, please keep that in mind."

"But that's not entirely true," Ray said.

Glasse waited before responding. Was that annoyance passing over her face?

"What do you mean, Raymond?"

He held his hands together and shifted in his seat, leaning forward to rest his palms on the edge of her desk.

"We're not safe here."

The words echoed around the edges of the room, like a voice calling a sleeping person back to the waking world.

"What do you mean?"

"A friend of mine," Ray said. "From one of my dead-end jobs. Grocery store. Knew her for years. She started working there out of high school, saving up money for college with shifts as a cashier. I guess she never found her way to school, because she was going on five or six years there when I started. Anyway, we became friends. Kept in touch, even after I bailed, or got fired, or whatever happened. Always took time to catch up, maybe once a year, twice a year, we'd have these good phone calls where we just talked about our lives, you know? Except one year I miss the call, because I'm busy or whatever. Drinking, mostly, I don't really want to hear a friendly voice, too busy chasing my tail, feeling depressive, whatever my problem was, take your pick.

"So, it's a few months later. You know how when you're drinking a lot, time gets kind of weird? Like, three or four months can drift by, all at once, all of a sudden?"

Glasse shook her head, *no*, but Terra chimed in with

an enthusiastic *yes*.

"So, I call her a few months later. I send her a few emails. Get a reply back from her sister. Brain aneurysm." Ray snapped his fingers. "Just like that. Dead. Not like she was unhealthy or anything. Liked to exercise, didn't eat meat. Sure, she drank, but I didn't know anyone our age who didn't."

Ray went quiet, his gaze drifting back up to those oddly shaped books, sticking out from the shelves of medical texts like a pre-cancerous growth.

"What I'm saying is that you can't promise us that we're safe right now. Because we're not. Not really. Mike's slaughterhouse tunnel—we're all in it, all the time. We're always tumbling toward those buzzsaws."

Glasse leaned back, her teeth moving behind closed lips, considering her next words carefully.

"Do you think about dying often? Do you have your own version of the slaughterhouse?"

Ray considered this. He closed his eyes. The images of those books lingered, ghosts drifting over his retinas.

"No, but I know what Mike's getting at," Ray said. "It's just that he's brave enough to acknowledge it."

"'Brave' has nothing to do with it," Mike said, laughing. "Wish it wouldn't crop up when I'm trying to get some damn sleep."

"Is that why you drink?" Glasse said. "Is that why you, any of you, use drugs or alcohol?"

Ray breathed in, slow and hard.

"I guess it's all on the table here, huh?"

"It is," Glasse said. "Time is short, and you're low on opportunities to get well. That's why you're here."

Ray nodded.

"I think... I think there's something wrong with my brain," he said. "Like, medically speaking, some sort of imbalance or whatever. The Army didn't cause it, but it certainly didn't help the goddamn situation." He looked at Mike and Terra, who nodded, encouraging him to continue. "I'm paranoid, anxious, insecure, always sure that I'm a failure and everyone knows it. My deployment confirmed what I always suspected: life's cheap. People don't give a shit. The big institutions we've created to protect us don't care about anything beyond themselves. I knew the Army could use people up, but I didn't think it would just... you know, *waste* your life or your body for some officer's PowerPoint slide. 'We did X number of patrols, which accomplished jack-shit except get a bunch of soldiers killed. Promote ahead of peers.' When I pointed out that we were just doing the same patrols over and over, talking to people who weren't listening to us, giving money and guns to people who kept losing it or giving it to the enemy, the officers just said, 'you don't see the bigger picture.' Then I came home, and I tried to talk about what was going on—the waste, the fraud, the death—and I heard the same thing. 'You don't see the bigger picture.' Do you know what that's like? Trying to talk to your friends and family, and they just tell you that you're wrong about what you just experienced? All the hard work and the missed opportunities and the injuries and the death, all the horror, because some staff pukes in the Green Zone decided your life was less valuable than one more pointless combat patrol to mention on a PowerPoint slide. I think I'm depressed *because* I see the bigger picture."

"There is a certain streak of nihilistic thought that can be appealing to a person who is suffering from depression," Glasse said. "Do you feel that life has any meaning at all?"

"Sometimes," Ray said.

"What about right now? In this room, with these

people? With this program?"

Ray considered the question for a moment.

"I'm not sure. I'm giving this a chance."

"Giving this program a chance is all we're asking of you," Glasse said, smiling her warm smile, but slipping in a glance at her wristwatch. "Thank you for sharing, Raymond. Terra, we haven't heard much from you. Your perspective is important to me. To us."

"You work with a lot of soldiers, right?" Terra asked.

"It's been the focus of my career."

"You work with a lot of women?"

"Proportionally, they make up a much smaller segment of the servicemember and veteran population, but yes, I do. In fact, I make it a point to include them in my research."

"What's it like being a woman doctor?"

Glasse shrugged.

"I enjoy my career, I've found success in my field, I get to pursue the research I'm interested in. What's the real question you want to ask?"

"Do you know what it's like being a woman soldier?"

"No, I don't, no more than I know what it's like being a man who is a soldier. If you would prefer, Terra, I could assign you to an all-female group. Would that be helpful to you? I want our patients to feel comfortable as we tackle these difficult topics."

"No, these guys are alright," Terra said. "So far, anyway. But being a female in the military—that's a whole *thing*, right? You gotta laugh off harassment, flirting, remarks about your body. And I know the guys have to put up with a lot of shit, too. One of the dirty little secrets about our proud-fucking-military is how much it relies on hazing, physical and mental intimidation. There's a difference between humiliation and discipline, but most of the NCOs I've worked with certainly didn't know the difference. But it's on another level when you're a woman."

"I am familiar with the unique challenges women in the military face, yes," Glasse said. "I can cite the statistics on mental health issues, and on the greater likelihood of female veterans to suffer assaults, rapes, murders, or disappearances. I know that they are underrepresented in senior NCO and officer positions, especially at the levels where policy and doctrine are generated. But no, I can't claim to directly understand your lived experience, even if I might have a better perspective than the average American."

"Sorry, you guys," Terra said.

"This is what we're here for," Mike said. "We got your six. Say your piece."

"So, you've got the baseline military stress that everybody deals with, most of it really unnecessary, right?" Terra continued, not missing a beat. "But then add to that officers or NCOs or whoever getting kind of handsy, maybe not all the time, but often enough to keep you on edge and alert. Then you got assholes telling you that maybe you made rank because of a diversity requirement, not because you aced your PT test or rifle qualification. Then head downrange, where it's even less safe, less regulated than your average military post—which is bad as is—and now you've got this, like, scent of death hanging over everything. Maybe the casualties are in your unit, or maybe they are in the units to your left and right, and you gotta think about that. You gotta think about the troop you used to see at the gym working out a couple times a week, they don't got legs now, or half their brain got sprayed across the roof of their Humvee. And pretty soon, you might not have legs or brains, either. That's assuming that you're not left for dead out there on some road because the convoy commander ordered a retreat, leaving your overturned vehicle behind, while the Taliban fighters crawl up to your position. You'll be lucky if you're bleeding out at that point, because you don't want to know what they do to captured soldiers, let alone *female* soldiers. *'I will never leave a fallen comrade.'* What a fucking joke."

Terra looked out the window, not wanting the others to see the tears gathering at the edges of her eyes.

"I made it out, and so did all my friends. Doesn't mean I don't wake up in the middle of the night soaked in sweat. Doesn't mean I don't snap awake, lunging to turn on the light, because I don't know where I am. I don't know whether I'm in my apartment in Colorado Springs or if I'm downrange five years ago, getting up early to go on a convoy mission that'll cost someone their eyesight or their fucking life."

Glasse set her pen and notepad down, giving Terra her full attention.

"Sometimes, I'm dog-ass tired, but I can't sleep because my brain is going a thousand miles a minute," Terra said. "It's like Mike said. I lie down and it's like, here's a documentary on all the embarrassing and painful shit you did years ago. Remember how you drink too much? Remember that person who loved you, and you hurt them? That maybe it was *you* who deserved to get blown the fuck up, that maybe it was *you* who should be dead or scraped back together in some VA hospital somewhere, living out the rest of your life in constant pain. Love being trapped by my own brain, which thinks I'm the worst person on earth."

"You are not the worst person on earth," Glasse said. "None of you are. You are all valuable, to yourselves and others."

"I certainly don't like who I am, who I've become,"

Terra said.

Glasse nodded, letting the words hang, letting the wind have its say by softly rattling the window.

"The key is to acknowledge your past, not to bury it, but also not to let it dominate your present or determine your future. Learn what you can from your mistakes and live the way you want to live going forward. Find a purpose again. That is what we hope you will find during our short time together. Purpose. Does that make sense?"

"That's easy for you to say," Terra said. "You're a doctor, a professional. You've made the right choices. I'm a fuck-up at an Army retreat for basket cases, seeing ghosts and living in fear of the demons in my brain." She tapped her right temple.

Glasse's eyes narrowed.

"What do you mean, 'ghosts?'"

Terra stole a quick glance at Ray.

"Nothing."

Glasse checked her watch.

"We have about ten minutes left in our session, which has produced some excellent conversations. I want to thank the three of you for your willingness to be vulnerable, to examine the pain, to bring it up among your peers, especially considering you haven't known each other that long."

Mike nodded. Terra wiped at her eyes, trying to find something interesting to see out the window.

"Can we talk about those videos?" Ray said.

Glasse almost let a smile slip. Almost.

"We can talk about whatever you want in the time remaining."

"Why do we got to wait until the end to talk about the videos?"

Mike and Terra shifted in their seats.

"I'll turn that question back to you," Glasse said. "Why wait until the end of the session to bring them up?"

Ray hesitated, considering her response.

"Didn't seem appropriate."

"Why not?"

"Not sure."

"Has someone here at the program dissuaded you from discussing them?"

"No."

"Quite the opposite, in fact, correct?" Glasse said. "I asked you to take notes, to reflect on the feelings conjured by the images on those tapes."

"Okay," Ray said, holding up his hands. "Sorry."

"No apologies necessary, but I want you to understand that we are not in the business of repression. Is it possible that your hesitancy to bring up what we saw on those videos stems from some cultural taboo? Perhaps you have biases and beliefs that prevent you from discussing the high strange."

"The what?"

"The *high strange*," Glasse repeated. "Paranormal, Fortean, the supernatural. A confluence of non-normative events that defy rational, mundane, or material explanations. What I meant to say was, do you think your reluctance to discuss what you saw on those tapes and how they made you feel is because of our cultural stigma against acknowledging high strange phenomena?" Glasse leaned forward, eyes locked on Ray's, not letting go. "Have you experienced events similar to or somehow resonant with those of the tapes? Are you too afraid to discuss those experiences because of the social pressure to discount their validity? *Your* validity?"

"I don't know," Ray said, feeling off-balance. He

looked to the window, suddenly wanting to throw his chair through it and make his escape, to run out of this office as fast as possible. "I feel like there might be something there, but I can't grasp it."

"What about the rest of you?" Glasse said. "Are you beginning to remember, or allow yourselves to remember?"

"It's just—I can't figure out why you'd show us something like that," Ray said, finally. "Like, okay, this session is good, group therapy or whatever, shared trauma, show us we're not alone. I get that. But that stuff you showed us earlier. Medical experiment footage meets *The Blair Witch Project*. What the hell."

"Our methods are unorthodox," Glasse said. "But I can assure you that everything we are doing has very clear and definitive goals. What you will experience here—the skills you will develop, the progress you will make—will have long-lasting impacts. I just need you to trust the program. To trust me."

"It's not just the videos," Mike said. "What was with that weird-ass psych eval on the computer?"

"That was a highly refined diagnostic tool, one critical to our efforts here at the reintegration program," Glasse said.

"This place is haunted, isn't it?" Terra said.

"The ghosts you mentioned," Glasse said. "Is that what you mean?"

Terra shot a look at Ray, like, *are you gonna back me up here?*

"This place is kind of spooky, right?" she said, when Ray said nothing. "I don't think it's an accident you showed us those videos and asked us those questions about entities and paranormal stuff."

"No part of this program or what you experience here is an accident, no," Glasse said.

"It's a little weird, Doc," Mike said. "Off-putting. I'm a Christian man. I don't like this spooky stuff. Never even liked Halloween much."

Dr. Glasse clicked her pen, took her notepad back in hand.

"What *have* you seen here? I am putting the question to all of you. I cannot ask anything more specific, because I do not want to influence your response. If you want to talk about something you saw here, I would very much like to listen."

"People," Terra said, suddenly. "Others. Not members of the cadre or medical staff."

"They were glowing," Ray said. "Like, from *within*. Not carrying headlamps or flashlights or anything."

Glasse remained still, her eyes moving from Terra to Ray and back again.

"And there was something... something in the air, last night, I think," Ray said. "We saw those—glowing people—moving along near the fence line of the camp. I was walking back to the male barracks, and there was a rush of air. Something in the fog above me."

"A bird?"

"Maybe, but that's not the feeling I got."

"What do you mean?"

"Hard to explain," Ray said. "It was like there was a dark presence lingering over my shoulder. When your hair stands up on the back of your neck, that sort of feeling. An electrical charge. It bleeds into how I'm remembering the events. Like I'm going to remember something I don't want to remember."

"I've seen them every night so far," Terra said, her voice flat and quiet. "I've been stepping out, late, to have a smoke. To look for them. They're usually out there, walking in the distance."

"Are you sure they are not Sergeant Major Haaster's

cadre?"

"I'm not sure about anything," Terra said. "But I don't think that's who they are. I've talked to him about it."

"What do you think they are?"

"I don't know."

"You said the word 'ghosts' earlier," Glasse said.

"I know. I feel stupid now for saying that."

"I'm not here to talk you out of anything," Glasse said. "But I need to be careful about how we treat your encounters. I don't want to influence your perceptions and memories, or exert pressure on you to exaggerate or embellish the experiences or phenomena you witness."

"See, you say something cryptic like that, and I can't help but get suspicious about this whole operation," Mike said, pointing at Dr. Glasse. "What 'phenomena,' Doc? I didn't come here to experience *phenomena*. I came here to get my drinking under control and learn how to get a decent night's sleep again. What exactly are we talking about?"

"Now that we are nearing the end of the first evolution, we can start to be more forthcoming with you," Glasse said. "Your honesty is noted and appreciated, especially concerning these encounters."

The doctor closed her eyes for a moment, as if conjuring the right words; as if consulting with the spirits who would tell her what to say next.

"The selection of Camp Winter Falcon as the site of this program was not arbitrary, and neither was your recruitment for it," she said. "You are here because of your trauma, because of your addiction and behavior issues, because of your post-traumatic stress, yes—but there's more to it than that. Tonight, over by the fire pit, we're giving Class Zero-Zero-One a briefing, of sorts, on what to expect from Evolution Two."

"And what can we expect in Evolution Two, Doc?" Mike asked, asking for them all.

Dr. Glasse smiled.

"Are any of you familiar with the concept of extra-sensory perception?"

POSSIBLE SIDE EFFECTS

The dark settled in over Camp Winter Falcon, held in place by a wall of clouds leading a vigorous cold front. A heavy fog rose up from the damp earth to cloak the facility's grounds, reducing visibility to a few hazy yards.

The patients' headlamp beams probed the vaporous, indefinite distance. Sergeant Major Haaster led the loose formation of veteran-patients north, a green glowstick in his left hand serving as a guidon. Three derelict buildings appeared in the murk ahead, a stone fire pit set between them. A grey anchor point in the dark.

Haaster brought them to a quick-time march with a sharp command, then called for a halt.

"You will form a half circle around this side of the fire pit. Medical staff will take command for this exercise. Keep your mouths shut and do as you're told. And keep those dang headlamps turned off, you're gonna blind some poor doctor and their very expensively educated eyeballs. *Fall out!*"

Headlamp beams clicked off, one by one. Figures emerged from the fog, standing in off-set rows just beyond the fire pit. People wrapped in grey fabric and grey fog, faces hidden within the folds of overlarge hoods and shadow. One of them stepped forward, then dropped her hood to reveal the face of Dr. Glasse.

"Let's form a crescent moon shape on your side of the altar," she said, that last word hanging in the air like ash churned up by the wind.

A hand grasped Ray's elbow from behind.

"How many staff and cadre you count since coming here?" Terra said, her voice hushed as the patients spread out in the dark.

"A dozen?" Ray whispered. "Maybe more?"

"There's at least three times that here, now, not including us patients," Terra said.

Torches flickered to life, sputtering and roiling in the creeping fog. Blurry amber light revealed figures wearing ash-grey robes and wielding long candles or torches.

"Maybe they're building up the staff as the program goes on," Ray whispered, hoping his voice didn't carry. "Replacements for soldiers cycling out to new duty stations. Maybe the contractors who run the chow hall, stuff like that."

"Dressed in robes and hanging out in the dark around an altar?" Terra said, hissing the last word. "Something doesn't feel right."

"You're hurting my arm," Ray said.

Terra relaxed her grip, but didn't let go.

"Welcome, falcons," Dr. Glasse said, her voice echoing off the nearby buildings. Faces lit from below drifted in the dark like apparitions summoned for night rituals.

"You've successfully navigated the initial psycho-emotional rigors of Evolution One. Congratulations." Glasse smiled and held up her arms. A sudden geyser of light and flame shot up into the air as the fire pit sprung to life. "From fourteen, you are now twelve," she said. "We're sad to lose any patient from the program, but happy that you have chosen to remain."

"Twelve?" Terra whispered. "There were thirteen of us, I thought, after that dipshit mouthed off and got booted on Day Zero."

"One of the guys in my barracks left," Ray said. "Someone named Nowinski. Left a couple of days ago, I think."

"What happened?"

Ray shrugged, but his gesture was lost in the haze.

Dr. Glasse made an odd, quick gesture with her left hand, and grey-robed specters marched forward to distribute white candles with paper hand guards and small, thin wafers to the assembled patients.

"Just like late-night mass, eh?" Terra said, accepting one of each. The man put a finger to his lips, the upper half of his face hidden behind that grey hood, and kept moving. A woman appeared in his place, carrying a candle of her own, dribbling wax from a stuttering flame. She offered the flaming wick, and soon their candles were alive with a desperate light of their own.

Ray held his candle up to illuminate the small wafer, which was cool and rough between his fingertips. It summoned up a memory of being young and hungry for a snack at his grandparents' house. They had offered him a roll of unblessed communion wafers. They explained that it wasn't the body of Christ, not really, not yet, because it had not undergone the sacrament. Now it never would. So, he could eat them as a snack, yes, and not worry about profaning the body of the risen Christ. Should he ever come across communion wafers in church, however, he must never eat them unless a priest said it was okay. They were dry and the taste was flat. The crackers turned into thick paste that stuck to the roof of his mouth and lingered between his gums and cheeks.

Terra held up her own wafer, the white, circular disk imprinted with an almost illegible pattern, revealed in part by the light from her candle. Numbers.

3 2 2

"The program's efficacy is exceeding our initial models," Glasse said, her words echoing across the space between the buildings as if amplified by unseen speakers. "Not all who started the program will complete it. You've demonstrated integrity, honesty, and a willingness to be brave in the face of intense psychological and emotional work. I thank you for that."

The fire pit before her erupted in another dramatic burst of flame, causing those patients closest to it to back away a half step. Glasse remained unmoved, her face serene, appearing as stone in the dancing flames beneath.

"Would you join me in a small ritual? A breaking of bread, the sharing of a meal. A symbolic act. Symbols are important."

Glasse held up her own wafer, her hands coming together to elevate it above the flames. She waited, patiently and in silence, as the others mirrored her action first, followed soon by the patients. She brought the wafer to her mouth, laying it on her extended tongue. Ray and Terra—along with the others—followed suit. The wafers tasted of salt and ash.

"Evolution One was only the first step," Glasse said. "For Evolutions Two and Three, we must dig deeper. We will excavate the trauma you have spent so much time burying. You are not here just because you are veterans who have failed to re-integrate. You're here because you are special. Because *special things* have happened to you. Things that you are only now beginning to recall. Things that, should you have never come to this place—to this holy soil—would have remained buried and forgotten. And what a loss that would have been for you and for your country."

Flames pressed against the limits of the pit, a beast attempting to escape its cage.

"Together, we will uncover those terrors that have stalked you in misremembered dreams and your shadow-haunted subconscious. We will reconnect you with those forces that even now are present in and among you and bound to the very earth beneath our feet. Forces that continue to shape our lives and the destiny of this country. Forces that, once untapped and rekindled, will shape the destiny of humankind itself."

New flames emerged to join the torches and sputtering candles. Dozens of lights appeared in succession all around them, in the space between the buildings, on their roofs, in the murky depths of the rolling fog enveloping them.

Terra squeezed Ray's elbow again. He didn't flinch. The pain was welcome, grounding, real.

Flames reflected off the silver surface of a mask Glasse brought up to her face. An owl's exaggerated visage: small, sharp ears angled back; a slight beak protruding forward. Eyes wide, black concentric circles absorbing the light of seething fire. She pressed the mask against her face, securing it within the folds of her hood. The gaze of those wide eyes swept across the patients gathered in the fog, pausing only to linger on Ray.

He took a step back. Instinctive. Sweat along his forehead. He tried to keep backing up, but Terra held his arm in place, squeezing hard, *harder*, her mouth hanging open, eyes gone wide and white.

"Magic, true power, means to focus one's force of will, one's thoughts and desires, through the use of psychotropics and authentic ritual to influence and channel the forces at work beneath the superstructure of normative material reality," Glasse said. "Psychotropics like the ones we have just consumed, together."

Ray swallowed hard, imagining the crumbs of the wafer stuck in his throat, trailing down God-knows-what through his esophagus, chemicals absorbed into his bloodstream, too late to spit it up, to cough it out, to opt out of whatever was in store for him next.

Glasse held up her hands, palms wide, fingers pressed together.

"The medication was necessary for this event. You have all been carefully screened and approved for ingestion of the medicine. *Good* medicine. It will begin to take effect shortly and, when it does, I think you will find that it has an agreeable effect. Does anyone have any concerns before we continue?"

"With all due respect, ma'am, but what the hell?" Mike said, stepping forward. "You can't just dose us with something without our consent."

"Captain Dodonna. You may recall the forms you signed upon your application to this program, and subsequent disclosures provided in your intake packet." Glasse paused, letting the flames snap and lick at the air between them. "It was quite explicit: you consented to accept all proscribed forms of treatment, including but not limited to the use of experimental medications and therapies. The possible side effects and risks of said medications were outlined on pages sixty-four through ninety-one."

"That's—I didn't get through all that, I just thought—"

"You *thought* yourself able to trust the qualified, professional, and empathetic medical staff here, yes? You assumed we would have your best interests at heart? That we wouldn't do anything that would bring you to harm?"

"Yes."

"Yes. This is part of your treatment, based on advanced research and the best practices developed and codified by the experts on my team. This gathering, this program. This *place*. I am asking you—asking all of you—to trust yourselves for having made the decision to trust us."

The fire snapped and hissed. Candle flames grew long and hot, reaching like wizened fingers.

"Has anything about my conduct or that of my staff indicated anything less than professionalism and competence?"

Mike thought about her question for a moment.

"You're wearing an owl mask."

Ray wanted to burst out laughing. To point and cackle and dance around the flames. To let the madness of the moment overtake him. He wanted to run off into the dark, away from this place, never to return.

"Yes, I am," Glasse said. "And like the medication administered to you just now, like the course of treatment and therapy you have thus far received, like the staging and presentation of this very carefully considered exercise, everything here has been calculated to elicit positive mental and emotional health outcomes for you and the rest of your cohort. If you wish to withdraw from this event—if any of you are uncomfortable and do not want to see what terrors and wonders come next— our staff will escort you to a safe place where you can rest before your dismissal from the program. I believe we can schedule another bus to return you to Colorado Springs as soon as tomorrow morning."

Mike held his tongue.

"Is that what you want?" Glasse said.

"No. I just—I wish you had told us."

"Would that have changed your decision to take the medication?"

"I don't—you didn't give me the choice."

"Here is your choice, then, Captain Dodonna," Glasse said, religious fervor animating her exaggerated body language and her voice. "A choice for all of you. Participate in this exercise or receive summary dismissal. You are here because traditional forms of treatment have failed. You are here because your substance abuse, depression, anti-social behavior, and trauma have led you here, to this moment. Time is of the essence, now, Captain, for you and your future. For the future of our country."

Glasse looked up to the clouds. They broke in a sudden rush of wind and smoke, revealing the moon hanging low and heavy over the camp. She held up her arms in supplication.

"It begins!"

THE FIRST RESONANCE RITUAL

Mike looked to the other patients, suddenly unsure of himself, realizing how quiet and lonely the whole world had become.

"I'll stay," he said, finally. He walked back towards Ray and Terra, who couldn't muster the courage to look him in the eye. He fell in next to them, head held low.

"You will not regret your decision," Glasse said, her voice muffled behind her owl mask. "Captain Dodonna's courage is an example for us all. What we are doing here tonight requires trust and bravery."

The others raised their candles and torches high, the flames sputtering and growing tall, fiery towers cultivated by the cold wind blowing in off of the snow-capped mountains.

"What you might understand as 'magic' or 'sorcery' is more accurately known as *pharmakeia*. True power, channeled through the use of mind-altering substances in the context of rigidly executed rituals designed to unlock the latent energies of objects, places, and astrological formations. Of people. These rites facilitate the formation of neural pathways that unlock the true powers of the human mind. Powers hidden and denied to you by the machinations of the religious and civil elite, powers they themselves call upon in their dealings with the spiritual realm."

Glasse turned her owl-face to the fire and waved a hand over the flames. A powder fell from her palm and the fire roared in heaving green and blue towers of heat. The patients closest to the fire pit retreated several steps.

"We can turn our desires and our thoughts toward specific, attainable ends. That is true magic."

Ray's stomach gurgled. He put a hand to his belly,

feeling the sudden roiling of his insides. He looked up to see the stars swaying above, the cosmos responding and resonating with his own upset digestive system. Shared rhythms of vibration. Signal and anti-signal in a nauseating feedback loop.

"Are you okay?" Terra whispered, her grip on his arm becoming a stabilizing hold, keeping him upright. Ray turned from the stars to her face, and found her concern for him—illuminated by moonlight emerging through broken clouds—beautiful. She had concern for another living thing. For him, just another sputtering ember at the edge of great and jagged mountains, at the edge of the world. He had lost his balance somewhere in those stars, but found it again with her.

"I think we're all okay, now," he said, smiling. Terra's eyes cycled through confusion to amusement. Now it was his turn to help her reclaim her balance from the stars. Some of the other patients weren't so lucky, discharging unpleasant burps before collapsing to their knees, only to be helped back up by wobbly-legged comrades.

"It's not like being drunk," Terra said, watching the clouds parting like curtains on a stage to reveal the shimmering cosmos. "It's nothing like that." The fog rose up, adding another layer of movement and color to the celestial procession.

"There are a variety of methods to trigger the emergence of pliable psychospheric energies," Dr. Glasse said, the fire swaying before her. "As the wafers begin to manifest their manifold effects, mind the candles."

Ray became aware of the candle in his hand, the warmth of the flame inches from his thumb and forefinger. The light fluctuated from yellow to orange to red, then gained a soft, flickering coat of blue spooklight. In the depths of that flame, eyes opened, bright and inhuman.

"The veil wears thin," Dr. Glasse said. "The permeable film separating the *within* from the *without*, the personal from the universal."

Ray nodded, *yes, exactly* as if she were speaking directly to him. Terra emitted a low moan.

"It will pass soon," he said, finding the sudden warmth in his core a pleasant counterpoint to the initial indigestion. But Terra's eyes were closed, and she made no indication that she heard him. She swayed back and forth, her lips moving not in a moan, but in a chant, her voice joining others. Their words were indistinct within the harmony of the rising chorus, nonsense maybe, or an echo of Latin, rhythmic and laden with meaning lost to him, but somehow resonant with the thoughts and feelings flowing through new pathways opening and alighting the dark, swirling higher-dimensional energies they might understand as their own minds.

"Do you desire healing, lives of purpose, life itself, anew?" Glasse shouted over the confluence of chanting. "Do you seek to leave behind the shame of what you have been made into, what you have allowed yourselves to become? Would you instead seek transcendence and power?"

Ray's vision went blurry. The ground shifted beneath his feet, but he was held in place by roots grown up from the hard, dark soil. Roots, indistinguishable from human bones. Painful memories bobbed in the roiling waters of his mind, emerging from abyssal depths like waterlogged corpses:

Crying in front of his father, whose face showed not empathy, but disgust and disappointment.

The face of a woman he loved, realizing that the man she wanted him to be would never exist.

Having another beer when he should have stopped.

Punching a barracks wall until his hand went numb.

Blood on his uniform.

Sticking a gun in his mouth, wishing he wasn't such a coward, wishing he could just get it all over with.

The ground pulsated with speckled blue light, illuminating the fog in short, soft bursts and disappearing again. Hands ran down his arms and took his hands, flesh-on-flesh, grip tight. Figures in grey robes standing before him, mouths moving in the dark, faces hidden behind their hoods. Eyes, glowing purple, the color of the cosmos, boring into his soul.

"*YOUR THIRD EYE BEGINS TO OPEN,*" they said, their many voices speaking as one, words reverberating and echoing.

A woman smiled bright and cosmic-purple, before leaning in to kiss his cheek. A religious gesture, a stage-kiss out of a passion play. They moved on to Terra, their words lost to the shouting of Glasse and the chanting of the crowd. Ray commanded his arm to release the candle, as the hot wax dripped over the paper guard onto his wrist, but realized there was no distinction between the candle and his hand, between the flame and the life-ember of himself. One in the same, all of it, just temporary fluctuations producing near-indistinct variations in an interlaced particle field. Vibrating now, here, in a temporary pattern, soon swept away, replaced by something else, something new, made from the same component parts. Rearrange the set. Swap the actors into new roles. Change costumes. Cue the lights. Raise the curtain once more. The audience will applaud all the same.

Spooklights appeared over the altar-fire pit. Small, glowing spirit orbs sputtering illumination, smears of light appearing first in the mind and then in the visual spectrum. The lights heralded the arrival of the shades, who appeared in the stretches of darkness draped between the dilapidated buildings nearby. They shuffled forward, spilling anti-light, distinct from the black of natural night, their eyes aglow with blue radioactive energy from an unseen and lifeless realm, eyes of the impatient dead returning to the material plane and finding it a grotesque disappointment.

The stone and roots holding Ray in place shifted and drew him toward the shades. The earth, air, and bodies of the patients and robed congregants sped by in a procession of furious light, their essential salts turned to energy from matter and back again by forces beyond comprehension. The earth went still and solid. Ray was face to face with three of those terrible spirits.

Their shapes held the vague outline of the human form, but were composed of fleeting shadow that glowed and rippled like the surface of water disturbed by invisible forces. Above them, the air churned with the familiar *whoosh-whoosh-whoosh* of a helicopter coming in low and hot. Maybe for a MEDEVAC. Maybe for an attack run.

They reached for him. Extensions of shadow became bone, muscle, and flesh, became arms. Arms soon covered with olive-drab or pre-War on Terror-era BDU camouflage uniform sleeves. The arms sprouted hands and errant radio transmissions danced along the whirring rotor wash. The voices of war, the voices of the dead, calling in contact reports, calling for support, calling the names of those gathered here for occult purposes.

The arms gripped his own, holding him still, and exuded a spectral mist, not unlike the fog that encircled their dark gathering. The spirits revealed their faces:

formless, limitless darkness coalescing into familiar contours and configurations.

Someone screamed—a scream picked up and echoed across the space between the three buildings. A scream whipping back and forth over the dancing flames of the altar, shuddering and repeated by ghostly mouths capable only of expressions of hunger and terror.

The scream was Ray's. The terror was his.

The chanting ceased. Glasse's shouted prayers and obscenities were no more. The churning air grew still as the phantom helicopter dematerialized. The spell was broken.

Skeletons' hands released their death-grip on Ray, pulling back into pools of inky black, waving and billowing like strands of ribbon. The dead withdrew, their claim on this patch of earth broken. For now.

EVOLUTION TWO

REPRESSION

Sergeant Major Haaster didn't show up at the male barracks until just after 0730, affording the patients the greatest luxury a soldier could ever hope for: more sleep.

Ray was the first one awake. Haaster moved down the center aisle, striking a broom handle against the metal poles of the bunks, *clank, clank, clank.*

"Rise and shine, sleepy-heads," Haaster said. "First formation is in fifteen minutes, followed by PT and breakfast chow, so we gotta move. The ladies are already up and waiting out front. Let's see if we can't be at least as professional as our female comrades, shall we?"

Ray offered a limp thumbs up as Haaster walked by his bunk, just like he used to do for his squad leader or platoon sergeant. He resisted the urge, as he always did, to raise his middle finger instead.

Haaster stood before the assembled formation, the patients adorned in hoodies and running pants, hands pressed into pockets against the cold—something they wouldn't have been able to get away with on active duty, of course. It was the small things that made being *out* worth it.

The sun hovered low over the distant plains to the east, its rays barely penetrating the blanket of fog that covered Camp Winter Falcon.

"Last night, you got a taste of the potential this program—this place—has for you," Haaster said. "You saw what we're working toward. Something special. A force you're connected to, whether you realized it before last night or not."

Ray risked a quick glance behind him. He caught sight of Terra, staring ahead. Staring into nothing.

"You may be scared," Haaster continued. "But like I would tell my soldiers when we were down range: fear is part of the job. Being afraid doesn't mean you've failed in your duty. Figuring out how to do your duty in the face of fear—that's bravery. That's what it means to be a soldier for this country.

"I'm sure you have questions. I know I do. But we still have our duty. We're still going to do PT this morning. We're still going to hit breakfast chow and conduct personal hygiene. We're still going to be on time for the activities and training of the day. We have our next program event at Building 12A at 0930, sharp."

He paused a moment, looking at their weary faces, his voice softening. "What you're facing here is stranger and scarier than anything I ever did in the sandbox. You have my respect. Keep moving forward, falcons. Platoon, atten-*tion*!"

The patients sloppily snapped to.

"Riiight, face!"

The patients turned to their right in unison.

"For-ward, *march*!"

With the light burn of a one-mile run in his legs and the aftertaste of cold mountain air on his tongue, Ray felt a shadow of normalcy begin to reassert itself. The chow hall coffee was acidic but drinkable with enough cream and sugar. From the moment the DFAC staff threw the eggs and bacon onto his tray, his body thrummed with hunger for fat and salt, as if reminded it did, in fact, have to eat.

He joined Mike and Adams at a small square table at the far end of the chow hall. The other patients milled about or sat quietly, speaking in hushed voices. He meant to greet Mike and Adams, but skipped the formality. Instead, he found his hands shoveling over-buttered toast into his mouth, followed swiftly by whole strips of bacon and shaking spoonfuls of eggs.

"That's how I felt, too," Mike said, sipping coffee from a white foam cup. He gestured to his tray, already empty. "Seconds seemed to help. They're being generous with the portions today."

Ray finished the last of his eggs and toast in record time, then slammed down the orange juice waiting for him in a plastic cup. He let out a belch, caught his breath, then shoved his tray back a few inches.

"Feel better?" Adams said, spearing an errant piece of toast into his mouth.

"That was super fucking weird last night," Ray said, tongue pushing at a bit of bacon stuck between his teeth. "I mean, Sergeant Major Haaster was very motivational this morning. Like we were coming back in from a long field training exercise, rather than waking up from a night of summoning the devil or whatever-the-hell that was. Jesus Christ." The bacon finally dislodged. Ray slugged down his coffee.

"I mean, it *was* weird," Adams said. "This is an 'alternative' program, right? That shit was *alternative*, man. How many people were out there, besides us? A couple dozen in the fog? Who were they?"

"I didn't like it," Mike said, looking over his shoulder to ensure Haaster and the other cadre weren't around.

"I don't think those were people out there."

"What's that mean?" Ray asked.

"Can't you feel that?" Adams asked. "That energy on the air? Can't you feel that weight just falling right off your shoulders? It turns out I *have* experienced weird shit like this before, but I just couldn't—couldn't face it, couldn't talk about it. Definitely not in the Marines, you don't want to say you've been touched by God or seen spirits or been bewitched by a bruja. You leave that shit alone. Here, though. I feel like maybe I can talk about it. Maybe even learn what it is."

"I don't know if I want to learn anything about what that was," Ray said. His mind conjured images of approaching his bedroom window, that terrible light pouring through the cracks in the blinds. His fingers parting them, revealing that bright light—

"The military's always had its little culture and customs," Adams said. "They probably did shit like this at the academy. You gotta be connected to the Illuminati to make colonel or above. They're just pulling back the curtain for us lower enlisted and junior officer types."

"Dressing up in robes and summoning ghosts doesn't strike you as weirder than change of command ceremonies or drinking grog out of a boot?" Mike said. "Seriously?"

"It's just New Age shit, maybe," Adams said. "I don't know what all that was, what caused it. The drugs they fed us, maybe. Magnetite in the soil, radiation from the uranium they used to mine out here. All I'm saying is that we got, what, two weeks left? We just need to adjust our expectations, do whatever weird stuff they want us to. Go with the flow."

"I need this program as much as anybody," Ray said. "But last night..." He trailed off, trying to dredge up more than the errant signal of confused memories, and failing. "It's just not squaring with what they told us this would be."

"That's because most of this stuff is classified," Mike said, leaning forward and lowering his voice. "I went back through the paperwork Glasse was talking about. You signed a non-disclosure agreement. We all did. Whatever we saw last night, we're not supposed to talk about it outside of Camp Winter Falcon."

Ray considered this as he finished his coffee, the last drops bitter and full of grounds. He swallowed them anyway.

"Then they're not showing the best judgment," Ray said. "We're alcoholics, drug users, bad with money, worse with relationships, burnouts. Maybe we could rate secret clearances when we were in, but we don't now. No way. Why would they show us something classified and expect us to keep quiet? Better than even odds about a third to half of us go back to our old ways, get plastered, and start blabbing about the laser light show they put on for us. Doesn't make sense."

"You ever talk about your experiences with anyone else?" Mike asked. "I'm not talking about what happened down range. I'm talking about the *other* experiences. The ones the medical staff are really interested in. The ones like those videos they showed us." He tapped his fingers against the surface of the table. "Those experiences are the real reason we were selected for this program. Not our boo-hoo PTSD that everybody has, or the fact that you can't keep a job stocking shelves because you're too much of a drunk. I'm talking about that spooky stuff that got you noticed by someone. And they made sure to get you—us—here."

Window blinds parted by his shaking fingers. The form rising up to meet him, impossibly, in the air outside his second-floor window. A wide, dark head, cloaked in shadow, ringed by terrible white light.

DO NOT LOOK. YOU MUST NOT SEE—

"I didn't talk about this to my VA shrinks," Mike said. "I didn't even... didn't even remember myself, I don't think, until I came here and they started to dredge it up."

"I might have told my parents, a couple times, I think?" Ray said, swallowing hard, the coffee grinds still working their way down his throat. "Maybe before I learned not to."

"Repression," Adams said, nodding. "Screen memories and repressed memories. That's what we got going on. Not just us three at this table. The whole damn class. Whatever they're doing to us, whatever we saw last night, it's bringing that all back up."

"Wait, I did talk to someone about it," Mike said, rubbing his eyes. "I remember now. I was, I don't know, nine or ten. I wanted to talk to my pastor. I thought to myself, maybe they were angels. Maybe demons. I told him..." Mike paused, commanding a quivering hand to wrap around his coffee cup and bring it to his lips. He took a sip and lowered the foam cup back to the table.

"My grandmother called them fairies." He held out a hand at the edge of the table, then lowered it toward the floor. "Couldn't have been more than yay high. Two, maybe three feet tall. Faces like Halloween masks. Blue. Glowed blue. Didn't light up what was around them, but I could see their faces. Frozen in these weird, scrunched-face expressions. Eyes blacker than night. Didn't so much look at me as *through* me. Like they didn't even see me at all. I made the mistake of telling my pastor about seeing them around grandma's farmhouse the one time. Asked him what they could be. He listened to me ramble on, then he took his belt off. Told me that if I ever told lies in the house of God like that again, he'd never stop beating me."

Ray and Adams found something else to look at.

"I never mentioned the—the sightings, the encounters—to anyone after that," Mike said. "Not even my wife or kids. I guess that's why I never brought my family to the old farmhouse. Maybe on some level I was afraid they would see them, too."

"I've just seen ghosts a few times," Adams said, nodding. "Just someone walking through the wall, plain as day, looking as solid as you or me. Dressed in old clothes, though, like from the 70s. Tight pants, unbuttoned shirt with a psychedelic pattern. White guy with big hair. My dad was a Marine, too, so we moved a lot. But that ghost haunted every dang house we ever lived in. Mom didn't want me talking about it."

The table fell silent, save for the scraping of plastic silverware on plastic trays.

"You seen Eckart?" Mike said, suddenly. He looked around the chow hall, eyes flitting from one face to the next.

"I know the name, just not the person," Ray said, happy to talk about something else.

"Haven't seen her since last night at the... the ritual," Mike said, trying the word out, not liking the feel of it. "She wasn't at first formation. And I don't remember seeing her on the walk back to the barracks last night."

"I don't remember anything after all that," Ray said.

Adams glanced at his watch.

"I'm gonna hit the shower before we head over to 12A," he said, pushing back from the table and standing up. "I'll see you guys out there."

"Roger," Mike said, raising his fork in mock salute.

"I'm gonna have a little more coffee," Ray said, looking around the chow hall, searching the faces of the patients he recognized, and counting.

Eleven. Eleven patients, down from fourteen.

REASONABLE RESPONSES

The computer room's warmth was a welcome escape from the morning cold. The medical staff, wearing white lab coats and blank faces, gestured for the patients to enter.

Ray found his name scrawled in black marker across a white label affixed to the wooden panel of a computer station on the far side of the room. Terra found her way to the station set opposite Ray's, her back to the wall.

"Welcome back to the computer lab here at scenic building 12A," Glasse said. "As you finish taking your seats, I would ask for your attention and your silence." She offered a beaming smile as the last patient took their seat. "Last time we were in this room, you completed a psychological evaluation attenuated to your individual pre-intake profiles. We have collated the resulting data and determined that the person sitting in the station across from you is likely your best match for the experiment we are about to conduct."

Glasse paused and caught Adams' attention, tilting her head apologetically.

"Mr. Adams, regrettably, your match has since left the program. An AI will be your partner for this experiment. That is not ideal, but with an odd number of patients remaining, we decided that your case would be a variation, an outlier. We are interested in the results nonetheless."

"What are we doing here, doc?" Adams said.

"Good question. We are attempting to generate a small-scale psychic resonance field between patient pairs, or, in your case, between a patient and a computer system."

The room fell into silence, save for the whirring of computer fans and the soft, almost imperceptible buzzing of the blank screens.

Mike raised his hand.

"Captain Dodonna."

"Dr. Glasse," he said, the formality coming naturally to the former officer, "please understand that I'm not trying to be rude here, and I am game to participate in this training event."

"I understand. You are a motivated patient—and inquisitive, your voice often serving to ask the questions that others may be afraid to ask. Which I appreciate."

"We're just going right into, what, psychic experiments? With no explanation as to what the hell happened out by that altar last night?"

Ray wanted to burst out laughing. The absurdity of the whole situation was beginning to become terrifying on a deep, instinctual level. Laughter seemed the only appropriate response. He brought his fist to his lips and gave his index finger a quick, nervous bite instead.

Keep it together, Ray.

Dr. Glasse smiled.

"Fair question, Mike. Last night, you participated in one of three resonance rituals that we will attempt. These rituals are meant to draw up the valences of both this location and of you, our patients—our honored guests, without whom this entire project would fail. We are still analyzing the footage and biometric data captured during last night's events, but based on our initial observations and projection models, we believe it to be a resounding success. It was far more spectacular than I anticipated, if I'm being honest, but that simply speaks to the hard work and open-mindedness of you, our patients. Our catalysts."

"'Valences'? 'Catalysts'? What's that all mean?"

Glasse laid a hand on his shoulder.

"I'm sorry, I don't mean to confuse the situation,"

she said, holding him quiet with her touch. "I would ask that you focus on the event before you, now. Everything else will be revealed in time. Let's see if we can cultivate a small-scale resonance between patients, here, right now. A microcosm of what we began to achieve last night."

"How will any of this spooky shit make us better?" Terra said suddenly, poking her head up from behind the wood panels. "No offense, doc, but why are we screwing around with magic stuff when we've got real problems to deal with? The war? The baggage we're all carrying? All that?"

Glasse took her time offering a reply.

"Confusion and anger are reasonable responses when undergoing intensive treatment and therapy."

"I think that's the point," Terra said, all eyes on her. "When does the 'treatment' begin? Far as I can tell, none of this is really therapy. Not like any I've ever seen, and I've been bounced around the system for a while."

Glasse's eyes met Terra's, her smile on the verge of a frown—but her voice remained friendly and soft.

"That's why you're here," Glasse said. "The traditional methods simply do not work for you. So, we have to get creative." She cut through the rising tension with a soft voice and confident smile, addressing the entire group. "You relied on one another while in the military, right? You had to count on your battle buddies to survive. Keep that sense of comradery in mind for this experiment. Building the resonance connection between patients is critical to our work. And while I greatly appreciate the respectful candor communicated by you here today, I must insist that we proceed with this experiment. Yes, last night was traumatic. You will have time to process it. But we must strike while the iron is hot."

As if on cue, the computer fans began to spin up. Electronic clicking and humming grew in volume. The screens warbled, then snapped alive with a hiss of static and a stink of ozone. Green bootup code cascaded down those bulbous, black screens, and the hazy lights dimmed. The green text reflected on the faces of the patients, radioactive runes writ on pale flesh.

The computers, now roused from their slumber, displayed the login text fields, a blinking cursor keeping cadence in the username box.

"Please log in with your first and middle initial, followed by your full last name, all in one string," Glasse said. "The passcode is the last four of your social."

Ray, typing quickly, input his information and hit ENTER. The screen froze before its text disappeared in a descending curtain of black.

"Please put on your headphones," Glasse said.

Ray retrieved the headphones from a hook set on the divider wall. They were a tight fit. They flooded his ear canals with the distant sounds of radio static, of dripping water, of voices whose words were lost in the susurrus.

A COUPLE OF WAVY LINES

The monitor flashed green, then went black again, before revealing a series of five symbols, glowing bright and verdant, manifesting line by line, arranged across the screen:

A hollow circle.

A plus sign.

A set of two vertical wavy lines.

A square in outline.

A star.

There was a series of clicks and thumps in the signal coming through the headphones, until a sonorous male voice spoke.

"Good morning, falcons," the voice said. "Please follow my instructions carefully. For this exercise, we will designate *transmitters* and *receivers*. For the first set, those of you sitting on the inside rows, you will be *transmitters*. Those of you sitting on the outside, closest to the walls, will be *receivers*.

"An image will appear on the transmitter's screen. If you are a transmitter, you must concentrate on that symbol. Do not communicate in any way with the receiver across from you. Do not make noise, tap your toes or fingers, move your feet, et cetera. Make every effort to remain as silent and as still as possible while concentrating on the symbol presented."

Ray's screen went black, then flashed each symbol individually, in sequence.

"Those of you on the outside rows will be the *receivers*. Each symbol will be displayed on your screen, in random order, with a number or a letter selection code. For each transmission attempt, there will be one minute of time. Please do not simply guess. Please do not rush to make a selection."

The voice went quiet. The errant signal noise and mechanical static washed over Ray. He suddenly felt very, very tired.

"The experiment will now commence. Transmitters, once the symbols appear on your screen, focus on them. Receivers, give yourself time to receive the signal and make your selections. You may begin."

Another series of muffled thumps and shrills buzzes marked the end of their instruction. The first symbol appeared.

A square in green outline, the image slightly blurred by some effect of the display and the curvature of the screen.

A square, Ray thought, turning those word-thoughts into shape-thoughts, seeing the form and holding its image in his mind. *A square.*

He had it. He began to push it outwards, picturing it moving in a very real, physical sense toward Terra, through the divider, through her face, through the walls of her skull, into her mind.

A square.

He had no way of knowing whether she had made her selection or not. He half-imagined the *clicks* and *taps* of fingers on bulky keyboard keys, but his headphones muffled everything and supplied its own cadence of mechanical noise and static.

The square faded away, its image dispersing, dissolving into wisps of threaded energy spreading across the screen like blood in water. Then they began to come back together to form a new shape.

A circle.

A star.

A star.

A couple of wavy lines.

A plus sign.

A square.

A plus sign.

A star.

Wavy lines.

The screen went blank. Something beneath the floor rumbled, like the diesel engine of a Humvee turning over. The sounds coming through his headphones were like the wet, soft snaps of a moist mouth, struggling to form words in the dark.

The symbols appeared on his screen, all five, all in a row:

A circle.

A plus sign.

Wavy lines.

A square.

A star.

The star, on the far-right end of the row, flickered out, replaced instead by a new symbol—an oval, with two tear-drop eyes within, and a grimacing mouth set below. A face. A gargoyle's visage, one that could have been leering down from the heights of an ancient stone church.

The square disappeared next, only to be replaced by the image of a burning candle, the flame strangely animated by alternating pixel configurations.

The wavy lines went, too, reforming into a rectangle... no, a VHS cassette. The plus sign became an American flag, or an approximation thereof, the lines and stars all wrong, too few and too haphazard, as if scrawled on the inside walls of a portajohn by some bored grunt. Finally, the circle sprouted a head along its upper curve, its open mouth full of teeth, a snake swallowing its own tail.

Ray, having fallen into the rhythm of the exercise, tried to focus on the shapes, tried to hold them all in his head, to share them, somehow, with Terra. His mind buzzed with the effort as these new shapes implied uncomfortable meanings and associations. His blood hammered through his veins. Something terrible was coming, he was sure of it.

Ray pulled his headphones off, trying to catch his breath, trying to ease the coming panic attack, the sensation exactly like snapping out of a deep sleep and flailing until the covers came off, terrified of a threat in the room that hid in the darkness. Grasping for the light switch.

The screen glitched out, becoming shards of green light and jagged lines, elements of the images smeared across the glass in pulsating, vibrating patterns attuned to the panicked rhythm of his own heart. Something was wrong with this station. He raised his hand and turned around to let the medical staff or cadre know.

No one else was in the room. Between the time he had donned his headphones and now, everyone had cleared out. Had he fallen asleep? Had he missed the transition to the next activity?

How long have I been here?

He stood up to peek over the edge of the divider. Terra should have been sitting there, headphones on, staring at her own screen, receiving the thought-transmissions from Ray. Building a *resonance field* together.

Something else sat there, instead.

Red eyes glowed back at Ray. Eyes set within a wide head and flat face, its inhuman skin the texture and consistency of melted plastic.

Ray stumbled back a step, sending his chair over, steadying himself with a lucky grab at the edge of the partition. He caught his balance and then circled wide around the computer station, fists balled, breathing heavy, sucking in oxygen in preparation for the fight-or-flight decision point.

Nothing. An empty chair. An empty chair before a blank screen in an empty room.

"Ray."

He sighed in something like relief, but not quite.

"*RAY*. Raymond Parnell."

The voice was tinny, quiet, like the buzzing of an insect at the edge of his ear. He looked around, but the room remained empty, save for him, save for his own elastic sense of time and place and paranoia.

"Ray. Over here."

Ray found himself picking up his headphones and bringing them to his right ear, not wanting to put them on again.

"*Ray. Please continue the experiment.*" A mechanical-man's voice, tortured into forming human words. "It's important that we continue to build the resonance between you and your partner."

"My partner's not here," Ray said, realizing there was no microphone on his headset. The voice seemed to hear him just fine anyway.

"Isn't she?"

Ray peered over the edge of the partition.

"No. She's gone."

"She's right where she needs to be for this experiment. Why aren't you? Are you unable to follow simple instructions, or are you being purposefully defiant?"

"There's something wrong with my screen," Ray said. "Strange symbols. No one else is in here. There's something wrong with this experiment. I want to stop."

There was a long pause before the mechanical voice spoke again.

"You're here because you realized that there's

something wrong with *you*," it said. "Everything was working as planned. Until you decided you had to stop. Did you see it, Ray? We have to know. For our experiment notes."

"Did I see what?"

"Did you see an entity in Terra's seat?" it asked, emphasizing each word. "Did you make eye contact with it? Did you speak to it? Did you give it anything that it may use to find you again?"

"I don't understand."

"We won't be able to stop it from finding you again, Ray. We have no control over what it does. Do you understand?"

Ray dropped the headphones and made for the door. He wanted *out*. He feared that the door would be locked, that he would find it secured against his hasty exit. He was sure it wouldn't open, but it did, thank God, and he kept walking through the next room and passed through door after door, until he was outside in the late-morning cold, watching his breath turn to vapor, the mountains obscured by clouds above and mist below, not another soul in sight.

SCREEN MEMORIES

The chapel had changed. Not the walls, or the ceiling, or the floor, which remained static and grime-ridden as ever, but the spiritual aesthetic of the place. The vibe, the *tenor*, the frequency of the feelings the place emitted, encouraged, and reciprocated—they all had turned sour.

The additions to the décor probably had something to do with it: animal skulls mounted along the walls, stripped bare of flesh and laden with runic carvings etched into old bone; long, fleshy candles set in elaborate, highly detailed candelabras like many-limbed trees; bizarre silver plates and bowls set atop wooden display cases, their polished surfaces twisting the reflections of the patients into warped, flickering inversions.

The patients waited quietly or murmured secretive conversations in the first rows of pews, faces set over steaming foam cups of coffee, half-hidden in shadow, partially illuminated by those unnatural golden candelabras gripping finger-like candles. Sickly grey light flooded the chapel as the main doors opened. A shadow walked in. Heads turned to see. The shadow walked down the center aisle, pale face revealed by the flickering, golden flames, becoming familiar. Ray, eyes wide and haunted, found Terra among the group. He slumped into the pew behind her.

"Where were you?" she whispered. "I think they've been waiting for us all to get together."

"I was with you," he said, his voice utterly flat. "The symbol transmission thing. Only it wasn't you, after we started. It was something else."

"Something else?"

"Not human."

"Jesus Christ," Terra said. "Are you okay?"

Ray leaned against the pew, head tilted back. Shadows moved among the cobweb-strewn rafters above him, furtive and impatient.

"I think I'm still a little lightheaded from the resonance thing last night," he said. "Whatever they put in those wafers."

"We've been waiting for you for like, an hour."

"I think they call that *missing time*. I should probably report it to the medical staff."

"You should go to sick call."

"This whole thing is one big sick call," Ray said. He had lost sight of the shadows, but they were still up there. He could feel it.

The floorboards groaned in front of Terra, drawing her attention to a uniformed cadre member handing her a set of paperwork.

"No talking," he said. "Complete this packet on your own. You can discuss this with your peers after you have completed this set." He leaned over the pew to hand Ray a stack, then moved down the row, giving the instructions in the same flat, monotone voice.

"Later, if you need to talk," Terra whispered over her shoulder. Ray was already flipping through the pages of his packet, oblivious. The instructions were ALL-CAPS, as if the paperwork felt the need to shout.

```
FOR EACH IMAGE CONTAINED WITHIN
THIS PACKET, RATE IT WITH A 1,
2, OR 3, WHEREAS "1" REPRESENTS
NO RECOGNITION, "2" MEANS SOME
RECOGNITION, AND "3" MEANS
STRONG RECOGNITION.

FOR EACH QUESTION, ANSWER "Y"
```

FOR YES OR "N" FOR NO.

YOU MAY ADD BRIEF NOTES TO
PROVIDE CONTEXT TO YOUR ANSWERS
AS NECESSARY. THESE ARE NOT
REQUIRED.

Well, that cleared things up.

"You have thirty minutes to complete this packet," a voice said from somewhere within the chapel. Terra looked around the space, but saw only her fellow patients, heads down and working diligently on the handouts. The newly mounted skulls stared at them with darkness in place of eyes.

She flipped to the first prompt: a greyscale forest scene, a photograph transposed into the packet and copied a dozen times over. Heavy, thick branches laden with leaves and offshoots, upon which a set of three owls sat, claws grasping the old wood, eyes staring forward, staring at Terra.

Something stirred deep within her memory. A camping trip, maybe? She couldn't place it, but she had learned that if she felt something, *anything,* in regards to this creepy shit, they wanted to know about it.

She circled "2."

The next page was a collage of images: more blurry photographs manually photocopied onto a single white sheet, some set at angles and overlapping with each other, all depicting isolated and ill-lit alleyways, backyards, or dark houses. The perspective was always from a moderate elevation, as if from a drone buzzing through sleepy, isolated neighborhoods to snap photographs.

Terra selected "1."

She flipped to the next page. Her breath caught in

her throat and her eyes went wide. She breathed in, heavy and slow, and looked around the chapel to see if anyone had noticed her reaction.

They're all too absorbed in their own crazy to notice mine, she thought to herself. The thought was exactly no comfort at all.

A grainy photograph—complete with water damage and wrinkles in the material preserved by the photocopying process—depicted a tall figure, covered by a thin, white sheet, complete with two black holes crookedly cut out for eye holes. The low-effort Halloween-costume ghost stood in a long hallway of cobwebs and old wood. A stately grandfather clock stood to the figure's left, its face obscured by shadow.

She wanted to choose "1" and then be on to the next picture in this stupid exercise. At least the last time they reacted to weird images, she could just press a key and let the computer decide if it liked her answer or not. This whole thing was a big waste of time. She wanted to move on and forget this costume gag that had absolutely *zero* to do with her.

Except, she couldn't. Except, she was sure she had seen this before. And not this photograph—but this person, this figure, this *ghost*, lingering in a hallway.

One night, decades distant, when she was sleeping over—her father was drinking again and mom didn't want her around—except, Gramps and Gigi didn't have a big clock like this, and their home was a doublewide trailer, not an old Victorian mansion big enough to have a hallway this long and ornate. But she was sure this was the same white-sheeted ghost that had been lingering outside of the guest bedroom door, silent and patient, waiting for her to wake from a deep, rigid sleep with a full bladder and a long journey to the bathroom through the dark ahead of her.

Her hand drifted down to the blurry "3" at the end of the row of numbers beneath the image. She circled it with a hurried scrawl and then made to flip the page—but held her hand.

Crawling out of bed, opening the door, seeing that sheet floating before me. The scream came, eventually, but only after I realized there was something under there, and that thing moved, and it didn't have feet or socks or shoes poking out from beneath.

Terra had let loose, her scream reverberating through the trailer. The sheet collapsed in on itself, settling down into a pile like abandoned skin, like someone had simply stepped out of the body they were inhabiting.

Her grandparents finally got through to her. *What's wrong, niña? Why are you yelling? Are you hurt?*

Why did you drag a sheet into the hallway?

Terra buried that corpse of a memory by flipping the page. Its fingers poked up through the soil of her mind, refusing to be forgotten.

The next image was a rectangle of grey contours framing a familiar sphere set amongst the blackness of space. Earth, as seen through an artificial portal. Terra was eager to make a selection and move on to the next page.

"1"

The final image was a low-angle shot of a door, tall and imposing, set against the dark interior of an abandoned house. The door was swinging open, revealing a swirling, illuminated fog beyond, not at all unlike the glowing bank that accompanied last night's bizarre outdoor activities.

Terra stared at the image, trying to make sense of it, trying to determine if it was in fact an illustration rather than a photograph, when she noticed the hand in the gloom. The hand *emerging*. Long, inhuman fingers crowning a pale, grey palm, open wide to grab, to take, to pull her into another realm entirely.

"3"

She turned the page, revealing text-based questions, the photos mercifully at an end.

HAVE YOU EVER CONSUMED FOOD OR DRINK OFFERED TO YOU BY NON-HUMAN INTELLIGENCES, TO INCLUDE BUT NOT LIMITED TO: TALKING ANIMALS, FEY FOLK, INSECTILE CREATURES, MACHINE ELVES, OR "NORDIC" ALIENS?

"N"

ARE YOU FAMILIAR WITH THE WORK AND WORKINGS OF ONE JOHN "JACK" WHITESIDE PARSONS, ROCKETIST AND DEGENERATE WIZARD?

"N"

WOULD THE SCIENTIFIC COMMUNITY'S ACCEPTANCE OF THE "UFO/UAP" PHENOMENON/A HAVE AN IMPACT ON YOUR BELIEF IN GOD?

"N"

DOES YOUR WAR-RELATED TRAUMA CHALLENGE YOUR SENSE OF SELF-WORTH?

"Y"

DO YOU OFTEN FEEL WORTHLESS, PATHETIC, OR NOT WORTHY OF LOVE?

"Y"

DO YOU FANTASIZE ABOUT SELF-
HARM?
"Y"

IS THE ONLY REASON YOU HAVEN'T
KILLED YOURSELF YET BECAUSE
YOU ARE A COWARD, TERRIFIED OF
DEATH OR OF THE JUDGMENT OF A
GOD WHOSE JUSTICE ON EARTH IS
WHOLLY ABSENT IN THE FACE OF
THE ABSOLUTE MORAL DEPRAVITY OF
HUMANKIND?
"Y"

DO YOU SOMETIMES SUSPECT THAT
GOD IS MAD OR BLOODTHIRSTY?
"Y"

ARE DEPRESSION AND ANXIETY
RATIONAL RESPONSES TO THE
INSANE CONDITIONS UNDER WHICH
WE LIVE IN WESTERN CULTURE AND
CAPITALIST ECONOMIC STRUCTURES?
"Y"

HAVE YOU CONSIDERED THAT THE
PATIENTS OF CAMP WINTER FALCON
ARE THE SANE ONES, AND THAT
THOSE NOT REQUIRING INTENSIVE
PYSCHIATRIC TREATMENT ARE, IN
FACT, MAD?
"Y"

HAVE YOU REALIZED THAT YOU
ARE SPECIAL, NOT BECAUSE YOU
ARE VETERANS, BUT BECAUSE OF
YOUR PSYCHIC POTENTIAL AND
SUPERNATURAL CONNECTIONS AS
REFRACTED THROUGH THE TRAUMA
OF YOUR MILITARY TRAINING AND
COMBAT EXPERIENCES?
"N"

WOULD IT SURPRISE YOU TO LEARN
THAT YOU ARE REPRESENTATIVE OF A
SMALL BUT SIGNIFICANT MINORITY
SUBSET OF THE POPULATION THAT,
SINCE THE EARLY 1950S, HAS BEEN
EXPOSED TO PSYCHOTRONIC AND
GENETIC MANIPULATION BY FORCES
BEYOND THE UNDERSTANDING OF
MAINSTREAM HUMAN SCIENCE?
"Y"

DO YOU BELIEVE THAT THE MEDICAL
STAFF WILL BE SUCCESSFUL IN
LEVERAGING YOUR FRAYING MENTAL
STABILITY TO CONTACT THE
ENTITIES THAT HAUNT CAMP WINTER
FALCON?
"???"

COULD YOU SEE YOURSELF
PARTICIPATING IN FURTHER
RITUALISTIC PRACTICES THAT WOULD
BE ANATHEMA TO THE TRADITIONAL
RELIGIOUS PRACTICES OF YOUR
UPBRINGING AND CULTURE?

"N"

YOU WILL PARTICIPATE IN FURTHER
RITUALISTIC PRACTICES THAT MAY
BE ANATHEMA TO THE TRADITIONAL
RELIGIOUS PRACTICES OF YOUR
UPBRINGING AND CULTURE. DO YOU
BELIEVE ME?
"N"

WHY WON'T YOU JUST ACCEPT WHAT
YOU'RE BEING TOLD?

WHY WON'T YOU BE REASONABLE

WHY WON'T YOU LET
                              US

IN?

VIDEO #3

The lights went down. Soldiers collected the packets. No one spoke.

The VCR accepted a new tape provided by a woman in a pristine white lab coat. The gears and switches buzzed behind the player's faded plastic casing. The drive mechanism extracted the magnetic tape, winding it through rollers and the rotating head drum. Chemicals applied to the tape's surface were converted into electronic signals, delivering sounds and images of moments in the past. Moments that would shape all to come after.

The screen buzzed to life with a sharp *pop* of static.

The spookshow began.

A spare, grey room, bricks painted over with a colorless paint. The footage is in black and white, and the image shakes and stutters, as if this is a transfer, the recording originally shot on film but brought over to VHS sometime in the 80s or 90s for posterity's sake.

The camera is set just about chest-level on a figure sitting behind a table, facing the camera, head held low and bent forward. There's a pair of Army MPs standing to the sides, bodies half-in and half-out of the camera's view, holding long rifles across their chests. They stare forward and stand still with the discipline of an honor guard, even as the moments drag on into minutes. The audio track rises in volume until there are dull, static-laden undertones, harsh and overwhelming, white noise not unlike that produced by the brain in the falling-sensation moments before deep sleep.

Metal hinges click and shift and a door opens off-camera. A man in a white lab coat steps into the shot, his footsteps loud and echoing in that cramped room.

"Twelve," the man says, too loud, his voice clipping, the speakers cracking.

The figure raises its head—its long, wide head, revealing a blank, grey space where its face should be. Only the dimmest impressions of eyes and a mouth are present, covered by flesh like pruned fingers in the moments after a long, hot bath.

Distortion descends. Fingers of a dead hand, reaching from above. Film frames and tracks become visible for a moment, until the strip slips away, and we're left with a stark, white-hot glow on the screen. There's no soundtrack, save the hiss of heat and the whirring of internal, unseen mechanisms.

Cut to a graveyard, its tombstones standing at odd angles like teeth in a shattered mouth, covered in moss and speckled with wet blackness. The grass is overgrown and sways peacefully in the breeze, creeping over a footpath that has lost most of its integrity to time. White fungal towers push up through the dirt and gravel. In the distance, the round, green hills—ancient mountains smoothed down by glaciers long since gone south to die—are laden with trees, green and vibrant, indicating a climate much wetter than Colorado's, especially in recent years, when the fires begin in the early spring and burn through forest and field and neighborhood, well past the holiday season, and the droughts last even longer.

There's a peaceful stillness to this scene, an idyllic Gothic atmosphere. It's the comforting guarantee of death, the promise of true quiet to come, of the consumption and reintegration of human structures and bodies back into nature, into the world itself, from which we are never truly separated, but believe we are, if only for a short while.

A *pop* precedes the emergence of a new film strip, the image shaking and struggling for clarity before settling into a rhythm in harmony with the workings of the human mind. The graveyard is gone now, replaced by something far less comforting.

A wide-bodied aircraft descends to a strip of desert runway, bobbing as its wheels make contact with the earth before wobbling to a slow halt. It's a military plane, American.

Cut to the side of an oval door, now open, a metal staircase on wheels brought up to receive its passengers. Men in military uniforms, chests laden with awards and decorations for their service in the Second World War or Korea, judging by the style of uniform and the apparent age of the film. Highly decorated and lauded for the many and frequent deaths and dismemberments under their command.

Another general—a former general, *the* general, in this case—emerges, recognizable even without his uniform. His wide, bald head and failing smile is a sight known to every person in the world with access to newspapers, television, or news reels. President Eisenhower follows his coterie down the stairs and is received by more military officers.

Cut to a darkened interior, soon revealed by sputtering movie-set lights come to life. Multiple cameras are set up here. There's a series of fast cuts revealing more people—more soldiers, government men in suits, scientists wearing white lab coats and heavy-framed glasses—arriving, or having already arrived. A *thud* of distortion, and everyone is standing, the room filled to the brim, the president at the center of the table, standing, giving a speech, head turning to make eye contact with the dozens upon dozens of important men who are packed in to hear him speak.

He leans forward across the conference room table, and another hand meets his own: limp and thin, papery skin draped over hollow bone, almost completely devoid of muscle. Photography bulbs flash and help hide the cuts to a new scene: Eisenhower and his military staff standing before a wall decorated by a massive, bronze eagle, on each side an American flag. Among them, dwarfed by them, is the grey entity, its head no higher than the shortest man's medal-laden chest. Its papery flesh, round stomach, and oddly proportioned hands hang in dull contrast to the colorful peacocking of its human hosts. Its wide, flat mouth remains motionless.

They stand for photographs, the flashbulbs causing the men to blink but having no discernable effect on the creature with them, whose black eyes are still and ever watchful. There's no audio track, but clearly something is wrong, as looks of horror pass across the faces of the military men, and President Eisenhower begins shouting and pointing before G-men in black suits emerge to separate him from the grey creature and usher him off stage. The camera jerks to the right to reveal a uniformed Army MP dropping his rifle and removing his helmet before vomiting onto the floor.

Other MPs approach him—one of the generals stomps forward to berate him for having the audacity to get sick in front of the president—but the vomit doesn't stop coming until it turns to a stream of dark blood. And we know it's blood, even in black and white. Blood, and then chunks of meat, and then a stream of flesh, and then a pillar of muscle tissue and marbled fat, flakes of bone, too, a goddamn *arm* with a hand and fingers sprouting out of his mouth. He's falling back and the arm swings and grabs around, knocking away the raised rifle of an MP. Its fingers grow long and the palm of its skinless hand grows wide, wrapping around the head of a fuming-mad general and squeezing until it pops like a gore-filled balloon.

The film strip is pulled up through the top of the screen. White-hot light, like the dumb glow of a movie projector.

Cut to an ornate ballroom, wood-panel framing complimented by tall, striking artwork of pastoral mountain scenes, stretching to the celling. A fireplace roars as heavy snowflakes land against the tall windows looking out on a dark, winter-swept night. The austere trees and great lawn of the hotel grounds are covered in white. Shadows dart between shaped bushes, visible in fleeting glances. Musicians paw at their instruments, eyes closed, as men in black tuxedos and women in extravagant dresses cling together on the great polished wooden dance floor at the center of the room. Wait staff circle the periphery, offering glasses of champagne or wine, or trays laden with hors d'oeuvres.

President Eisenhower is here, too, sans generals, but still in the company of staff and heads of the federal bureaucracy, who cluster around him and his wife, Mamie. It is Mamie, in fact, who first sees the apparition. Her reaction is captured by the cameras present at this soiree: her face goes slack and pale. She drops her glass and a few people step back to avoid the splash. Ike sees it next, pointing, shouting for the attention of his security detail. There's a rush of people fleeing the dance floor. The musicians scramble back to the far corner of the room. The wait staff presses back against the far walls or disappears through the kitchen access doors. The guests flee back into the opulent hotel lobby.

There are two cameras working now, and we cut back and forth between them: one set up near the glass doors leading to the snow-covered garden outside, the other standing behind Eisenhower and a small crowd of G-men with guns drawn and trained on the thing that floats above the center of the room.

It's a head.

Orders of magnitude greater in size than your average human specimen, yes, but a head nonetheless. Masculine in appearance, with bronzed skin, wide, murmuring lips, flat ears, and long ropes of scraggly hair spider-webbed across its scalp. The eyes are bright gold and shining.

The head parts its lips to make some unheard pronouncement. We rapidly cut between the two cameras, seeing the remaining people cringing in horror at whatever is being said, and then backing away, further, when the snakes appear: glowing cylinders of light that emerge from somewhere behind the floating head and wrap around its scalp and forehead like glimmering halos, the light searing the film, trailing ghost-scars. A neon-bright legacy of terror, seared across time.

The shot returns to the president and his security detail. Eisenhower, ever the soldier, steps forward, much to the apparent distress of those around him. He holds his hands high, his words lost to us. The great head takes notice, its massive, golden eyes shifting to focus on him with a gigantic, stupid glare, and the head soon follows on a slow turn along its axis, bringing itself face to face with the American president.

There is apparently some back and forth—perhaps introductions, perhaps negotiation, perhaps nothing so formal, but merely the soft words spoken between thinking beings across a vast gulf of alien natures.

Eisenhower lowers his arms. The head, still floating in place, nods, and the beams of light snaking around itself sputter out, like sparklers going dark at the end of a long night of partying. Eisenhower turns his head over his shoulder to say something to his aides, who lower their guns but keep their attention fixed on the entity before them.

The head tilts back as its jaw falls open. Its eyes go unfocused and roll to the sides. Skeletal hands, soaked through with bloody gore and the muck of the grave, emerge from the yawning maw of the great head's mouth, reaching and grasping the chapped, flaking lips and pulling a skeleton head and torso forward. This is death emerging in a mockery of birth, complete with placental gore pushed out in a liquid wave by a malformed tongue.

The skeleton tumbles out, head-first, to clatter onto the floor, awash in afterbirth.

The security detail has had enough. Four men rush the president, seizing him from behind and shuffling him back, toward the exit, toward the camera, as the skeleton rises up behind them, all wide shoulders and grinning death's head. They push the cameraman aside, and the device tumbles to the floor as the others flee the ballroom. The camera, still rolling film, lands at just the right angle to capture the leering skull from below as it comes alive with a burst of flame. The fast-moving licks of unnatural fire spark and release embers into the air.

Its mouth opens, its arms stretch wide.

VIDEO #4

Another tape. A fresh stage for a beautiful parade of horrors. The image emerges, grey and bright, from the dark wash of nothing. This is security camera footage, complete with a date and time stamp in the lower right-hand corner:

12/18/17 04:32:20 MT

A mountain spur, stretching down to meet an unpaved road leading from the left-hand side of the screen. There are single-story buildings in the nearby distance, buffered against the dark by a wash of floodlights. This could be any military base built in the mountains. This could be Camp Winter Falcon.

A light emerges from the darkness of the mountain, illuminating the contours of a cave, a space stretching up from within the rock itself. The light passes beyond the cave's limits to hover above the road, slow and pulsing. This is not a headlight from a vehicle or a flashlight held by a soldier. This is an orb of terrible, eye-irritating energy, too bright and too caustic, even for a black-and-white image appearing on a cathode ray tube television screen.

The orb disappears in a plume of static. The camera, some distance away, is suddenly blinded with a burst of light and an emergent spiderweb crack along the surface of its lens, marring the image but not halting the recording.

More lights appear, coming from the opposite side. Headlights from Humvees drowning out the dark. Two of the vehicles slide into frame and grind gravel to a halt, doors popping open as soldiers in full battle kit step out to poke their rifles around the edges of the armored doors. The gunners up top pull back the charging handles on their M240 machine guns, then angle them down toward the open mouth of the cave.

Someone shouts an order. The machine guns and rifles erupt in a sputtering concert of light, their muzzle flashes leaving afterburn images in the digital film, their tracer rounds simmering and flying into the dark to help guide their aim.

What they are shooting at emerges from the righthand side of the screen, one grotesque appendage at a time. Great strands of dripping flesh push through the hail of gunfire, only to erupt in geysers of blood and bile before falling, shredded and limp. But more come, tentacles of exposed muscle and sinew, their fleshy, organic consistency unmistakable even at this distance.

The soldiers' fire becomes more sporadic as magazine and belt changes become necessary. They've been shooting for a long time, relatively speaking, and whatever mass of writhing, organic matter is rolling out of that cave isn't slowing down, even if it is hurt, even if its limbs and great, pustulating sacs of flesh rolling forward are rendered into gore by a wall of NATO-standard 5.56mm rounds. But the momentum is on the creature's side—and so is its great mass, emerging and pushing through the destruction of its probing limbs, rolling forward until the soldiers on the ground retreat back into their vehicles and the gunners on top of the Humvees spray the wave of flesh with an indiscriminate storm of fully automatic fire.

One of the soldiers throws a grenade in a wide arc. It lands in the muck of the living abyss roiling forth, swallowed by it, accepted without protest, just as the first tendrils reach the hood of the lead vehicle and begin to search for purchase.

The grenade explodes with a flash of heat and light. Flames follow. The organic mass is apparently a good fuel source as the fire begins to consume it beneath a rising column of steady black smoke. The flames grow taller than the Humvees. The grisly tide of flesh and meat is halted in its advance for the first time, whole sections of its body aflame, tentacles and huge, fleshy nodes writhing in helpless agony.

Whatever vomited that mass forth begins to swallow it back inside, leaving a trail of smoldering flesh and smoke, until only ash and blood slicks remain.

A woman screams, her cry coming up through her throat like a knife, cutting through the stillness and the dull, droning static of the screen.

Other voices join her cry of sorrow and pain, shouting obscenities, shouting for help, *oh my God oh my GOD, there's blood everywhere.*

The lights come back on and the television screen goes dark, taking with it the fleeting possibility of context or resolution.

Terra joined the other patients around Kairns, who wouldn't stop screaming, her throat hoarse with the effort. She clutched at her stomach and at her crotch, where her grey Air Force sweat pants had soaked through, red.

"They wanted my baby, now they can't have him!" she screamed, eyes wild and meeting anyone who would look at her. "He's safe now!"

The other patients backed away as she held out her hands, blood lining her fingers and palms. Terra thought about the purple ink they used to put on Iraqis' fingers to show they voted, and what a big PR coup that was so many years ago for some public affairs unit.

Somebody got a promotion for that.

Kairns' eyes caught Terra's and she stepped forward, fingers outstretched in bloody offering. Tears streamed down her face. She pointed one of those wet fingers at the television screen.

"*That* can't have him. Not now."

Haaster appeared with two soldiers at his side, blue medical gloves on their hands. They touched Kairns' shoulders, slowly, letting her know they were there. No rough violence for her, but a reassuring, intentional progression of presence and voice guiding her toward the chapel doors. Kairns offered up mild protests, but walked with them, eyes wild.

Terra realized she was holding her breath. She exhaled, letting out a low moan as she did so. The lights hanging from the chapel's rafters flickered and buzzed. Terra looked back at the TV screen, which remained black, reflecting the retreating shapes of Kairns and the cadre leaving the chapel.

"Some places are cursed," Dr. Glasse said, suddenly appearing next to Terra. Two other soldiers wheeled the television away. Just another a prop in a stage play between scenes. "Camp Winter Falcon is tied to suffering and history in the same way a haunted house is. Generative cycles of violence. Self-perpetuating. Oscillating between dormancy and tragedy." The doctor placed a hand on Terra's shoulder, lightly turning the patient to meet her gaze.

"You're starting to see the connections now, aren't you? You're starting to feel it."

FREEDOM TOAST

Ray joined Terra and Stacey at a table in the far corner of the chow hall during Sunday's extended brunch. The same food and bad coffee, but with a nice French toast bar from 0800 to 1000.

Ray took his seat and went to work on his stack, the toast dusted with powdered sugar. The women stared past him over steaming cups of coffee and their own trays of food, barely touched.

"I feel like I'm going insane," Terra said, flatly.

Ray nodded, his fork delivering a chunk of syrup-dripping toast to his mouth, then spoke between chews. "We're all insane, or we wouldn't be here," he said.

"They're trying to make us crazy," Stacey said, leaning over the table and running her fingers through her hair. The blonde dye had retreated further from her scalp, the base of her hair darker than before.

How long have we been here?

Ray looked over his shoulder. To his relief, there were only patients at the DFAC. No cadre, no medical staff. Even the kitchen crew had retreated behind closed doors in the back.

"Two weeks, I think?" Terra said. "Almost, anyway."

"What?" Ray said, turning back to his French toast.

"We've been here for two weeks."

"Why'd you say that?"

"You asked."

"No, I didn't."

Terra focused on him, frowning.

"I guess you're not doing so hot, either."

Ray shook his head.

"Maybe it's like basic training, you know?" Stacey said. "Break us down to build us back up again. That's why they're hitting us with all this oddball shit. Keep us off balance."

"I'm remembering more and more oddball shit the more they poke at it," Terra said.

"Yeah," Stacey said. "Me too."

"Do you guys remember the computer test, where they showed us symbols on the screen, matched us with partners?" Ray asked.

Terra canted her head at a confused angle.

"I was your partner, Ray."

"Right. And do you remember how it ended? Because I do."

"Yeah, of course," Terra said. "They cut that weird spooky music in the headphones, and then they announced our results."

"That didn't happen for me," Ray said, his voice louder and sharper than he intended. He stared down at a pool of syrup congealing on his tray. "I was left there. Alone. Working with the computer, and you—and everyone else—were gone. Except there was... there was this *thing* in the seat across from me, where you should have been."

No one knew what to say to that. Ray didn't know how to follow it up, either.

"That video they showed us yesterday," Terra said, breaking the silence. "It was filmed here. There's a cave on the west side of the base. That's where that horror show played out. I'm sure of it."

"How do you know that?"

"Because I've spent a few lonely midnight hours exploring this little slice of heaven," Terra said. "You know those brick buildings with all the weird shit on the roof?"

"What about them?"

"A couple of the buildings have busted door handles and locks," she said, leaning forward on her elbows.

"There's an archive. Classified files and maps some spook forgot to shred when they closed this place down. Maybe we can learn something about Camp Winter Falcon. Fill in the blanks a bit."

"You mean breaking and entering," Stacey said.

"I'm not here because I made all the right choices in my life," Terra said. "Better to beg for forgiveness than ask for permission, my squad leader always told me. Of course, he had three or four Article 15 disciplinary actions before he made rank, so take that with a grain of salt."

"I don't know about this," Ray said.

"They've got nothing scheduled after final formation tonight," Terra said. "We could sneak off, just say we're going for a walk if any of the cadre catch us in their security sweep, which, I mean, they won't. The three of us will be less suspicious than one or two. Maybe we can learn something about those videos they keep showing us, or those apparitions I keep seeing. Maybe what you say happened to you might start to make a little sense." Ray nodded. "And it might make us feel better to find out if the soil's radioactive or there's chemical weapons leaking somewhere, driving us all crazy."

"Okay, I'm in," Stacey said. "What's the worst they're going to do? Send us to Afghanistan?"

Terra leaned forward to touch Ray's wrist.

"What do you say?"

SÉANCE

When Sergeant Major Haaster dismissed the remaining patients after final formation—Kairns was noticeably absent—Terra, Ray, and Stacey broke ranks and began to jog together down the road toward the main gate. Their reflective PT belts shined under the sputtering streetlights, making them clearly visible to anyone who bothered to look. If Haaster noticed, he certainly wasn't bothered by three of his troops headed out for some extra PT.

Soon they were in line of sight with the main gate, the lone guardhouse lit up with cell phone screens and a green light within, while a burning cigarette tip bobbed in the dark just outside the door. Terra led them at a jog away from the gate, turning north down the footpath winding along the perimeter fence. They clicked off their headlamps and removed their PT belts after moving some distance away.

"Some of the buildings we'll slip past are occupied by the medical staff and Haaster's soldiers," Terra said. "If we get caught skulking around, we'll just start jogging again, but let them catch up to us. They can probably figure out who's running out here, anyway. We just play dumb, say we were trying to shake things up with a new route."

"I can play dumb," Ray said. "Infantry guys are good at that."

Stacey snickered and gave him a friendly shot on the shoulder.

"Let's go," Terra said. They stepped into darkness, putting the outer fence—and the rest of the sane world—behind them.

Terra crouched low and Ray and Stacey followed close behind. They gave a wide berth to any building with lights on and voices and music emanating from within, until they were well beyond those islands of human activity.

Soon enough, the great, reaching hand of a derelict satellite and antenna rooftop array was before them. Red lights glowed from within the superstructure—twin pairs keeping watch. As they approached, Ray tried to make out what they were. Part of him feared the lights existed only in his mind, some refracted projection of the last few days' strange events. The more rational part of his mind assured itself that those were simply red aerial warning lights, and there was nothing to be concerned about. Another, more insistent voice offered up sputtering, nonsensical alternatives.

Terra led them up the building's nearest side. She risked switching on the red light from her headlamp. The plastic-on-plastic sound of the switch was louder than it should have been. It jarred commotion from above. Air churned and wings flapped. A shadow the size of a person dove from the lip of building over them, darkness blotting out darkness. The cold, sharp air went thick and humid with a wet-cardboard taste and smell.

The shadow was gone, and the flapping of great wings with it.

"What the fuck was that?" Stacey whispered.

"An owl, I think," Ray said.

"Too big to be a goddamned owl," Stacey said. "Must

have been a crane or something."

"It was an owl," Ray said, his tone harsher than he intended. "I'm sure of it."

Terra looked at him, her red light illuminating his face. He didn't blink.

"We should get inside."

"How do we do that?"

"Door's unlocked," Terra said. "I told you, I've been doing some exploring." She slipped around the corner and pulled a heavy metal door open. She entered quickly, pausing only to hold the door for Stacey.

Red beams swept across the interior, revealing computer consoles, derelict office furniture, and piles of abandoned paperwork layered in years of dust.

"This place is a tomb," Stacey said.

"How do you know we're going to find anything in here?" Ray said, last in, softly pulling the door shut behind them.

"Anything classified or important should have been swept up by Army intel when they mothballed the post," Stacey said.

"How competent does the military seem to you these days?" Terra said, leading them to a stack of boxes overflowing with manila folders and stacks of computer printouts. "Let alone military intelligence. What's their track record for success the last 20-30 years?"

Ray flipped through a stack of papers on a nearby desk. "Memos on uniform policy, supply logs, packing lists for training exercises," he said, shaking his head. "Nothing worth saving. Or policing up by intelligence, anyway."

"Same," Stacey said, flicking through a pile of paperwork on top of an old-style computer console. "What am I looking for, exactly? Secret files that reveal the hidden history of Camp Winter Falcon?"

Movement—either shadows shifting, or the natural blurry interplay of rods and cones in his left eye struggling to make sense of the dark—caught Ray's attention. He swung the beam of his headlamp to the far side of the room.

"If I were going to store secret files," he said, "I'd probably put them behind a door like that."

Stacey and Terra followed his beam, which he kept trained on the same spot as he crossed the room. He ended up in front of a great, silver door with a textured metal frame. There was no handle or knob, just a keypad, covered in dust, embedded in the frame on the right-hand side.

Ray bent down to study the device. He cupped his hand over his headlamp and switched to white light. He blinked for several seconds until his eyes adjusted.

The pad held ten grey, concave keys—0 through 9—and one longer red key reading INPUT. Dust clung to them in layers as thick as fungal growth.

"The 2 and 3 keys aren't as dusty," he said. "Or the INPUT key, for that matter. Looks like someone pressed them, maybe not too long ago."

"Just those two numbers?" Stacey said. "You're sure?"

"Seems unlikely the code is just made up of 2s and 3s," he said.

"Everything here seems unlikely," Terra said. "Even if we assume the keypad code only uses those two digits, we still wouldn't know the combination, or how many to input. If this is used to guard classified material, it'd be a pretty long combination."

"Or it'd be short so the dummy officers and senior NCOs wouldn't forget it," Stacey said. Her smirk faded. "Wait." She held up her right hand, as if stopping the others from doing something. "Yes. It *is* short. Only three digits." She extended her right index finger, then let it float just above the keys. "Three digits..."

"What are you doing?" Ray said.

"Two of us know the combination," Stacey said, voice flat. "No. Maybe all three of us? Or two. Two of us. That seems..." She shook her head.

"Are you okay?" Terra said, putting a hand on Stacey's shoulder.

"I..." Stacey closed her eyes for a long moment. When she opened them again, the confusion was gone. "We should attempt a resonance cascade. The information is here, in the air around us. I feel like I almost have it. We can find it, if we work together."

Ray and Terra considered this is silence.

"You two already have a resonance connection, right?" Stacey said, finally. "You were paired up for that computer symbol reading test."

"I don't want to talk about that," Ray said.

"Yes, go on," Terra said.

"Then focus on the symbol," Stacey said.

"We don't know the symbol, or in this case, the code," Ray said. "How can we focus on something we don't know?"

"But you already have its primary components," Stacey said. "A two and a three. Focus on those numbers, and on the keypad, and project that to one another."

"We'd just be projecting confusion," Terra said, shaking her head.

"Maybe," Stacey said. "But don't think of it that way. Don't *believe* it that way."

Her words echoed around the room, as if whispered back by ghosts.

"This is crazy," Terra said.

"Everything here is crazy, including us," Ray said. "I'm game if you are. Stacey, you might as well try and join our resonance connection."

"Will it work with three people?"

"Couldn't hurt, right? Glasse and the others seem to think it will work with all of us."

"Right."

Terra held up her hands.

"Okay, okay," she said. "Slow down. How do we start?"

Ray shrugged.

"We can try holding hands, like a séance," Ray said. Terra gave him a sharp look. He returned a smile. "It doesn't mean we're engaged or anything."

"*I'll* hold hands with both of you, so as to diffuse some of this pathetic sexual tension, okay?" Stacey gave them a big grin, clicked off her headlamp, then clasped their hands in her own. Ray and Terra clicked off their headlamps, then joined hands to form the circle.

"Let's close our eyes and concentrate on the code, with its component parts of 2 and 3," Stacey said. "Focus on the memory of the code in the air, in the walls, in the ether between us."

Ray and Terra shut their eyes.

Inside, in the dark, their hands holding one another tight, they began to concentrate on a number they couldn't know.

The hair on Ray's neck and arms stood up.

A cold draught overcame them. Terra saw numbers like smoke in her mind, struggling to form.

Their breathing matched in rhythm and cadence.

Their heartbeats synchronized.

Their eyes remained closed but their mouths fell open, their tongues rising to meet the words given them.

"Three," Ray said.

"Two," Stacey said.

"Two," Terra said, opening her eyes and releasing her grip. Ray held on to her fingers, but she pulled back, pulled away from the circle to wrap her arms around herself, suddenly very cold.

Ray turned and punched the code into the keypad behind him: 3-2-2. Then he hit the INPUT button.

Unseen mechanisms whirred and clicked in the wall. A layer of dust fell from where the door frame met the ceiling. A shrill, electronic beep made them jump—and the door clicked open, its edge swinging out from the frame, slowly. Ray caught it in his right hand and clicked his headlamp back on as he pulled the door open wider. Inside was a small, cramped room, piled high with more boxes overflowing with paperwork and thick binders. Shelves laden with electronic equipment—radio consoles, computer towers, bulky handheld devices—were stacked against the walls.

"How did we do that?" Terra asked, already knowing the answer.

"Resonance cascade," Ray said. "I guess the training here is paying off."

"We're supposed to be getting mental health care, not training," Stacey said. "But I can think of a lot of times where the military *should* have given me something, and it gave me shit instead."

"A wise soldier expects nothing except pain, and is therefore never truly disappointed," Ray said.

"We shouldn't stay too long," Terra said. "I figure we got maybe ten minutes before we need to head back to the barracks."

"How are we going to find anything useful in that time?" Ray asked.

"We could do another séance," Stacey said. "No reason it won't work again, right?"

"I'm worried about what happens if we keep doing

it," Ray said.

"Why?"

Ray turned away, then thumbed the edge of his lips, nervously.

"The convocation. The ritual at the altar. It drew something to us. Something that wanted to reach out to us, specifically. Not Dr. Glasse or her robed weirdos. *Us*."

Stacey snapped her fingers. "Except, they had us all drugged up, right? Doc Glasse was leading that ritual. Lot of ceremony involved. And a lot of *us* involved. It wasn't two or three of us. It was all of us, in one place, with spooky theatrics. They didn't seem so concerned when it was just pairs of people thinking about images on computer screens, right?"

"You've got a point," Ray said. "But something did find me when I was matched with Terra, in the computer lab."

"Nobody else experienced that," Terra said. "I think you fell asleep, dreamed the whole thing."

"What's the difference between a dream and what we just did?"

Terra gave him a defeated smile. "Okay. So, we try it again. But we keep it short. We focus on a single question, maybe, then cut it off before any goblins show up."

"What made you say 'goblins'?" Ray asked.

"Just a figure of speech," Terra said. "Why?"

"Those things outside, on the roof. They weren't owls. Not really. I know that now."

"You're creeping me out," Stacey said, stepping forward to shine her headlamp beam into the room. "How about, 'what the hell is up with this place?' Good as any other question to ask."

Terra grabbed their hands, the circle formed once

more.

"Close your eyes and cut the lights," she said.

EPISTOLARY

CLASSIFIED 2009/12/15
DIA: RDP550-0080R0040011-3

MEMORANDUM FOR: Adjutant General
Reginald Shank, Colorado Army
National Guard

FROM: Deputy Director Suzanne M. Grey

SUBJECT: Camp Winter Falcon Change
of Command / Property Authority
Changeover

REFERENCE: National Guard Bureau
Change of Authority Special Order
79-A4A-CO-US-2009

1. DIA-CIA working group PROJECT
EIBON personnel will arrive on-
site at CAMP WINTER FALCON no
later than 2010/1/5 for official
grounds inspection and assumption
of command. No formal change of
command ceremony or decommissioning,
folding of colors, etc. is to be
performed. Colorado Army National
Guard personnel (with exception noted
below) on-site must vacate premises
NLT 2010/1/7 0900 local. All keys,
property books, and sensitive items
are to be transferred to working
group control within 24 hours of
arrival.

2. Special Detachment Zero (SDZ), Co. B, 5th Battalion, 19th Special Forces Group (Airborne) is to remain on-site for continued security operations in vicinity of Tunnel 6. 5-19 HHC (Watkins) will maintain operational and administrative support of SDZ. OIC and NCOIC of SDZ will report directly to the incoming working group control officer. All SDZ direct and support operations are to remain classified.

3. This memorandum and Special Order 79-A4A-CO-US-2009 supersedes all previous change of property authority orders on record and available to ODNI at the time of records request: 1948 Army Air Corps to Air Force authority; 1958 Air Force to CIA authority; 1962 CIA to Army 10th Mountain Division authority; 1989 Army 10th Mountain Division to Colorado Army National Guard authority.

Deputy Director, DIA
CLASSIFIED 2010/02/28
DIA: CWF004-0000A-1002-1

MEMORANDUM FOR: OIC & NCOIC Special Detachment Zero (SDZ), Co. B, 5th Battalion, 19th Special Forces Group (Airborne); HHC 5-19

FROM: Director, PROJECT EIBON Control Group

SUBJECT: Expansion of Operations at Tunnel 6

REFERENCE: National Guard Bureau-DIA Cooperative Agreement for Special Projects

1. This is formal notice that PROJECT EIBON Control Group (formerly "working group") traffic in and around the vicinity of Tunnel 6 will be increasing as of 2010/03/01. SDZ personnel should be informed and adjust operations accordingly.

2. All non-PROJECT EIBON personnel, including SDZ soldiers, are restricted from entering Tunnel 6 and vicinity beyond the control access point and Final Protective Line. Access will only be granted to PROJECT EIBON personnel carrying special badge access card Type II. Type I access is now rescinded. Logs with timestamps, personnel requesting access signatures, and sergeant of the guard signatures

must be maintained and subjected to
leadership spot checks.
SDZ HHC support group will continue
to maintain and operate video
systems for visual digital records of
personnel access and anomalous events
occurring in vicinity of Tunnel
6. Temperature checks and visual
inspection by team medic must be
conducted on all personnel entering
or exiting Tunnel 6 regardless of
time spent "below deck." Control
Group is in the process of consulting
with USARMDC on permanent assignment
of medical staff to PROJECT EIBON
for follow-on research and clinical
trials.

3. Anomalous atmospheric events,
Unidentified Aerial Phenomena,
or "high strangeness," pursuant
to SDZ Camp Winter Falcon INDOC
brief adapted from "Meta-Cognitive
Reflective Phenomena in Isolated
Locations" (Hyman, Slatsky, Jones,
Holesapple, 2009) must continue to
be reported to Control Group via
Observer/Experiencer Form A1. Reports
must be made as soon as possible.

4. Control Group recognizes and
appreciates the capabilities and
dedication of SDZ. As Green Berets,
your training and professionalism are
not in question. In-ranks grumbling

about "glorified guard duty" are to
be kept in-house, not expressed to
PROJECT EIBON personnel attempting
to access Tunnel 6 and complete
their critical work. Control Group
would remind OIC and NCOIC that this
matter is of the utmost importance
to the DIA and the Secretary of
the Army. SDZ was selected for its
combat abilities, professionalism,
security clearances of its personnel,
and proximity to the site. Future
reports of disciplinary infractions,
disrespect, failure to adhere to
containment protocols, etc. must
be handled with the utmost urgency
by the SDZ OIC and NCOIC. It is the
Control Group's desire to maintain
a professional and amicable working
relationship with this detachment.
SDZ personnel who do not share that
vision will find themselves at risk of
formal disciplinary action including
but not limited to revocation of
security clearance, reassignment out
of SOCOM, summary dismissal, and/or
formal UCMJ action.

5. Containment breach is unlikely
due to "below deck" security
protocols and safeguards, but SDZ
must be prepared to enforce the Final
Protective Line.

We appreciate your cooperation and

contribution to this mission.

Director, PROJECT EIBON Control Group

"Where's Tunnel 6?" Stacey asked. "I haven't seen any Green Berets on post."

"These documents are over a decade old," Terra said. "Project Eibon is probably finished."

"I don't believe that, and neither do you," Ray said. Terra tilted her head and gave him a puzzled look. He tapped his forehead, then softly touched hers.

"We could probably find this Tunnel 6 if we spent a little time on the mountain side of the base," Stacey said.

"Not tonight," Terra said. "We've been gone too long. We need to get back to the barracks. Preferably covered in sweat from a long run."

"Tomorrow then," Ray said.

"Tomorrow, okay," Stacey said, nodding.

"I'm not sure what we're going to find," Terra said.

"Maybe some answers," Ray said. "Maybe nothing. This could all just be nonsense. Disinformation."

"You don't believe that," Terra said, tapping his forehead.

RITES OF CONFESSION

"The American project is a failure," Dr. Glasse said, standing behind the chapel's altar. "How do you feel knowing that you sacrificed your time and energy in the service of institutions that failed to achieve even a modicum of strategic success in Iraq and Afghanistan? And what success they did achieve was at the price of blood, of birth defects in the children born there since the American invasions, of generational trauma and terror, to say nothing of the atrocities you facilitated in Syria and Libya. How do you feel about that?"

The chapel's furnace rumbled to life with a burst of dust from the vents and a grinding of metal from below. Ray, sitting at the far end of a pew near one of the vents, held his hand down to feel the lukewarm air. He struggled to keep his eyes open, even after two cups of chow hall coffee.

Terra sat next to him in the pew, and Stacey beside her, just as bleary-eyed. The other patients didn't look to be faring much better. Mike sat up front, his dead-eyed stare trained on the floor in front of him as he kept hold of a foam cup. Adams, sitting next to him, had lost the test of wills with his own eyelids and was leaning forward, in danger of falling. There was Calhurst, former sniper, training his marksman eyes on Glasse but shaking his head every few minutes to stay focused. The rest—Boskins, Garcia, Halloway, and Robertson—weren't in much better shape.

"You spent years—some of you a decade or two—serving a system that brought only pain and misery to people, not the least of whom were yourselves," Glasse continued. "Knowing all this, would you serve again? Knowing that the population doesn't care about your heroics or lack thereof, that they don't care about the pain and wounds you carry, mental and physical, that they don't even care about the results of your campaigns? That the military operations in which you took part—and were often almost killed for, or your friends *were* killed for—amount to nothing more than bullet points on some future AP history course?"

Someone coughed. Ray snapped his head up, almost drifting off again.

"Would you serve again?" Glasse asked. "If what I just said was true, would you serve again?"

She produced a long match and its book, then snapped a flame into existence. She leaned forward over the altar to light the tall, twisted candles at either end. The air went thick with the taste of grey smoke. Antelope and elk skulls leered from the high walls. Glasse dropped the sputtering match on the altar and walked back to the front of the stage, her high heels clicking against groaning wood planks.

"That's what we're really doing here," she said. "We're building you back up. Giving you the tools to be useful again. To be whole again, and something more. To serve, even in the face of impossibility, of disappointment. Of horror."

She realized, then, that perhaps her patients were not fully engaged.

"Raymond," she said, her gaze falling on him like a hammer.

"Yes," he said, straightening up. He *had* been paying attention. It had just been a bit of a struggle.

"What's the worst thing that you ever thought about someone else? I'm not talking about idle violent or sexual adolescent fantasies, either. I'm talking thoughts that you had, fully in control of your faculties, about harm coming to another person. Perhaps by your hand. Perhaps not."

That got the patients' attention. Ray felt their bleary eyes on him. He felt too warm suddenly, as if the heating system were up to its task.

"Um," he said. He caught Terra and Stacey's eyes on him from the side, something accusing in their faces. Something hostile. "Well, there was this one time. In-country. Over there."

Glasse smiled.

"Go on. I think this is something your fellow patients may be able to relate to."

Ray puzzled over that comment for a moment before continuing.

"We were a few days into an extended field operation. There were parts of our area of operations that were Indian Country, so to speak. Sorry, I know I shouldn't use that term, but, old habits and all."

"The Army was instrumental in the genocide of the native peoples of this continent," Dr. Glasse said. "Isn't that right?"

"Yes, I suppose it is."

"Then it's only natural that vestiges of its settler-colonial mission would remain within its culture, even if the original context or intent has merely become a metaphor for new imperialist projects."

"You sound like one of my old history professors, Doc. I didn't peg you for a lefty."

"I'm not a 'lefty,' Mr. Parnell. I am in a senior position where I am afforded the luxury of my own opinions on certain topics—as long as I deliver results. Please, continue."

"It was a valley under the control of the Taliban," Ray said. "Nobody really disputed that. There were two roads in and out of the mountains. Go up one, you're going to get into a firefight, most likely. Go down the other, you're going to run into bombs in the road. Well, we took the route in with the bombs."

"What kind of bombs?"

"IEDs or mines," Ray said. "This one was a mine."

"How does your anger fit into this?"

"We knew that going down that road meant someone was going to get hurt or killed," Ray said. "That's soldiering sometimes, right? But the rub was—and I don't know how common this was for you folks—" he gave a hasty glance at his peers around the rest of the room, "but our commanding officers and NCOs, they couldn't really give us a mission objective most of the time. Like, at all. It was usually 'go meet with a person that we hope is in this location,' or more often, 'just drive around for a while.' Like, none of us had a problem facing danger. We just had a problem when we were facing danger for nothing. For no tactical reason. No threat brief, no intel, no route clearance support package. Just get in and go."

"Maybe you couldn't see the bigger picture," Dr. Glasse said. "Maybe you weren't privy to the mission objectives or the broader strategy."

"I sat in on their planning sessions, when they bothered to have any," Ray said. "I saw the reports they put up to higher. What they *said* we were accomplishing—training X number of Afghan National Police, conducting Y number of combat patrols with our coalition partners—didn't have anything to do with reality. We were joyriding, rolling the dice. Wasting fuel. Not accomplishing anything. Every goddamn day."

"And?"

"And people were getting killed around us. Dismembered. Blown the fuck up. You ever get so much blood on your hands from someone else, that you have a hard time cleaning it off? Little bits of it stick under your fingernails for a while."

Glasse leaned her head forward, a subtle gesture to continue.

"So, you start thinking: it would be better if some of these insane officers and NCOs who can't even clean their own weapons, don't know how to operate the radio, don't bother filling up their trucks after a mission—it would be better if they were *just fucking dead*."

Was that a smile creeping along the edges of Glasse's lips?

"And you focus that hatred into a beam, onto the truck ahead of you, onto the dumb-fuck captain commanding this suicide mission, and, *boom*." Ray clapped his hands together. "Chunks of road are rising into the air. Flame and black smoke. The truck rumbles to a halt, spitting out fluids and missing its fender, its tire shredded. You can't see what's going on and they are not moving. Your truck commander shouts out 'fives and twenty-fives!' and the driver slams on the brakes. You start looking for IEDs nearby, AK fire, RPG bursts in the distance. And when the enemy mortars start to fall, you realize that you *wanted* it to happen."

Ray went silent. He rubbed a palm across his forehead.

"Did you make that explosion happen?" Dr. Glasse said. "Did you will it so?"

"Sometimes, it feels like I did. Yeah."

Glasse nodded. She held her hands out wide and spoke to the group.

"That is a good place to stop for now. We have small group counseling sessions this afternoon, followed by resilience training for an hour after dinner. You have chow in thirty minutes, so take a little time to yourselves. Good work today, everyone." She turned her gaze back to Ray.

Especially you.

NIGHT LIGHTS

Terra, Stacey, and Ray reached the site of the first resonance ritual. The clouds above the altar broke, revealing a heavy moon weighing down the sky. The three patients kept their headlamps off, finding one another as dark shapes touched by the lunar light. The air tasted of ash.

"I think Tunnel 6 will be somewhere in the spurs to the west of here," Terra said. "If it's the same place we saw in that video of the one-sided firefight, we can follow the streets until we find it."

"Why would they show us a video of a classified location?" Stacey asked.

"I don't know," Ray said. "But I think that was the 'containment breach' the memorandum mentioned as a possibility. Those were the Green Berets holding the line against... whatever it was."

"Let's see if we can find the tunnel and if it's still under guard," Terra said. "If it is, I guess that's the end of our field trip."

"And if it isn't?" Stacey asked.

"Then maybe we take a peek inside. Whatever was going on in there then seems to be connected to whatever is going on here, now. I don't think it's a coincidence we were able to get into that locked room and find those documents."

"Maybe they wanted us to find Tunnel 6," Ray said.

"You're being paranoid," Stacey replied.

"The only way we could have opened that lock and found those files was by using these resonance connections we're creating," Ray said. "They must know we'd start creating those connections on our own." He tapped his temple. Stacey nodded, but kept her gaze on the fire pit.

"The others are starting to talk about these powers, too," she said. "Isn't this whole thing co-sponsored by a defense contractor? Malthus. They ran logistics for us in Iraq. Charging $48 a tray for turkey sandwiches and potato chips."

"I thought they did consumer products," Ray said. "Fridges connected to the internet. Microwaves and coffee makers."

"Definitely military R&D," Terra said. "Bombs and drones, optics and radios. They do a lot of arts and sciences grants, too. Probably a tax write-off. I think I saw some made-for-TV vampire movie they sponsored for Halloween years ago."

"All of the above," Stacey said.

Terra led them past the fire pit to the face of the middle barracks. She stopped suddenly and held out her hand, gesturing for them to hug the wall. Ray and Stacey crouched low behind her.

"What is it?" Ray whispered.

The answer came in a flash of light from ahead. A beam cut across the road beyond the barracks, blinding them for a half-second before swinging away. Ray's heart jumped and the cold excitement of adrenaline flooded his body. His hands longed for the reassuring cold metal and hardened plastic of his M-4 rifle, even though, rationally, he knew he was not in any real danger. It was probably just cadre on security patrol, or maybe even the Green Berets still assigned to this side of the post.

When the beam broke into two separate, pulsating pillars and began to ascend into the dark sky, his mind gave up attempting to generate a rational explanation.

Stacey cursed; Terra moaned in an involuntary expression of fear. The lights sped overhead, heading east. The air rushed by with them, kicking up dirt and pebbles that pelted their faces and upturned hands. The lights swirled around one another, shifting from white-hot light to soft blues and warm purples and back again, ascending high, higher, until a bank of grey-purple clouds hid them from sight.

The world exhaled. The night was quiet again.

"Christ, help us, Christ, save us," someone was saying, over and over again.

"Ray."

"Christ, help us, have mercy, Christ, Christ, Christ—"

"*Ray.*"

The prayers ceased. Stacey and Terra crouched close, their faces all wide-eyed concern.

"You okay, man?" Terra asked.

"What?"

"We lost you for a second there."

"What the hell was that?" he asked. He shook off their hands and stood up, desperately searching the sky.

"That was different," Stacey said. "I haven't seen something like that here before."

"But you've seen it elsewhere," Terra said, a statement, not a question. Stacey nodded.

"That's why we're here," Stacey said. "We've encountered this stuff before. Ghosts, UFOs, whatever. Maybe we attract it."

Ray tried to catch his breath, his nose and mouth sucking in cold air. Air that should have been fresh, coming in off of the mountains, but that instead held a tinge of burning-plastic and wet tissue paper. Spoor of the damned.

"Maybe we create it," he said, the words automatic, dredged up from his subconscious. "Maybe it's coming from us."

"That's worse," Stacey said. "That's definitely

worse."

"Come on," Terra said, taking his hand in hers and pulling him forward. "Let's keep moving."

ON TIME IS LATE

The moon provided enough light to guide them through the western reach of Camp Winter Falcon. The roads and buildings thinned out the closer to the mountains they went, until they followed an isolated gravel path leading them deep into shadow. A thin mist clung to their ankles, rising and flowing along the surface of the cold earth. The mountains were dark leviathans ahead.

Terra, leading the way, held her left fist up for a halt.

"Dismount, two o'clock, one hundred meters," she said. She took a knee. Ray and Stacey crouched low behind her. They strained to see through the murk. A pale figure loped ahead, just close enough to be recognizable as a shambling human form, but too far out to be recognized in detail.

"Come on," Terra said, standing up and making a straight line toward the figure.

"What are you doing?" Ray whispered, but Terra was already a dozen meters away. The fog rose with each of her footfalls, hiding her behind a curtain of phantoms.

"Shit," Stacey said. "Wait up!" She plunged ahead into the rising murk. Ray followed after.

Terra almost lost sight of the figure ahead. She quickened her pace, inhaling heavy, wet air and exhaling just as fast. She drew close enough to recognize clothing: grey Army sweats, not unlike her own. The figure slumped forward with slow, painful steps, clutching at their abdomen and breathing in shallow gasps.

"Hey," Terra said, stopping a few meters behind, but close enough to be heard. "Hey, are you—"

The figure stopped, raised their head, and turned back.

Kairns. The woman they pulled out of the chapel, after the video of the... the *thing* emerging from the mountains. From Tunnel 6. Kairns' face was pale, her expression flat.

"Are you—are you okay?" Terra asked. The others caught up to her, struggling to catch their breath in the humid, heavy air.

Kairns glanced at the others, then turned back to the dark ahead.

"I have to go," she said.

"Go where?" Terra asked.

"I'm expected. I need to report. On time is late. Always be early. A good NCO told me that, once." She shuffled forward a few more feet.

"You don't look so good," Ray said, approaching her. "We should get you to sick call—" Ray stopped mid-sentence and mid-step.

Kairns wasn't alone.

Emerging from the fog were two soldiers—or collections of light and smoke temporarily assuming the form of soldiers. Old BDU-style uniforms, possibly from the late 90s or early 2000s. They fell in step next to Kairns—rather, they floated and congealed in line with her, assuming the upper torsos, shoulders, necks, and heads of soldiers wearing camo soft caps, rifles slung over their right shoulders. Everything below their waists was swirling mist and nauseating light.

The ghosts escorted her through the rising fog ahead, out of sight, as if they had never been there at all.

TUNNEL 6

They continued west. Terra got the sensation they were traveling in circles. She had flashbacks to land navigation exercises where the maps were 30 years out of date and the terrain changed due to erosion and the footfalls of thousands of lost troops over the years—or the range cadre had maybe screwed up the location of an objective point or two.

Just as Terra was going to suggest they go back, that the fog rolling in from the mountains was a bad omen and maybe this wasn't such a hot idea after all, great, dark monoliths emerged from the vapor ahead. She risked turning on her headlamp to get a better view. The structures were concrete pillars, wide and tall, adorned with shining reflective tape.

"We're still on a road," Stacey said, kicking at the heavy gravel beneath her feet. "*The* road. From the video."

"This is an entry control point," Terra said, walking past the first pillar to discover more set in a winding formation to force incoming traffic to slow down. "That's a guard post up ahead." She clicked her headlamp over to white light and the broken glass windows of a guard shack glimmered.

"It's not under watch," Ray said. "Unless those special forces guys are going to rappel out of the sky."

"We've seen weirder things happen," Stacey said. "Any sign of Kairns?"

Terra swung her light around the control point, spying rolls of concertina wire, concrete blast pillars, and abandoned piles of sandbags, many burst from years of neglect.

"No," Terra said. "I don't think anyone's been manning this post for a while."

"She might be further up ahead," Ray said. "They might have…" He trailed off. Just admitting there had been a *they* felt like a bad idea, as if acknowledging the spirits might conjure them back.

Terra suddenly clicked off her headlamp. "Take cover!"

Headlights emerged from behind them, muted and dull in the fog. A Humvee made its way down the gravel road. Ray and Stacey sprinted to the far side of the nearest concrete pillar. Terra crouched low and moved to the far side of the abandoned guard shack.

The Humvee's engine fouled the air with diesel-driven exhaust. The vehicle was painted desert piss-yellow, but all of its armor plating had been stripped off. It had a flatbed in place of a closed trunk, in which open-topped wooden crates were set, secured by stretches of fraying rope. It rumbled past the pillar behind which Ray and Stacey hid, snaking its way carefully around the concrete obstacles until it reached the guard shack. The rear brake lights came on, staining the fog blood-red. The brakes whined as the truck shuddered to a halt. The engine died and the Humvee's doors groaned open.

A lighter sparked and a cigarette tip glowed in the murk. Voices. Footfalls leading back down the gravel road. That glowing red cigarette tip approaching, passing, heading away. The two soldiers, their duty fulfilled, faded away into the darkness of the camp beyond.

Ray and Stacey waited until the gravel footsteps were out of earshot, then snuck around the concrete pylon and headed to the abandoned vehicle. Terra was already at the back, leaning over the bumper, the light from her headlamp revealing its cargo.

"Tapes," she said. She held up a pair of black VHS

cassettes, their stark-white labels home to black marker scrawl. Ray examined one.

"Calhurst, Kairns, and Nowinski," he said, reading the names. "This is dated a week ago."

"Here's you and me, and Mike," Terra said. "Dodonna, Morales, Parnell."

Stacey moved in to examine the crates herself. She picked up a handful of the black tapes, checked their labels, set them aside, then went back to dig up more.

"This one's got my name on it," she said. "They never said they were recording us." She set the tape down and picked up a few smaller cassettes, holding them close to read the labels. "There's a bunch here labeled 'Resonance Ritual #1,' with alphanumeric strings."

"They must have had cameras set up around the fire pit altar," Terra said. "Why would they bother to record this stuff, just to leave it out here?"

She set the tapes back in the crates and stared off into the fog, not sure what she was looking for.

"The cave's gotta be dead ahead, right?" Stacey said, pointing beyond the abandoned Humvee. "This looks like the spot from the video. Which means Tunnel 6 is at the end of this road."

"We should go back," Ray said.

"No," Terra said. "We need to see what's inside."

"We shouldn't..." Ray paused, then instinctively put a hand on Terra's shoulder. "There's someone coming."

"The soldiers?" Stacey asked.

"No, from the mountains, from the cave," Ray said. He pointed ahead, where dim purple lights floated within the heavy fog. "Come on." He led Terra and Stacey away from the road, taking cover behind the nearest concrete pylon. They crouched low as the lights approached.

The illumination seemed to be a trick of the fog. But

it soon coalesced into a pair of distinct, glowing orbs, accompanied by slow, patient footsteps on gravel. The fog bank broke just ahead of the darkened Humvee. Two figures emerged, wrapped in black cloth from head to ankles, hunched over and carrying strange, hexagonal black lanterns that spilled out a miasma of gloomy, violet light.

Ray, Terra, and Stacey held their breath as the two robed creatures shambled forward, moving with short but quick steps. Lantern light reflected off of bullet-proof glass windows as they passed. At the rear of the vehicle, they raised long arms and skeletal hands to open the flatbed and withdraw the boxes. Plastic tapes shifted against one another. Tepid fog glowed purple around their lanterns, wrapped tight like a funeral shroud.

Ray shook his head, hoping to clear his vision, trying to reset the bizarre visual data set forming in his mind. But when he looked back up to the Humvee, the robed creatures were still there, just a few meters past the front of the vehicle, heads tilted skyward to stare into the dark firmament. The sky held a peculiar darkness. An anti-light that pulsed to some unknown and unheard rhythm—concussive waves of energy passing through an otherwise formless spheroid of matter, suspended in the air directly overhead.

Stacey and Terra gasped, their brains registering the impossibility at the same moment, hands held against ears, shivering bodies instinctually pressing together in dread.

Hoods slid back to reveal skulls. Skulls, slick with a green, glowing slime smeared over leering bone picked clean of flesh, eye sockets empty save for the terrible light that bled out from within like a radiation leak. Their jaws opened and they groaned in pain and prayer, until their dead voices reached a fever pitch with that bizarre, psychic vibration localized above them, building to a harmony that would boil the brains of their hidden observers if left unchecked.

Floating orbs appeared in a brackish explosion of blue and green lightning, all ozone and wet paper smell. The skeletons' lanterns glowed purple in rhythm with the pulsing of those spheres above, which spun in mad, shallow, concentric circles. Celestial bodies or particles in a gravity-directed dance number.

The lights went dark and the air went still, as if they were never there at all.

The three hidden watchers blinked or rubbed at their eyes in vain attempts to see anything beyond an overwhelming, burning slash of fading light. Terra was the first to regain some semblance of vision, risking a step out from their hiding place to find the creatures gone and the crates with them. Stacey and Ray joined her at the back end of the Humvee.

"They took everything," Terra said.

"I don't like this," Stacey said.

A crunch of gravel caught their attention. They froze like deer caught in a spotlight.

"What was that?" Ray whispered.

"Sounded like a footstep," Terra said. "Someone's watching us."

"The soldiers? Those... things?" Stacey said.

"Shhh," Terra hissed. "Quiet."

Terra cast her headlamp beam out to probe the dark.

"This fog is too damn thick," Ray said. "I can't see anything beyond a few feet."

"Look," Terra said, clicking off her headlamp. She pointed ahead of the Humvee. At the end of the road the fog began to part, revealing a straight line of gravel leading into the dark maw of a great, open tunnel, in which the faintest ghosts of purple light receded, inviting them to follow.

in which the faintest ghosts of purple light receded, inviting them to follow.

UNDERHALLS

Tunnel 6 welcomed them with a stream of cool air that flowed out from somewhere deep within the haunted earth. Terra took the lead, the red light from her headlamp sweeping across the carved-out walls and low ceiling. The tunnel had once been a natural formation, but crews had cut through its heavy, grey rock to make room for the railroad tracks that ran straight down its throat. Those tracks had fallen into disrepair, the wood boards splintering, the rails heavily worn and covered in a layer of rust the color of blood. Wires stretched along the walls, leading into the dark.

The narrow tunnel opened up to reveal the interior of the cave, its ceiling high and riddled with stalactites. There was a thin layer of moisture over the high walls and ceiling, glimmering red. At the back of the cave, a set of guard rails led up to the skeleton of an elevator shaft: great pillars of metal held together in crosshatch, leading down into the darkened abyss. Shrill, buzzing lightbulbs spilled out illumination to either side of the elevator's entrance, which was held shut by twin slabs of awkwardly cut sheet metal. Terra approached the structure and found a metal case on the right, which was home to a single call button.

"We've come this far," Terra said, pressing the button. Unseen mechanisms began to grind and squeal. Great cables and wires shifted. The elevator began to rise.

"I'm not sure I want to follow those things we saw," Ray said.

"Then you can head back," Terra said. "But I want to know what's going on here. Don't you?"

"It feels like we're *supposed* to know," Stacey said. "The way we found those documents—the way we used the resonance field that we created—none of it feels like chance."

With a relieved groan, the elevator ascended into place, coming to a halt. The metal doors retracted a few inches. Terra grabbed the handles and pulled them apart, revealing the service elevator, empty and patient.

When the elevator reached the bottom of the shaft, the doors slid open halfway. Ray and Terra pulled them apart to reveal a long, concrete hallway, lit by errant light spit out by unevenly spaced bulbs connected by exposed wires. The hall was broken up by metal doors with brushed-silver knobs and keypads covered in dust. Ray tried the first door they came across, and the next, but they were locked. The handles were warm in his palm.

They continued forward until they reached a T intersection, with the choice to head left or right down identical halls. Terra didn't speak—she didn't have to— but merely held out her hands. Ray and Stacey took them in her own. They closed their eyes and, instead of having to concentrate, pray, or meditate, the hallway to the right simply went dark, the lights suddenly flickering out. The hall to the left saw its bulbs burn brighter.

They broke their connection, but the path remained bright and welcoming. They took the path they were meant to walk.

A hum of machinery vibrated through the floor and walls. Stacey brushed her fingers against the concrete walls, as if to keep her balance, as if to keep from losing her way. Soon that wall changed from rough, exposed concrete to natural stone. Obsidian, cool and smooth like glass, glistening with light from the buzzing bulbs overhead. Streaks of velvet cut through its uneven surface, pulsating—wet strands that Stacey was careful to avoid. The air carried that fleshy, wet-paper smell. Communion wafers and stale bread.

Turn back, Ray thought, in a voice not like his own.

"We must go on," Terra said.

The ceiling grew low and close and the walls drew closer, until the patients moved in a slight crouch, bodies turned sideways to avoid contact. The wires and bulbs snaked overhead, the lights pulsing arrhythmically.

Terra maneuvered around a bundle of wires hanging from the ceiling, alive with the shrill buzz of exposed electrical charge.

"Watch your step," she said. "Don't get shocked." Ray, following close behind, paused to examine the wires. He discovered they were not wires at all, but warped lengths of gummy pink matter, dripping down from a vein of deep crimson in the ceiling above. Moisture like diluted blood slid down its surface to pool on the smooth black floor.

"Hey," Stacey said, several meters behind them. Her headlamp splashed white light against the black wall. "This looks familiar." On the wall before her was a cascading series of interconnected shapes— curves forming concentric circles, interlaced with sine wave formations of disturbing familiarity. DNA double helixes. Interconnected solar orbits. Expansive, accusing eyes, cut in thin, sharp lines, staring out at them from the reflective black surface. The deep red veins of pulsating tissue gave a wide berth to the carvings, content to grow in vines along its perimeter.

Ray and Terra shuffled back just in time to watch the

holograms emerge. New patterns continually presented themselves out of the scrawl of interconnected, nauseating geometry. Inhuman faces in outline; star charts and ley lines of cursed topography. A living, ever-redefined tapestry of intersection and negative space, all working to present incalculable combinations of form. The lights above dimmed, the power suddenly drawn elsewhere.

Ray forced himself to turn away. Terra half-turned her face from the lines and shapes and wonders as the black rock glowed with some eldritch, interior light, like a muted television signal splashed across a living room wall as seen from the street outside.

"I don't think we should look at this too long," Terra said, but not meaning it, not wanting to leave. She put a hand on Stacey's arm, and through a great force of will, gently pulled her away and further down the tunnel.

The promise of fresh bursts of serotonin-wonder and delight were hooks in her mind, but instinct or psychic resonance warned Terra away, winning out, drawing her to lead them deeper into the earth where another rendezvous with horror waited. They left the holographic glamours of the alien rock behind.

The tunnel terminated at a great, grey door set in a concrete frame, its grey-silver brushed metal reflecting the bobbing light of their headlamps. There was no handle or knob, no keypad or security device. It yielded to Terra's open palm, swinging inward on a smooth, easy arc.

Beyond the door was a great, open cave not unlike the antechamber above—save for the composition of its walls. Fleshy, pulsating insulation spread across the cavern ceiling, floor, and walls, arrayed over smooth, black rock too rigid and straight in angle to be natural. The air was heavy with a sharp, metallic stench, like breathing through a bloody nose. Great, black bundles of fleshy wire coursed through the organic deposits spread across smooth obsidian surfaces, wires alive with synthetic energy, delivering power to the glowing floodlights erected around the cavern's center.

The light arrays spat polluted illumination across a mass of pink and purple organic matter held between great metal pylons set up to support and contain its sloshing bulk. Electrified mesh spread across all sides. Wires from the makeshift Faraday cage-prison to deliver power to a dozen or more television monitors on mobile consoles set around the containment apparatus. Flat screens, big and small; old-style CRTs with their bulbous glass—all of them likewise connected to the power network of flesh and matter covering the walls like a fungal explosion.

Just a few meters away, a twin set of control consoles were alight with flickering buttons and data readouts. Each console held four horizontal slots—dark mouths the perfect size to swallow VHS or MiniDV cassette tapes, of which there were teetering piles set on the floors nearby, kept in stacked towers of wooden crates.

The screens flickered to life, the eyes of a great spider awakening. Alphanumeric bootup code, followed by a rush of static, then star fields churning through the rotted heavens, the currents of the universe—through the foundational radiation of creation itself.

The great, pulpy flesh-mass within the electrified metal enclosure shifted, pressing itself against the limits of its prison. Veins of connective tissue on the ceiling, walls, and floors popped and hissed with a hideous, reverberating wetness. The interlopers suddenly had the impression of being within the belly of a great leviathan shuddering to life as it sucked in air in desperate gasps.

The floodlight panels went low and dark. The monitors went blue screen, then grey—static crash and errant lines of distortion—until the wash dissipated, revealing a series of faces emerging from chaos. All eyes were on the trespassers cowering at the cavern's entrance.

Cracking bones and snapping sinew reverberated throughout the cave. One after another, the monitors dislodged themselves from the surface of the console arrays, guided out on fleshy stalks interwoven with black wires, floating through the air, projected by hideous musculature and an obscene trick of physics. The screens presented their horrors to their audience in terrible clarity. Familiar faces, eyes wide in terror, mouths open in terrible, silent screams.

Faris—the mouthy washout from day zero, who had gotten his ass kicked and put on a bus back to Colorado Springs. His sneering cockiness was gone, replaced with bulging, bloodshot eyes and a mouthful of broken teeth.

Nowinski—one of the first to disappear—the skin along his forehead and cheeks laced through and exploded out by jet-black wiring, drooling blue sparks of arcane power.

Eckart—missing since the resonance ritual, her long brown hair slicked back and wet with black gore, her mouth covered with a grey latex membrane.

Kairns—who had been ahead of them in the fog, leading them into the tunnel. She had arrived at her destination: the other side of that dreadful screen, an image of pale-faced fatigue, eyes unfocused and blood-shot, mouth locked open in a silent cry. Appendages appeared behind her, wielding sharp instruments in clutches of grey, chitinous fingers. The blades began their ghastly work.

The audio track warbled and rose in volume, until all four on-screen faces released dire screams of despair, echoing across the open mouth of the cave.

Two of the slouching skeletal creatures emerged from behind the great brain-like mass frothing against the limits of its cage, carrying handfuls of VHS and digital cassette tapes they let fall to the floor like the great petals of plastic flowers. Purple light spilled from their hexagonal lanterns and emanated from within the folds of their dark hoods.

Instinctual retreat followed, a fight-or-flight reflex that was no choice at all. Terra grabbed for the others and pulled them back through the door, which even now was swinging shut.

Veiny growths pulsed and pushed red liquid through transparent veils of thin flesh. Lines of ghost-light formed rectangles in the walls, revealing secret doors. They swung open, revealing darkness and pairs of purple eyes within—sputtering fluorescent lights set above paper-laden conference tables, piles of plastic cassette tapes, and the glowing faces of ghastly apparitions. Other phantoms sat strapped to chairs, screaming. Volunteers sitting at tables, blindfolded, scrawling coordinates and automatic writing on stacks of paper. Others, suspended in the air, floating with the power of their corrupted minds, while transparent researchers took notes behind the safety of two-way mirrored glass. Ghosts of ghosts.

And all the while, screaming.

They fled through the narrow tunnels, finally reaching the intersection, then the elevator beyond, reality going choppy, losing frames, lights flickering and those grotesque strands of flesh humming with vile energy, stretching out, *reaching* for them, as the goblins pursued them and the screams of their fellow patients echoed through the cursed earth.

They clambered inside and hit the button to ascend. The whole world shook and roared, but the elevator's mechanisms worked true, doors beginning to close as the horrors of that subterranean nightmare poured through obsidian stone and concrete tunnels to reach them—

"You blame your addictions, your trauma, your parents, your military leadership, everyone but yourselves, for all the things that have gone wrong in your lives," Dr. Glasse said. "I recognize the limitations of the DOD's mental healthcare programs, yes, but I have to point out that you have had multiple opportunities to engage with more positive-feedback counseling and therapy techniques. Here, your failures to engage with those systems are laid bare. You wouldn't be here if you had tried harder."

Glasse walked out from her position behind the chapel lectern, her eyes locking on Ray's, who found himself at the far end of one of the front-row pews. He sat up straight, his notebook and pen spilling to the floor.

"Have you considered that you're not entitled to anyone's love, compassion, or effort?" Glasse asked, releasing Ray from her gaze to address the room in a rising voice. "Perhaps in the days and moments leading up to your various and incompetent gestures at suicide—and you couldn't even get *that* right, could you—you have considered yourselves undeserving. You are entitled only to what you earn. This is the United States of America, where those that can, take, and those that will not, or cannot, are worthy of derision, of poverty, of pain. Of short, meaningless lives spent toiling for the benefit of their moral and spiritual betters. Are you incapable of earning respect, support, or love? Perhaps you are defective, of no use to anyone, let alone yourself, and the universe has marked you as such and behaved accordingly.

"I have seen or led your counseling sessions. I have studied your profiles. You project contempt and distrust, but really, you are scared. You have been rejected, mocked, ignored, marginalized. You are weak inside. Being weak is one of the only unforgiveable sins of military service and life in America. You are afraid everyone else will find out. You have never mattered to anyone. Not to your family, not to those whom you would love, not to your chain of command. The machine grinds on, with or without you."

Ray felt his hands shake. Glasse softened her tone.

"But here, at Camp Winter Falcon, you do matter. To me. To this program. We can teach you how to matter. How to become useful again. Useful to yourself, and to those whom we serve."

No response from the patients. Just blank stares, heads bobbing from exhaustion.

Dr. Glasse suddenly stood straight, then executed a form-perfect *about face* to stand at attention, facing the back of the chapel.

"Platoon, *atten-tion!*" came the deep-voice command. Sergeant Major Haaster's voice, projected through static-laden speakers. The patients, languid and passive, rose to their feet, some quicker than others, to join Glasse at attention. Ray risked a glance at Stacey and Terra, who stood along with the rest of the group, despite their obvious bafflement and disorientation.

In the rafters, the creaking of old machinery heralded the descent of a large, gold-trimmed American flag, held lengthwise by fishing wire. A pair of small spotlights clicked on, illuminating it from below as it came to rest high in the air. The other lights in the chapel dimmed low.

"Present—*arms!*"

Ray joined his fellow patients in snapping a smart salute. He—they—held that position for several awkward, unending minutes. Instead of a tinny rendition of reveille, taps, or even the national anthem, a low, rising murmur rose up from the chapel vents as they rendered honors to the flag.

The words became verses sung by a monastic undead choir slurring their Latin. Ray resisted the urge to scream.

MISSING TIME

Stacey waited for him outside the chapel. The other patients streamed by, headed to the smoke point or the chow hall. The smell of fried chicken was on the air. Ray's stomach growled and his throat cried out for water. His voice came out raspy and hoarse.

"What the *hell*," he whispered, or tried to. Stacey slipped her hand into his and led him forward, away from the crowd, toward Terra, who was stumbling away from the chapel, headed nowhere.

"Terra," Ray said.

She stopped, then lifted her head, as if just remembering something. She turned slowly to face Ray and Stacey. No one spoke for a long while, all three of them waiting for someone else to begin.

"What the fuck happened?" Stacey finally said.

"I remember going into that cave," Ray said, shaking his head. "Then there was an elevator, right? And tunnels. Underground tunnels, and I think there were people. We were following someone. Kairns."

"Videotapes," Terra said. "In my mind, all I see is a set of consoles. Fitted with tape decks. Computer systems and controls. Something beyond."

"Something being fed," Stacey said.

Terra doubled over. An uneven, tepid stream of vomit landed between her feet, bits of gristle and pale liquid spattering against her shoes.

"Christ, you okay?" Stacey said, holding Terra's arm. Terra nodded, or tried to, and pulled her hair back as she forced herself to expel more. When she stood back up again, Ray's eyes went wide.

"Whoa," he said. "Don't move." He pushed aside strands of hair from her forehead, revealing a freshly healed-over pink line, dotted with tiny bumps or cysts buried just beneath the surface of the skin.

"How long have you had this scar?"

Terra managed a pained gurgle as she cleared her throat.

"What are you talking about?"

Ray ran a finger over the line, finding its surface wet with diluted blood. Still fresh. He showed Terra, droplets of watery plasma dripping down his index finger.

"What the *fuck*," she said. "Did this... did this happen in the tunnel?"

"It looks like it's been healing," Ray said. "Like a recent injury, but you got it stitched up or something."

"*Or something*," Terra said.

"We should get you to a medic," Stacey said. "If you can't account for it, then we should get it checked out."

"And tell Sergeant Major Haaster what? That we were doing a little spelunking, came across a giant brain in a cage, lost 20 hours, and I got a mysterious scar on my forehead?"

Images flashed through their minds:

Television monitors.

Familiar faces, screaming.

A desperate flight back to the elevator.

The walls, alive with alien symbols and fleshy wires...

Stacey put a hand on Ray's shoulder, her face pale.

"Tell me if I have one, too, please," she said. She lifted up her bangs.

"Close your eyes," Ray said. He clicked on his headlamp.

"I've got one, too, don't I?"

"There's a line running across your forehead, like someone split open your skull."

"Don't say it like that."

"What about me?" Ray pulled off his headlamp and handed it to Stacey. He closed his eyes as the light moved across his face.

"Yes," she said. She clicked off the light and handed it back to Ray. "Maybe the other patients have the scars, too. Maybe it was something we all went through this morning and we just don't remember. Painkillers or anesthesia or something."

Ray touched the unfamiliar contours of the scar on his own skin.

"They're pretty hard to see," Terra said. "We could have had them for a while."

"There's just a blank slate, after the tunnel," Ray said, more to himself than anyone else. "Like I was drinking and I blacked out. This is kind of like that feeling, but without the hangover."

"I'm sorry I talked you both into this," Terra said.

"Don't start with that," Ray said. "We were in it together. We wanted to see." Stacey nodded in agreement.

"Whatever we saw below has something to do with the tapes here—the sessions, the rituals, all of it," Terra said. "Something to do with the resonances and the insight we're gaining." She tapped her right temple.

Ray reached up for her wrist. He moved her hand over to the front of her face, pointing her extended index finger to the center of her forehead—to the center of the thin scar.

"Insight from within," Stacey said. "A third eye, opening."

"It's some fucked up government mind control thing," Terra said. "Like MKULTRA. The CIA used to run experiments on hippies, mental patients, soldiers, their own personnel. Maybe they never stopped. Maybe that's what all this is. Weird drugs and weird costumes."

"What do you think was in those communion wafers at the resonance ritual?" Stacey said. "That might explain what we saw—what we *experienced*—last night. Why we've got missing time. We're having some sort of shared trip."

"I haven't taken any wafers or pills or whatever since the convocation," Ray said. "That was what, almost a week ago?"

"Maybe they're putting it in the food," Terra said. "In the coffee, in our water."

"No," Stacey said. "They're not." Her hand drifted up to her face, finding the center of her forehead. "What's happening to us is different. I can feel it."

"Then we need to get out of here," Terra said.

"And go where?" Stacey said. "I don't know what you've got waiting for you out there, but I've got nothing. I've told pretty much everyone who ever cared for me to fuck off. I don't have a job. I've a needle or a fucking gun waiting for me back out there." She pointed to the east, where the sky was dark. "I need this program, especially if there's like, a job or something at the end of it."

Ray thought through his own situation: his best hope was another few months on unemployment, if the state approved his application, which was doubtful. That was assuming he could even access the online or phone system, which usually required waking up at four in the morning to *attempt* to log in. Maybe he could beg for work back at Queen Supers, land a job as a weed trimmer, or start at one of those fast-food places paying $12 an hour. Even if that was the case, he'd still have to crash with someone he knew until he could get a better job or a promotion, because covering rent by himself was out of the question. And his parents... No, he couldn't go back to them again, this many years later, and say he was starting over. Even if they would take him in—which was doubtful—he'd wilt under their judgment, their disappointment. There was no support there. Just contempt.

"I have a cell phone," Terra said. "I keep it on me." She patted her waist. "I get reception on the north side of the camp, where there's usually nobody else around. I can get ahold of someone to come get us out of here. There's a service road that runs along the side of the camp, far enough away from the entry control point not to be spotted. We just need to get over the fence and we're gone."

"I'm in the same boat as Stacey," Ray said. "It's just like, what, one more week? Then if there's a chance at a job, or maybe a ticket to some other program where I can get some unemployment or welfare or whatever. Maybe one of those housing programs for vets, anything to get a roof over my head."

"You have your sanity," Terra said. "We can keep our minds intact." She absentmindedly scratched at the center of her forehead. "If we leave, we might have that, at least."

"What's this? Y'all malingering here on the military's time?"

The three of them turned quickly toward the deep voice, finding Mike approaching them from the direction of the chapel.

"Whoa. Did I interrupt something?"

"Mike," Ray said. "Mike, something's going on here."

"You're just figuring that out?" he said. "Sergeant Major sent me over this way to round up any strays. Chow hall is closing early tonight. We need to be assembled for formation in thirty minutes. If you want to eat, you gotta grab it now."

"What's the hurry?" Ray asked.

"They're saying it's time for another resonance ritual."

THE SECOND RESONANCE RITUAL

The clouds fled as night fell. The sky opened up to the limitless black of the cosmos, pockmarked by bright stars puncturing the dark like radioactive sores. The patients stood in formation on the road near the barracks, Sergeant Major Haaster at the head of the assembly. His cadre moved down the formation's ranks, handing out sets of white pants and white tops.

"Medical scrubs," Ray said, turning the clothes over.

"Uniforms for the inmates at the asylum," Adams said. "Been wondering when they were going to fit us with straightjackets."

"At ease with that talk," Haaster said. "Falcons, these are tonight's uniforms. You've got fifteen mikes to make the change. Footwear is shoes or boots. Sandals are not authorized. Nothing open-toed. Something with socks, you get me? We've got some walking ahead of us tonight. I don't need any scuffed-up pinky toes on the march over."

"March over to where, Sergeant Major?" Calhurst asked from the back row, holding up the clothes. "Are these gonna fit me? I'm kind of a big guy."

"We had to sew two of them together for you, but I think they'll fit," Haaster said. "Platoon! *Atten-tion!*"

The patients snapped to.

"Fall out!"

In the male barracks, Ray held the white uniform up to the struggling light. Something that could be worn by a nurse or doctor on duty, but white, which wouldn't have been appropriate, considering how blood and bile would show. He unfolded the top, pulling out the sleeves, the torso section. Symbols were etched across the fabric in jagged, black lines.

"What is this shit?" Adams said from the other side of the bay, echoing his sentiment. Adams held up his shirt. "Yours look like this, too?"

The others held up their shirts and pants—all the same stark white, yes, but decorated differently, with variations of fractal-pattern lines sewn in. Branches of sickly trees growing from white soil; straight lines and jagged branches spreading forth like infected veins. They possessed the countenance of folk hex symbols placed on barns to keep out marauding goblins and protect against the Evil Eye of petty grievances.

An image—a memory—kept trying to intrude back into the foreground of Ray's mind: a wall in a cave, far beneath Camp Winter Falcon, covered in concentric circles and strange, angular formations. Symbols upon symbols, framed by tendrils of pulsating flesh.

Ray doubled over in pain, his head giving three sharp, distinct pounds, like the onset of a migraine. When he recovered, he looked up to see Mike staring at him.

"You okay?"

"I don't know," Ray said.

"Yeah," Mike said. "I don't like this." He held up his own shirt, the lines and rays intersecting to create a nauseating patchwork. "We've come this far."

"Not far enough," Ray said.

Haaster led them through the darkness, their headlamps creating a fluttering perimeter of light. The patients' white uniforms stood out in the night, like ghosts in the distance. They marched west, toward the mountains, following the paved roads of the camp to their limit, then turning onto a gravel path that Ray, Stacey, and Terra already knew well.

They reached the concrete pylons marking the access control point for Tunnel 6. The guard shack was empty. There was no Humvee parked near the entrance of the cave, no crates of mysterious video tapes. No terrible goblin-things carrying oddly proportioned lanterns spilling out purple light. Just gravel crunching beneath the rhythmic steps of the formation and darkness ahead.

Torches sprang to life, flames emerging from all corners: from behind concrete pylons, from the guard shack, from the mouth of Tunnel 6 itself.

Twin torches met the marching formation at the end of the gravel path as Haaster called for a halt. Dr. Glasse emerged from the mouth of the cavern. She, like the others, wore white robes stenciled with threaded, interlaced patterns and occult symbols.

Sergeant Major Haaster turned toward the formation.

"Falcons, you will form a half-moon around Dr. Glasse. Fall out!"

No sooner has the patients broken ranks than Dr. Glasse reached them, her arms spread wide, sleeves of her robe long and deep. A dreadful wizard come to parlay with mere mortals.

"Welcome, falcons, patients, honored veterans," she said, words cloaked in warmth and excitement. Even the wind paused, allowing her to be heard clearly, the echo of her voice bouncing back at them from the cave's open mouth, only a dozen meters behind her. Ray kept an eye on that yawning portal into darkness, afraid to see weird lights floating out toward them—and yet hopeful, too, because seeing those strange creatures might prove he wasn't mad after all.

"It's too late for that," Terra whispered, next to him. "You don't come here unless you're already mad."

How did you—?

"Tonight's ceremony will be a little different, but no less important for you, and for the program," Glasse said, her voice rising to the occasion. This time, no attendants came forward with candles or communion wafers. The others—faceless under heavy hoods—seemed content to linger far from the patients, torches and their own candles burning brightly.

"We've achieved a great deal in a very short amount of time," Glasse said. "Your mental and emotional resiliency has increased. The unique nature of your memories, of your abilities, has begun to reveal itself to each of you in its own way." Glasse favored Ray and Terra with a wide smile. "But before we can proceed to heal and to grow as a group—the ultimate goal of the final resonance ritual—this second convocation will mark your transition from damaged individuals with occluded powers to conduits of functionally limitless psychospiritual energy."

She turned and made a series of strange, awkward hand movements toward the mouth of the cave. An ill wind rose from its depths in response, buffeting them with a strange but not-unpleasant warmth and the smell of wet paper.

Ray's mind flashed images of floating television screens, of the faces of the patients who had quit or been kicked out of the Winter Falcon program. Their eyes showed terror, and his heart held their fear.

Glasse's face went slack and pale, drained of all of its vitality. She held up her left arm and pointed north, to the right of the assembled patients. Only a few dozen meters away from the road, the creeping fog parted to reveal a long, isolated barracks building, framed in black shadow against a sky suddenly alive with a terrible green glow from over the horizon. Perhaps the building chose to remain hidden until this moment. Perhaps it simply manifested itself out of nothing. It was a single story high, with faded and chipped white wooden siding, shingles missing in odd patches along its sloped roof. It could have been any other building within the camp.

Except: none of the other buildings glowed from within with a pulsating, purple hue. None of the other buildings' doors opened to reveal the diminutive, crone-like creatures carrying hexagonal lanterns, bodies draped in corrupted black fabric. None of the other buildings radiated pure dread, set against that terrible sky.

Terra's hand grabbed Ray's wrist, squeezing hard until his fingers went numb. Stacey came up behind them and wrapped her own arm around Terra's.

"Don't look into their eyes," someone said. Haaster? Glasse?

Dr. Glasse led the patients toward those short beings, who held their lanterns aloft in greeting, their faces mercifully hidden within the folds of their rags. But their hands were visible, and their long, emaciated fingers held bronze lantern handles.

Two of Haaster's military cadre escorted the nearest patient—Adams—up to those small creatures, who stood no higher than the waist of the shortest patient among them. They lowered their lanterns and gestured toward the door of the building. Dark, shifting patterns of red and purple danced among the shadows. A low, creeping fog spilled out as the door swung open, trailing down the wooden steps in a river of heavy vapor.

"I don't like this," Adams said. Tendrils of fog wrapped around his ankles, as if to welcome him—or hold him in place. "Yeah, no, I don't want to do this."

"Mr. Adams," Dr. Glasse said, her voice firm and authoritative. "Thomas. You were a good Marine. You faced things far more terrifying than your own demons in Iraq. What lies in wait for you, in there, cannot physically harm you. What waits for you is the key to unlocking your full potential."

Adams placed his right boot on the first step.

"I don't know, Doc. What the hell even *are* these things?" He pointed to the creatures, who held frozen in their poses, pointing toward the door, lanterns aloft.

"Friends of the program," Glasse said. "Old allies."

"Man, I don't like this. At all."

But he ascended those stairs and stepped inside all the same. Ever the brave Marine, charging into danger.

The creatures lowered their fingers and lanterns. The door slammed shut, too fast to see until it was quivering in its frame, the air around it shimmering like heat off a mirage. Weird light spilled out of the building's thin, opaque windows, dull but fluttering with color and movement like strange fire. The ground vibrated beneath the patients' feet, almost imperceptibly, in concert with a great, low hum escaping from the mouth of Tunnel 6.

The door opened again, slow, wide, creaking on hinges in desperate need of oil. Inside, a wall of fog or heavy, white smoke obscured bursts of purple and green illumination. The air tasted of burnt cinnamon.

The creatures raised their lanterns, the purple lights growing sickeningly bright.

"Who is next?" Glasse said, her voice pleasant and encouraging. "You have all faced horrors before. Going to war, coming home again. Surely, entering a dark room provides no terror for you now."

Terra released her grip on Ray's wrist and stepped forward.

"No," he whispered.

"I'm next," Terra said, to him, and to everyone else. "I should have gone first."

"Ms. Morales," Dr. Glasse said, beaming with pride. "What do you hope to find inside?"

"I don't know," she said. "But I've been passing through membranes. I've been emerging into new spaces." She brought a hand up to scratch at the strange, impossible scar on her forehead. Ray and Stacey did likewise, the hum of the ground beneath their feet triggering a rhythmic itching sensation beneath their scarred flesh.

As Terra approached the steps, the light within grew stronger and the hum in the cold earth grew more persistent. Glasse reached out a hand to touch her arm—a gentle, familiar brush of palm and fingers that turned into a soft grip. She stepped forward and examined Terra's forehead, then turned back to offer Stacey and Ray a knowing smile.

"You are about to emerge from your chrysalis," she said, her words for them as much as they were for Terra. "You've experienced a drastic period of accelerated growth. I can only imagine what this second resonance ritual will do for you." Glasse broke eye contact with Ray and Stacey and spoke to the larger group. "For all of you." She turned back to Terra, hands on her shoulders, and whispered something to her, lips matching the volume and rhythm of the earth's dreadful frequency.

Terra ascended the first step. Glasse lifted her hands

from Terra's shoulders and kept them suspended in the air in a prayerful gesture.

The portal accepted Terra. She passed through the limits of the fog, as if she had never been there at all.

The door slammed shut. The creatures lowered their lanterns.

"Ray and Stacey," Dr. Glasse said. "You two will go next. It's important that you set a strong example for the others, considering your advanced conditions."

"I don't understand," Ray said, touching his forehead again. But his words were weak, empty. He *did* understand, of course.

Before Glasse could challenge his empty defense, her attention was drawn to the far side of the barracks. A man was screaming—words turned to gibberish by his rush to get them out.

"Mr. Adams has completed his portion of the second resonance ritual," Glasse said, voice rising with excitement. "I am impressed it took him so little time."

The patients turned their attention to the far side of the barracks, past the fluttering lights and roiling shadows. Some of Haaster's cadre carried a limp figure between them—Adams, with his head hanging low, his boots dragging along the ground, his throat and words failing and turning to desperate whispers, barely audible now.

"What happened to him?" Mike asked. "Where are you taking him?"

"He'll receive three hots and a cot," Glasse said. "Standard procedure after experiencing a traumatic event down range, right?"

"Is that going to happen to us?" Mike said.

"I cannot tell you what waits inside," Glasse said. "That's for the camp to decide."

"And if I don't go through that door?"

"We will schedule a bus for you in the morning," Glasse said, her tone neutral.

"Then do that," Mike said.

"What should we tell the Veterans Trauma Court judge who gave you the choice to attend this program or spend a year in El Paso County jail?" Glasse said. "How would your family feel about that, considering the circumstances of your arrest?"

"That's confidential," Mike said, his voice low. "You have no right to—"

"We are a little beyond such formalities, aren't we?"

The door swung back open with a rush of cold air. The lanterns rose and spilled their terrible light.

"Ray? Stacey?" Glasse said.

Ray stepped forward, a pit of ice where his stomach should be.

"I'll go," he said.

The two goblin-entities turned their hidden faces toward him, canting their heads in curiosity—or recognition. Ray refused to meet their terrible gaze. To do so would admit to the madness they represented.

Ray walked up the narrow steps, his arms shaking with adrenaline. The fog wall embraced him. Light fluttered ahead, puncturing the gloom, and the sound of creaking wood and great, heavy things shifting, moving, and groaning in the fog drowned out the sound of his heartbeat.

He didn't even hear the door slam shut behind him.

SPOOKHOUSE

Ray walked further into the fog, refusing to stop, knowing that if he did, he would be lost. The only way out was through. Time grew slow and laborious, his steps heavy and his lungs churning humid air. At one point, a shadow in the shape of a human form stood before him, several feet ahead and obscured in the gloom. Ray made for it, hoping he had caught up to Terra, hoping they could face the terrors ahead together.

He reached for the shadow, but his hand passed through the column of dark vapor. He turned back the way he came, or tried to, only to realize that he was disoriented, his sense of *forward* built on assumptions he no longer held. He chose a direction and started walking. Surely, he would reach a wall or a door soon. He held his hands out in front of him and took careful, slow steps, despite the anxiety in the pit of his stomach that threatened to boil over into panic.

Dim outlines of swaying forms appeared ahead. Ray stepped through a membrane of heavy, roiling mist, emerging into clear air on the other side.

A locker room. The familiar smells of sawdust, warmed-over plastic, and a whiff of motor oil rushed to him, centering him in place and time. The lockers were old and scuffed or bent, and between them ran short wooden benches along the floor. Beyond the lockers were storage cage walls set up to prevent access to the darker recesses of the floor, where riot gear and old, outdated equipment lay in shadow and dust. This was *the* locker room, set atop the mezzanine of his National Guard armory.

There were no soldiers here, busy prepping their rucks for a trip to Fort Carson for a long drill weekend. In their place, large, brown fabric-covered forms hung from the metal rafters, bound in twine and held by fraying rope. Bodies, upside down, mummified or wrapped up like cuts of meat from a butcher shop; half a dozen of them in this section alone. A quick glance to Ray's left revealed at least that number again, with more likely hidden by the lockers dividing the floor.

The ropes groaned as the forms swayed back and forth. Ray approached the nearest body, the earth-colored bandages wrapped at odd angles but held tight against contours of shoulders and head.

The rope snapped and frayed. The metal rafter above groaned under the strain. Dead, bulging eyes stared out at Ray from the parting folds of the funeral wrappings. Eyes dry and glazed over with death. Eyes suddenly shifting into focus, breath snapping into desiccated lungs, mouldering lips struggling to form words drawn from the ether.

Ray fell back, stumbling over a bench. He landed hard on his right knee, which cried out in a flash of red pain.

"*Parnell,*" the corpse said.

Ray tried to say something—anything, even a frightened *no*—but couldn't. He couldn't say *no* to this apparition, which swayed on a rope threatening to give, its gaunt arms crossed over its chest like a Gothic movie monster.

"It's me, your old pal Reine," the shade said. "Don't you remember me, battle buddy?"

Ray nodded, hoping that by agreeing with the revenant, it would somehow be satisfied and leave him in peace. He felt vulnerable and small, like when a childhood bully cornered him and demanded that he go along and *enjoy* the pain he was about to dish out, in those long, hard years before Ray learned to stand up for himself.

"It wasn't the war that killed me, but it might as well have been," Reine said, the words coming slow and slurred over a numb, dry tongue. "You think I would have gotten in that accident if I wasn't going to drill, if I hadn't joined the Nasty Guard? How many times have you driven drunk, Ray? Had a few close calls, maybe? But I'm the one who's dead from a stupid mistake, and you're not."

Ray held up his clenching hands, trying to block out the vision of his friend's corpse, trying to forget the face of the young man with whom he had endured the petty tyrannies and soul-numbing exhaustion of U.S. Army Basic Combat Training. Back when being a soldier had meant something to him. To them.

"It's not fair, what's happening to you, now," Reine said. "It wasn't fair when you were chosen, not because of something you did, but because of something in your brain, or maybe your spirit. That's what they want, you know. Not to heal you, but to use you. To make contact."

Ray nodded. He did know. He knew from the moment he arrived at Camp Winter Falcon. That he was here for a reason. To become something new.

"Veterans are special," Reine said. He struggled to move his limbs beneath the wrappings that held him in place, like a piece of salted meat hung up to dry and season. "That's true, you know. Not just a platitude. We volunteer. We stepped forward while everyone else stepped back. We gave our lives and our futures and the love of our friends and family over to our country, and we said to Uncle Sam, *do as thou will*. And boy, did he ever."

Low, pained moaning began to rise from the other bodies hanging nearby. Their bound arms and legs attempted to free themselves from twine and fabric restraints. The ropes began to fray.

"We don't have much time," Reine said, his eyes turning red as they filled with blood. "Suicides, these ones. Hangings, painkiller cocktails, folks who went to sleep in the garage while their pickups idled. Shotgun sandwiches, death-by-cops, murder-suicide double features. More than a few died of complications from excessive drinking, but those should still count, don't you think?"

Reine's face grew dark. "We're all dead because we volunteered, even if we didn't get killed in the sandbox. We're war casualties just the same, right, Ray? Except, suicides and the long crawl of years of self-destructive behavior don't get the 21-gun salute at football games, do they? Where's *my* Miller High Life, official beer of Support Our Troops Dipshittery? I'm really thirsty, Ray. My throat is killing me. I could use a fucking drink."

Reine bent his head down to reveal his neck, sliced open and through with shards of windshield glass. Blood—liquid and fresh—cascaded out of the gaping wound.

One of the bodies nearby shook itself free, the rope above snapping with a wet, organic *pop*. Others followed shortly thereafter, landing with unpleasant *thumps* that reverberated through the floorboards. Ray managed to stand up, his legs quivering.

"Tell that joke you used to crack in Basic," Reine said, his words hard to understand with all that blood pouring out of his throat. "When things got bad or tough and we were all dragging ass? What was that thing you used to say? Made me laugh every damn time."

Ray sidestepped down the aisle, heading straight toward the stairs that would lead him down to the drill hall floor. More bodies shook free of their ropes. Corpses pushed through the wrappings, freeing mangled limbs. Their fingernails had grown long and jagged, ready to tear into fresh meat.

Ray found the shallow staircase. He hurried down those short steps, careful not to trip over his own feet. A fog-wall membrane, pulsing with light, waited for him at the bottom. The cries of the dead echoed against the concrete walls of the old armory. The shuffling of dead feet in blood- and mud-stained boots approached the stairwell. Close, closer.

As he dove through the fog, into a new, unknown terror, Reine cried out after him:

"I remember the joke now, Ray! 'Should've joined the Air Force!' Ha, remember? *'Should've joined the goddamn Air Force!'*"

A kitchen, recently remodeled: white floor tiles; a central marble top island, upon which rested several plates piled high with pancakes and bacon; dark wood cabinets; a tall, black refrigerator, complete with a fancy water and ice dispenser combo.

Light streamed in from a wide window above the sink. A woman stood before the basin, running a stream of hot water onto a pan, letting it soak. Her long, black hair shined in the morning light, and when she turned to reveal her face in profile, Ray did not recognize her, but his heart ached for her all the same. She had an understated beauty, present even and especially in the inglorious task of soaking a pan, her large brown eyes possessing an underlying, simple kindness that grew into a devastating wash of love as a pair of children scrambled into the kitchen. They ran in at full speed, socks slipping over the tiles but keeping their balance.

A pair of twin boys, with short brown hair, brown eyes like their mother, but with noses and jawlines he recognized.

His own.

Ray walked into the kitchen. *Another* Ray.

"Slow down, please!" this Ray said. "No head injuries before breakfast. That's the rule."

The woman turned that warm smile toward Ray—the *other* Ray, the Ray that belonged—and handed full plates to the boys, who then scrambled away and out of the kitchen just as quickly. The other Ray went to the coffee maker on the far side of the room where he set his mug down and topped it off with a generous pour from the steaming glass pot.

"Smells great," he said.

"Your recipe," she said.

"Thanks for cooking this morning," Ray said.

"You do it so much. I wanted to give you a break."

"There's no break with the goblins scrambling around," Ray said, smiling. "But I appreciate the gesture."

"Maybe you can repay me later," the woman said, picking up another pair of plates.

"I would like that very much," Ray said, meeting her mischievous smile with his own.

"Would you grab the syrup when you come to the dining room?" she asked.

"No problem," the other Ray said. "Just gonna get some cream."

The woman left, and the kitchen seemed somehow darker without her presence or that of the boys, despite the sunlight streaming through those wide windows.

The other Ray made his way to the refrigerator and pulled out the coffee creamer, giving his mug a quick drop before setting it back inside. He made to follow the others, stage-left, but paused at the threshold, beyond which was only darkness.

The other Ray turned, slowly, to face himself. Their eyes met for one long, terrible moment.

Finally, the doppelganger broke eye contact. He turned to look back out the window set above the kitchen sink and the pile of pans soaking within.

The air came alive with a shrill, distant buzzing sound—blades cutting through the air, growing louder, coming closer. A sound somehow familiar, but frustratingly just out of the reach of memory, out of context.

Ray—the Ray at the window, of this family that he had built for himself, in another, better version of life—turned back in horror, all pretense of manly bravery stripped out and replaced by a howling, cold fear. He shouted something. Words too distant and cut too short to be of any help to the woman and children in the adjacent rooms—and dropped his coffee as he turned and pumped his legs, slow-motion, to escape the kitchen and reach those whom he loved.

The buzzing-droning sound was lost in the explosion of fire and shrapnel and wood and glass, the house coming down upon them all in a catastrophe of smoke and fire, the other-Ray's body destroyed in a cascading series of sudden, competing traumas of metal and flame. Although his death was quick, his last moments were full of terror and despair.

Ray shielded his face with his hands, but found that, as time slowed and the procession of structural collapse and incendiary explosions continued frame by frame, he was unaffected. He was a ghost, a voyeur, free to move about the house as it suffered through staggered detonations of ordnance, working as designed by the best engineers in the world.

Ray made for the next room, passing through explosive bursts of growing flame and clouds of flesh-rending metal he could see but not feel, all near-frozen in time. The other-Ray was dead already, his skin fried off of his bones, his muscles and fat liquefied and boiling into vapor.

The hallway led Ray to the dining room, which opened up to a high ceiling and large, wide windows that shattered in a waterfall of glimmering, broken glass, each of the hundreds of shards reflecting the terror unfolding in the room. The boys—or what remained of the boys' disintegrating bodies—were falling back, hands up and over their faces in instinctual reflex, their heads already succumbing to the trauma of explosive force, wood from the ceiling and shrapnel projectiles, and the corrosive touch of pillars of flame.

The woman's face was missing. In its place was a screaming skull, her eyes no more than yellowed sludge emerging from howling eye sockets. Dead and dark, turning toward Ray, the jaw cracking open, asking, if the mind had enough time to form and communicate a question that could have no answer: *why?*

Time resumed its normal course. The ceiling collapsed and flames consumed and metal chewed through children and carpet and toys and television set. A follow-on explosion rendered the accumulated possessions and hopes of this family (*my family...?*) that did not, could not exist into nothingness, into casualty statistics, into numbers on a report fed to a series of command staffs, all the way up the chain, for the benefit of careers and war-time public relations propaganda.

When the fire and the debris cleared, Ray's spirit moved among the smoldering ruins of the house, stepping over and through burning wood and plastic and charred bones. Overhead, that buzzing continued apace, carried on the winds off to the horizon, the faintest outline of that unnatural bird glimpsed only by some supernatural provenance, because Ray had to see—had to be made to see—that drone was of American manufacture, of American design, of American will, and its purpose was and had always been terror.

The cold came before the shift.

Ray found himself in a cramped, musty room, somewhere near the back end of the old barracks building. The windows were painted over with streaks of black paint, but faint, dim light revealed the contours of the shallow room. Illumination spilled from a television set on a wheeled metal stand, its screen a wash of silent static. A VCR and a single tape sat on the platform, the deck blinking its timeless digital clock in a dull and stupid rhythm.

Beyond the TV, a door waited in the gloom. He sidestepped the stand and made for the door. His hand found the handle, but it wouldn't turn. The door shook in the frame, but held its place, obstinate.

Ray moved back to the far side of the TV, making his way to the limits of the short room, where another door waited. For each step he took, he found himself two further away. Behind him, the TV and stand remained as close as ever. There was no choice here, then.

He slapped the cassette into the waiting VCR. The screen went from static-grey to blue to black. Once again, Ray saw himself.

This other-Ray was in a cramped room—not unlike this one, just with a couch and a coffee table, bathed in the sputtering glow of a TV screen. Other-Ray was seated, a glass in his hands, an open bottle of whiskey on the table nearby.

There was something else on the table, too,

something in his hands the moment he finished his drink and tossed the glass to the floor. A pistol—the .40 caliber that had been a gift from a friend for some occasion he couldn't remember.

The Ray on-screen opened his mouth. The gun found its way inside.

Gore splattered on the wall behind him, bits of teeth and skull and grey brain matter trailing down in a grotesque slash. Other-Ray slumped over, arms going slack, the gun clattering to the floor.

Static.

Other-Ray paced back and forth between the thin walls of a cramped apartment kitchen, stacks of dirty dishes obscuring the camera's view from the sink. He drank can after can of beer, and those empty cans appeared in the sink and on the counter. Ray moved about in sputtering, hard cuts, time condensed down into a short series of awful vignettes: throwing a half-full can across the room before cracking another and letting the foam cascade down his neck and shirt as he chugged; screaming into a cell phone at someone who most certainly didn't deserve it; emptying a bottle of pills into his beer-foam-full mouth; falling forward, arms not stretched out to absorb the fall; the camera shaking as his head struck the floor, followed by the rest of his limp body.

Static.

Other-Ray stood over a mountain ravine at the edge of a hiking trail, holding on to the twisted, blackened trunk of a small tree touched by a recent forest fire. Water rushed by below, foam tossed up like spittle over the rapids. Ray took off his hiking pack and set it in the dirt behind him, his eyes never wavering from the water. He took off his boots next—a pair of his desert tan combat boots, of course—and lined their toes up to the edge of the cliff.

There he stood, hand on the burned tree, toes on the edge, leaning forward by slow degrees, until his head dipped forward and low and the rest of his body followed.

The TV set clicked off. Something moved and snapped beyond. The door on the far side swung open on groaning hinges. Cold night air flowed in, threatening to freeze the tears splashed across Ray's cheeks.

Two soldiers caught him as he tumbled out of the back door of the barracks. They wrapped a blanket over his shoulders and kept him standing upright as the strength went out of his legs. His stomach lurched and vomit shot out of his mouth in a sloppy arc. They held his torso upright but let his knees touch the dirt while he emptied his stomach.

When he finished, Ray reached up to wipe away at his forehead. The back of his hand came back covered in blood and smeared with ash.

EVOLUTION THREE

PROPER IMPERIAL DECLINE

Mike Dodonna woke up just before 0600 as light snow drifted down like ash. The Army and parenthood had taught him if you wanted time to yourself, you had to get up before anyone else. Otherwise, your time became *their* time. This never bothered him, not really. But he had hoped that he might be able to sleep in a little this morning, considering how late he had been up—experiencing terrors and drinking stale bottled water in the chapel until the others had completed their part of the second resonance ritual.

The other men in the barracks slept the deep sleep of exhaustion and trauma. Mike had seen this before in the units he served with, usually after taking casualties or after long, days-on-end operations with only small pockets of rest sprinkled in, when you were so dog-tired that if you weren't driving or behind an M240 in the turret, you were likely to fall asleep.

The Army liked to preach that only four hours of sleep per night were necessary to keep a soldier performing at standard. Senior NCOs and officers liked to mention these "studies," but, of course, there were never any specific citations, and even if there were, those were studies sponsored by Army brass and carried out by researchers who were beholden to pre-determined outcomes. Experience had taught him that the human body and mind could go with reduced or no sleep for a time, yes, but memory—and the mind itself—began to degrade in performance after twenty-four hours without adequate food, water, or rest. The patients of Camp Winter Falcon's Class 001 needed more than four hours of sleep after the second resonance ritual. Much more.

That's how Mike dealt with things: he thought of others first. He thought of systems and procedures and policies and his training as an officer on the psychological effects of trauma. That's what had made him a good leader. That's what had stunted his career—that, and being a former enlisted black guy in a white boy's officer club dominated by ring knockers from West Point and elite ROTC programs. When he had nowhere else to go, no one else left to help, he simply didn't know how to help himself.

Maybe the final week of this program would help him unpack what it was he witnessed. Maybe the pain would mean something in the end.

Mike was relieved to discover the chow hall open, the self-serve breakfast bar piled high with steaming food. He wasn't particularly hungry but he filled a tray anyway, knowing he needed the calories.

Sergeant Major Haaster sat at a table in the middle of the dining hall, by himself, finishing his coffee while he looked over a newspaper.

"Any good news from the outside, Sergeant Major?" Mike asked. He gestured at a chair and the NCO nodded. Mike took a seat and went to work on his hash browns.

"Ongoing plagues and civil disorder," Sergeant Major Haaster said, folding the paper back. "Our military retreats from its quagmires. The weather's getting worse. *Everything* is getting worse. The people in charge don't seem too concerned, though. That means we're in the middle of what my old history professor would call a *proper imperial decline.*"

Mike gave him wide eyes over his eggs. Haaster smiled and shrugged.

"I'm retiring. I'm entitled to my opinion. Hopefully, the fall of the empire will be less bloody than its rise. But I'm not an optimistic man."

"You're full of surprises, Sergeant Major."

Haaster shrugged.

"Gotta make a living somehow. I'm good at soldiering. I just don't always agree with how I'm put to work, is all. But I tend to keep those opinions to myself."

Mike waited a beat before following up.

"And how do you feel about all this?" he said.

The door to the DFAC swung open, letting in a gust of cold air. Adams, Boskins, and Halloway stumbled in, faces slack with exhaustion.

"You're to report to the post theater at 1100," Haaster said, suddenly changing his tone as he handed Mike a copy of the day's itinerary. His first name, last name, and last four of his social were emblazoned across the top in big, bold letters.

"What are we watching now? More spookshow videos?"

"Not 'we,' you," Haaster said. "Individualized and small-group treatment schedules today."

"Sergeant Major?" Mike said, almost a whisper.

"Yes, Captain?"

"What do you think about all of this? About what we... do you know what we went through last night? The shit we—I—saw?"

Haaster shrugged.

"I've been in so long, nothing surprises me anymore, or at least I thought it didn't."

"What they're doing to us doesn't bother you?"

"I'm not privy to the plans of Dr. Glasse and the people she reports to," Haaster said, keeping his voice low. His eyes wouldn't meet Mike's. He kept them on the newspaper, folded up between their trays. "I'm not a religious man. I'm not spiritually minded. But I know the ways we try to treat veterans haven't been working. You retired out, right? That means you are probably connected to someone who took their own life. That means you know the VA, the Army, the civilian world—no one really cares, because if they did, they would have tried something different with us these past twenty-plus years."

He finally met Mike's gaze, having worked up to his justification. "Dr. Glasse is doing something different. She's tapping into the spiritual side of things—things I can't claim to understand because I'm not entitled to the finer points of her research, which is very much proprietary, under the aegis of the DOD." Haaster put an elbow on the table and leaned forward, keeping his voice quiet. "I've seen things here, Captain. Incredible things. Things I never would have believed had I not been a part of this project. It's remarkable. It's terrifying. And I'm thankful."

Adams walked by the table, exchanging nods with Haaster. The sergeant major sat back in his seat.

"We've got one week of this program left," he said. "You'll graduate, then move on to new jobs, clear criminal records, access to additional care through the VA. Whatever this program is doing, its primary goal is to take care of soldiers. To take care of you. Even if it's unorthodox. Even if it involves ghosts and strange lights in the sky."

Haaster glanced at his watch.

"I should get going. Remember, Captain. Eleven-hundred hours at the post theater, north side of the camp. There's a map on the back side of the schedule."

"Roger," Mike said. "Thank you, Sergeant Major."

"Thank you for wanting to get better," Haaster said,

standing up and collecting his newspaper and tray. "Because I've known more than a few guys who didn't want to get better. They all ended up dead."

MATINEE

Mike followed crumbling streets through blocks of abandoned buildings he had only seen in passing while on morning runs: derelict structures in serious need of repair, many with sagging roofs destined to collapse under the heavy snows soon to come. The buildings seemed to have a *smell* to them, too: a fleshy, wet paper and cinnamon scent dominated the air, accompanied by a faint electric ozone aftertaste that lingered in his sinus cavity.

The theater was in slightly better shape, the recipient of some small gestures of routine maintenance. It was a wide two-story building wrapped in simple white and grey siding, but with a traditional marquee overhanging the main entrance's twin glass doors. There were even inset windows for movie poster displays on each side. The marquee held a few stubborn letters like broken teeth, but Mike couldn't guess the title of the movie.

Empty, crumbling streets led off in each direction away from the theater. A strange, translucent fog began to roll off the mountains beyond, perhaps a cloud no longer content to view affairs on the ground from above.

He pushed the doors open and entered the lobby. Inside, the air held a tinge of humidity, the threat of mold in moist air. Beneath that, the smell and taste of burnt popcorn, or the sugary-sweet smell of spilled soda. Dim light fixtures offered some illumination, but the soft light gave the scene a blurry, dreamlike quality.

The lobby held glass display counters, cracked and covered in grime. Boxes and bags of old candy remained within, covered in shattered glass. Derelict popcorn machines and soda dispensers stood sentry on the far right and left limits of the countertop. Sets of doors sat on either side of the concession area, the number "1" above the set to the left, "2" above the right.

Mike checked the paperwork Haaster had given him. "POST THEATER @ 1100" circled on the Excel table on the front; some hastily scrawled directions on the map on the back. No mention of theater 1 or 2.

He caught his reflection in the broken glass of the display case. Several Mikes stared back at him, all pale and gaunt in the odd angles and bad light, eyes dark and hopeless.

Not hopeless, he thought. *Doesn't matter what I saw in that spookhouse. What matters is that I keep driving on.* Resiliency in the face of all reasonable evidence served him well during his military career. Even if the drinking—the *bad* drinking—started only a few years in, and got worse as he went... Well, that's why he volunteered for this project. Or, rather, he accepted the opportunity when it was presented. Because he didn't really *volunteer*. The judge saw to that.

The phantom Mikes frowned back at him from shattered glass. His hand jerked out involuntarily, striking the counter and shaking the broken glass within. He looked away from his reflections, suddenly afraid of seeing eyes, even if they were his own.

A moistness developed above his eyebrows. Probing fingers discovered a thin, red wetness in a narrow line across his forehead. He looked to the ceiling, assuming the roof had sprung a leak. The soft white sound-dampening ceiling tiles showed dust and discoloration, but no signs of water damage. His gaze dragged itself down from the ceiling, finding the doors leading to Theater #2 flapping on their hinges, as if someone had just recently passed through.

Mike wiped the blood on his PT pants and made for the doors.

Inside the theater, his eyes adjusted to the sudden

rush of dark, revealing rows of seats split by the middle aisle. Two narrower aisles bisected the far ends of the theater. Red Christmas lights held in plastic tubes ran down the floor, beckoning him to enter, to find a seat before the great blank movie screen, already revealed by velvet curtains pulled back to the sides, fluttering in the dark.

"Hello?" he called out. "Dodonna, Mike. Captain, retired. Here for... for whatever this is." The theater swallowed his voice and remained silent, save for the rising wind pawing at the building.

The air shifted and a shaft of light emerged from somewhere above and behind. The projector, springing to life. Black and white test bars, then a 3-2-1 countdown on-screen. The audio track kicked on with a flurry of static and *pops*.

Mike walked down the center aisle and took a seat near the front-middle of the theater. The projector rattled on. The audio track slipped and warbled, then landed on environmental ambience: soft wind and the soft crunching of feet on gravel. The screen revealed a swirling procession of smoke or fog, white vapor, barely parting to reveal three figures standing near a military vehicle, the shot zooming in on them, blurry and distant, but recognizable.

"They took everything," a woman said.

"I don't like this," said another.

Mike's right hand drifted up to his forehead involuntarily. He recognized those voices.

A loud crunch of gravel—the person holding the camera, taking a few tentative steps forward, then suddenly holding in place.

"What was that?" A male voice now, familiar. So damn familiar.

"Sounded like a footstep," the first woman said.

"Someone's watching us."

Terra?

His situational awareness condensed into a cone projected directly in front of him. He failed to notice the twin doors to the theater opening behind him, or the dark figures that stepped inside.

"The soldiers? Those... things?"

"Shhh. Quiet."

The camera was set a dozen feet away or more, far enough that their faces were obscured by the swirling fog and heavy dark. Beams of light attempted to pierce these vaporous walls—occasionally even passing over the camera lens itself—but the people on screen gave no indication they spotted it in the gloom.

"This fog is too damn thick," Ray said. "I can't see anything beyond a few feet."

Shadows entered the theater and moved down the aisles, their footfalls swallowed by the crackling audio of the bizarre, invasive scene playing out for Mike's benefit. They took seats many rows back, their dark faces focused on the audience of one.

"Look," a woman said, on-screen. Terra.

More shadows poured through the swinging doors, light from the lobby too dim and low to draw Mike's attention. New lights appeared in the theater: soft, glowing purple illumination from below, revealing the twisted and desiccated faces of the corpses now seated behind Mike, three rows back, two, one. Eyes bulbous or burst, teeth rattling behind ruined or missing lips, cheek-flesh remaining in rotten strands, revealing black tongues and snapping, impatient jaws. A dozen more entered, silent and purposeful, taking seats, filling rows.

On-screen, Mike's friends made their way down the gravel road to the mouth of a cave, ominous and familiar. It was near where they completed the second resonance ritual.

The audio track swelled in volume, footsteps on gravel loud, louder. The camera followed close behind, closer than should be possible—surely, they should have heard the footsteps—until the shot held in place, content to watch the trio pass beyond the limits of the open world and into the mouth of the underworld.

The image on-screen flickered and jumped, errant frames from disjointed scenes playing out in rapid succession: patients seated at computer screens, bizarre shapes appearing and disapearring before them; Sergeant Major Haaster leading them in formation on a morning PT run; Dr. Glasse, wearing occult robes, raising her hands to the sky before a great, roaring fire; Mike, in his bunk, thrashing and shouting out in a night terror; the whirring blade of a chainsaw, cutting through flesh and spattering blood in a wide, wicked arc; a fog wall obscuring a menagerie of horrors; a bus smashing through the camp's central gate, sending sparks and metal flying.

Mike closed his eyes. With the spell of the bizarre film broken, his instincts flooded back, demanding his attention. The sensation of being *watched*, so pervasive here at Camp Winter Falcon, became an immediate klaxon in the stress-fried portions of his brain, all warnings suddenly flooding back and cranked to 11.

He opened his eyes and stood up. For one drawnout, frightening moment, he was afraid to turn around, afraid to face and confirm what his spirit already knew. Self-preservation triumphed over preservation of sanity.

The theater was almost at capacity, with only a handful of empty seats left, conspicuous as missing teeth. Dozens of sets of glowing eyes—and eye sockets lit within fleshless skulls—were upon him. The dead had gathered for one last spookshow, and he was the star.

Joints and frayed sinew popped like popcorn as old bones found life again. Bodily liquids splattered against sticky floors like soda. The air was laden with the foul gases of decay.

The dead came for him.

Mike ran down the aisle, away from the encroaching figures. He cut in front of the stage and screen, heading for the dim glow of a red EXIT sign. He reached the door as the foul air shifted and forms spilled out of the seats and into the aisles. As his hands found the door's cold metal pushbar, the sign above went blood-red bright, then burned out with a slow fade.

The door wouldn't budge.

Mike put his considerable muscle power and weight behind his next push. His hands and wrists began to strain but the door held no matter how hard he pushed.

The projector ran out of film. The screen went black and then stark-white, illuminating the theater with a dead, pale glow that revealed the terrors stalking down the aisles.

White hands grasped through slats of projector-light. Jaws snapped rotten teeth together. Desperate, hungry moans were a chorus of horror. The army of corpses massed to clog the aisles, to roll toward him in a wave of inevitability.

Mike lowered his shoulder into a linebacker's stance, then pumped his legs forward. He collided with the nearest ghoul, who collapsed back, bowling over several of its comrades with a wheeze of escaping breath that left a cloud of stink in its wake. Mike gagged, pumped his legs forward, raising his arms out in front of himself to knock the walking corpses toward the stage or back toward the seats, where their limbs snapped off and their mouths disgorged streams of noxious, bright-yellow liquid.

By the time he reached the aisle leading back up to the theater entrance, the dead had managed to tear through the sleeves of his PT jacket. He had no idea what kind of undead these creatures were, or if they were undead at all, and not some symptom of the psychosis the camp staff had been cultivating in their patients. He had no idea if their attacks led to infection, and if infection would lead him to become one of *them*, like in those awful movies his kids liked.

My kids.

The aisle leading to the doors was full of shambling forms, all teeth and claws and leering skulls. The projector finally sputtered into death, the beams of white light fading out, the theater falling into total darkness. An endless row of green or purple-glowing eyes stared down at Mike from the aisle's incline, the air thick with their smell: heavy sulfur-tinged air, meat left out in the sun, a taste like iron.

Mike made a silent apology to his knees as he stepped up onto the first row of seats then leapt over, landing with a grunt on the next row. The press of the dead had been focused on the aisles to block his escape, and they were slow to adjust to his decision to vault over difficult terrain. Mike leapt over row after row of old-fabric seats, their metal backing wet with humidity and sticky with decades of spilled pop, discarded gum, and melted chocolate. He moved closer to the inner wall of the theater each time he cleared another row of seats. The tide of the dead shuffled toward him, clambering down the rows to cut him off.

The adrenaline kept him going. It kept the pain and fatigue quiet. He would pay that bill later. Time slowed down—as it always did in life-or-death situations, nothing unfamiliar about that—but he felt that he was moving too slow, their numbers too great, his chances diminishing with each passing moment.

But then he was over the last row. A clutch of doddering corpses waited for him near the exit, purple light emerging from the depths of their skulls, spilling out strange fire from black eye sockets and emanating from snapping mouths. A gore-slicked skeleton lunged for him as he stood on the precipice of escape. Mike swung an arm in a ferocious punch, splitting the death's head open, its skull giving in like wet paper mâché. A geyser of yellow liquid shot out in a clumsy arc, staining Mike's PT jacket. He pulled his fist back to examine the gore and liquid spread across his knuckles.

The others stepped forward, eager to receive him. Mike tossed his right fist wide, knocking two of them back. The others pressed back up the aisle, hands clawing over the seats, over each other, eager to claim their prize.

Mike charged toward the door, knocking limp bodies down, then headbutted the shambling corpse posted at the center of the exit. Its lower jaw went up through the bottom of its skull and released a slurry of melted brains like a fungal burst through rotted soil. Mike shoved it aside and shouldered his way into the lobby. The overhead light fixtures had filled with blood, casting the room in a dark, crimson glow. He found the doors to the theater unbarred and pushed out into Camp Winter Falcon's cold morning air.

The streets were still empty, but darker somehow. He turned around and stepped back, expecting the ghouls to come pouring out of the theater in pursuit. One of the glass doors swung back and forth, slowly, revealing the inner lobby by uncertain inches. Nothing came for him. No claws, no snapping teeth, no smashed-in paper mâché dummy face dripping with acrid goo. He stood his ground, arms raised at face level—keeping his guard up, protecting his eyes, nose, mouth and neck. His arms shook with the last vestiges of an adrenaline spike. He let gravity drag them back down before letting out a long, slow moan of exhaustion and relief. He didn't know what would be more terrifying: opening the theater doors to see an army of the undead shambling toward him—or seeing nothing at all.

His legs shook as he walked away from the theater. He looked up to the sky, expecting to see a storm rolling in over the mountains from the west—and saw the clearest night sky he had ever seen this side of the war. The stars were brighter than they had any right to be. The moon was missing. The spiral arm of some unfamiliar and malign galaxy stretched over the open heavens, alien stars pouring from its veins and shedding a multitude of strange and wondrous colors.

His head began to pound. Blood slicked down his forehead from a thin scar, split open. He doubled over as the spikes of a migraine threatened to burrow outwards from his skull. The alien cosmos swirled above, its stars all deep greens and deeper purples.

ON-SCREEN OCCULTATIONS

Terra and Ray reported to Building #322, one of the brick buildings some distance away from the chapel and within sight of the antenna array and archives. Inside, a pair of fold-out metal chairs waited for them on the open floor. Dust-covered office chairs and desks had been pushed back to the walls. Black metal bookshelves laden with binders and aging manila folders spilled out their secrets. The floor was an alternating black and white tile pattern covered in a layer of dust.

Set before the chairs was another TV and VCR combo on a rolling stand. Ray reached along the shadows of the wall to the right of the open door. He found a switch and flipped it up. A pair of long overhead light fixtures hummed to life. On each chair was a clipboard home to a sheet of paper and a pen. Terra picked up the clipboard on the chair to the left as Ray closed the door behind them. The paper held only one question:

HOW DOES IT MAKE YOU FEEL?

Terra puzzled over this as Ray took his seat next to her.

The TV buzzed to life. On screen, Terra sat in Dr. Glasse's office, the camera set somewhere on the other side of the doctor's desk, so that it held her in the center-right of the frame. Dr. Glasse's hands were sometimes visible on the desk as she leaned forward, but the focus was on the patient.

"Tell me about your relationship with Ray," Glasse said.

The Terra on-screen smiled. The Terra in Building #322 said simply: "What the fuck?"

"What is this?" Ray asked.

"They—they didn't tell me they were filming the one-on-one sessions," she said.

"I'm only hanging out with him because he makes me feel better about myself," the other Terra said.

Ray went totally still, as if trying to fold back in on himself.

"In what way?" Glasse asked.

"One, he's more of a basket case than I am," Terra said. "I thought I had problems, until I started listening to his traumatized ass." Glasse offered a chittering laugh in response. On-screen Terra smiled, then her face fell into a cartoonish mask of sadness. She brought her balled fists up to the sides of her eyes.

"Boo-fucking-hoo, I hate myself and had depression and anxiety before I ever joined the Army." Glasse emitted a shrill laugh, and Terra giggled as she leaned back in her seat. "It's good to have a guy around who wants to get into your pants, even if you're not interested. Good for morale, you know?"

Glasse *tsk-tsked* her.

"What?" Ray said, turning from the screen to look at Terra. His face was beet red, his eyes wide and beginning to water at the edges. "What the fuck?"

"Ray, I didn't—I swear to God..."

"Is that you?" He pointed to the screen.

"Personally, I think this whole program is wonderful," on-screen Terra said. "But he won't stop going on about how 'weird' it is. How this isn't 'real therapy.' I gotta tell you, Doc, I've never felt this good. And I'm not just talking about since the war. I'm talking about *ever*. My mind is clear. I'm open to the signals the world is sending me. I can receive them, retransmit them." She leaned over Glasse's desk, putting her elbows down and holding her index fingers to her temples. "My third eye is *wide-the-fuck-open*, Doc. All aboard the occult express, next stop, the motherfucking Ghost Apocalypse. I feel it and it feels good. And Ray's too wrapped up in hating himself and making excuses. He's missing out. He needs to get with the program."

"Get with the program," Glasse said.

Ray stood up, sliding his chair back with a frustrated slap. He started moving back toward the door. The lights overhead buzzed. The building groaned under unseen pressures.

"Ray, I swear, I never said those things," Terra said, her voice catching in her throat.

Ray reached the door, his face read, his vision going blurry.

The room went dark. The screen emitted a sudden burst of static, casting them in a shimmering grey light. The image shifted and frames slid together, forming a new scene.

"Oh, God," Terra said.

Ray turned back to see himself sitting in the chair in Glasse's office.

"Tell me about Terra," Glasse said.

On-screen Ray smiled.

"She's made being here a little more exciting," he said. "I'll admit that. It's a little distracting to the work we're doing, but..."

"Because you're attracted to her?"

On-screen Ray laughed.

"Because of how much better she makes me feel about myself. In comparison. You ever keep someone around because they're kind of your little pet project? That's Terra. Terra can't-get-right Morales. She's got the smell on her. Of addict. Of a fucking junkie. Because she's always just sort of... restless. Never satisfied. Always wants to be going somewhere or doing something. Dragging me or Stacey or Mike or whomever else she can guilt into hanging out with her. She's got a cell phone that gets signal, did you know that? Can't even stick to a few simple rules. Personally, I think she wants to get kicked out."

It was Terra's turn to feel a flush of red-hot embarrassment.

"You didn't," she said, all the emotion drained from her voice.

"She's been making calls," on-screen Ray said. "My guess is to her dealer, maybe some guy she can't get over. She offered me the chance to leave. But I'm not going to take it. No way."

"Why not?"

On-screen Ray smiled.

"Because if I went with her, I'd miss out on all this." He held his arms out wide, then brought them back in, placing a finger on his forehead. "I'd miss out on all the fun. Resonance rituals. Can you imagine leaving all that behind?" He held his hands up in fists, then opened his fingers suddenly, fireworks in miniature. "We're going to make *contact*. And after—"

Ray stepped forward and turned off the TV.

The lights flickered back on.

Ray reached down for the VCR. He hit the EJECT button. The device whirred in response, but nothing came out. He bent down and flipped the tape deck panel open.

"There's nothing inside," he said.

Terra wiped a tear away from her cheek.

"Do you believe me now? That I didn't say that crap?"

"Do you believe me that I didn't say all *that*?" Ray countered. She nodded. "Okay. Yeah, I believe you."

"I'm losing my mind," Terra said, standing up.

"Let's talk outside."

Ray flipped the switch to OFF as they stepped back out into the evening air. The dark sky was brighter than before. The clouds glowed with a shimmering grey light like television static.

"Ray, look."

Ahead of them, at ground level, was a ovoid of static wrapped in pulsing fog. The sphere grew and warped in size, until it threatened to consume the sky itself.

MANIFESTATIONS

Terra grabbed Ray's arm and held tight. He took an instinctual step back. A Humvee's desert-yellow hood and side-armor appeared in the crash of light and heat, leading the truck out of staccato bursts of static. Flames and smoke whirled inside the cab, visible through the cracked windshield. Black smoke poured from its turret, where an M240B machine gun sat pointing up at a crooked angle, its gunner nowhere to be seen. Scorch marks covered the Humvee's exterior. Glass was shattered in small spider webs of chaos along its windshield and reinforced windows.

Fully through the portal, the vehicle slid to a halt. It stood still, save for the flames and smoke within, and the shimmering wall of static behind it. Ray and Terra clung to each other, frozen in place.

The passenger door opened. Black smoke poured out, an inverted waterfall flowing into a dead sky. Cooked-flesh fingers wrapped around the outer edge of the armored door. A head emerged. Empty, black eye sockets. Chattering teeth set in a grimace, the flesh of lips and cheeks burned away. Scorched uniform, its body armor aflame. A crown of fire spun atop a charred skull. An enlisted soldier, likely poor or lower middle class, now finding a royal inheritance in death.

The other doors opened. Fresh mountain air rushed in to feed the flames. Soldiers in various states of fiery decomposition emerged, flesh sloughing off of young, ruined faces, white bones emerging from beneath glistening tissues, eyes popping and dribbling down leering skulls. Rifles held tight—a weapon is a soldier's life, after all—even as their rounds cooked off and exploded.

Three flaming corpses shambled away from the

burning Humvee toward Ray and Terra. The nearest revenant raised a quivering finger and pointed in accusation. It opened its mouth—a column of black smoke in place of words, communicating anger and assigning guilt, all the same. The other two skeletons pointed and moaned, too—crying out to whatever god or devil had laid claim to Camp Winter Falcon, to demand retribution for lives cut short by terror and fire. Ray and Terra had survived where they had not. Survival was guilt. Balance must be restored.

Ray turned to run, pulling Terra hard by her wrist. She came with him with some resistance, eyes locked on the closest skeleton's body armor. The way it carried itself, the rifle strap, the burning name tape affixed to its body armor—this was someone she lost. Someone who was left behind.

They ran away from the road and into the yawning dark. Their legs pumped and arms cut through the cold air. They carried on their clothes the stink of burning metal, plastic, and flesh. They carried with them the taste of the burn pits, the promise of cancer-to-come, the curse of birth defects in whole generations of Iraqis and Afghans. The empire's carrion legacy was with them, part of them, and always would be, no matter how hard they tried to atone.

Blinding lights appeared in the dark ahead. Ray and Terra stumbled to a halt, covering their faces with their arms. There was shouting and a rush of motion, the clinking of metal and plastic. Soldiers carrying rifles and wearing body armor and helmets emerged from the light.

"Are you alright?" A familiar voice. Haaster.

"Sergeant Major?" Ray managed. A headlamp beam cut through the dark to blind Ray.

"It's me, soldier. What's the situation?"

"Back there," Ray managed, the words not coming, his throat tight, eyes wet. He pointed behind him. To the living corpses shambling forward, still aflame, still coughing out black smoke.

"First Squad!" Haaster shouted, his voice calm and direct. "Skirmish line, fifteen meters out from the manifestations. Move it out!"

A group of soldiers rushed by. Sergeant Major Haaster emerged from the light, clicking off his headlamp. He held his rifle over his body armor. Just another soldier in a combat zone.

"You troops alright?"

"What is going on here, Sergeant Major?" Terra asked. "Just tell me the truth."

Haaster turned back.

"You've got your manifestations," Haaster shouted. "What now, Doc?"

More soldiers rushed by, wearing armor and helmets—but carrying video cameras instead of weapons. They took up positions just behind First Squad, who kept their rifles trained on the burning corpses continuing to shamble toward Ray and Terra. The camera operators went to work, flicking switches and popping off lens caps, red and green lights blinking in the dark, capturing terror on digital film. The Humvee continued to burn, and beyond that, the static-portal expanded in waves of pulsing radiation, growing with each visible burst.

"How are our star recruits?" Dr. Glasse emerged from the light and the dark. "Terra. Ray. I hoped we could produce a full manifestation with you two, but I did not think it would be so soon, so early. You continue to exceed even my most optimistic models for psychospheric resonance."

"What are your orders, Doc?" Haaster said, nodding

toward the advancing ghouls.

"We'll need to get the portal closed first, otherwise those bullets won't have much of an effect," Glasse said. She paused, then smiled wide. "Actually, let's test that hypothesis. Have your soldiers open fire."

"Yes, ma'am." Haaster moved up to the line of soldiers, who were slowly back-stepping as the creatures approached. "First Squad! Take aim! Check your angles of fire—I don't want any living soldiers in your line of sight! Once you have acquired a target, you are weapons free. I say again, *weapons free!*"

There was a delay—of uncertainty, of hesitation—until the first *pop* of a 5.56mm round out of an M-4 rifle. The discharge was a comforting sound amidst the chaos. It was soon followed by another, and another. More, until the line of soldiers held their position, pouring bullets into the shambling remains of fallen comrades.

This continued for less than a minute—a minute that felt like an hour—until Haaster called out new orders.

"Cease fire! Cease fire!"

The rounds stopped flying. Fire selector switches clicked back to *safe*.

The dead, still on their feet, had paused their advance. Smoke and vile liquids poured out from bullet holes spread across their bodies and shattered skulls, but they held their forms and stood their ground.

"Minimal effect, Doc," Haaster said. "We could try grenades, but we'll need to get behind some cover, first."

"Thank you for humoring me, Sergeant Major," Glasse said. She turned her attention back to Ray and Terra. "Our next course of action is to deny the enemy his supplies. We'll see if we can close the portal. Camera one, you're on the portal. Camera two, focus on our patients, please."

Two shouts of "Yes, ma'am!" came from nearby as a pair of soldiers broke off from the group. One approached the ovoid of static hovering over the road behind the flaming Humvee. It continued to grow in short, sharp bursts of energy. The other camera-person jogged back to Ray and Terra, clicking on a mounted light to spotlight them in the dark and the fog. A red light blinked on its side.

"I need you two to close the portal," Dr. Glasse said, speaking directly to Ray and Terra. "I need you to close it now."

"They're advancing again!" Haaster shouted. "Troops, keeps your weapons on them, but backpedal. Slow is smooth, smooth is fast!"

A chorus of *affirmatives* and *yes, Sergeant Majors* followed. The dead continued their slow, deliberate march. The living gave them ground.

"I don't know what the hell you're talking about," Terra said. "Dr. Glasse, I'm sorry, but I don't!"

"You two created that thing," Glasse said, pointing toward the fluctuating orb of light beyond. The cameraman kept his distance, but held the lens on the anomaly. "It allowed *them* to emerge, called and made material by your psychic energy. I had hoped to achieve such a feat by the third resonance ritual. But you've exceeded my expectations by a fair margin, Terra." There was genuine awe in Glasse's voice. Awe and wonder, even and especially in the face of terrors. "Now exceed them again by closing the portal."

"We're... *responsible* for that?" Ray asked.

"For those manifestations, yes," Glasse said. "Our work here—with our collaborators, with whom you've become acquainted—has been geared toward the exploitation of your latent abilities. The signals you are able to receive, to modify, to transmit."

"Like radio antennae," Terra said. "Translator systems, like in a network, right?"

Glasse looked impressed. "That's as good an analogy as any," she said.

"Why us?" Ray said.

"Pain is the important part," Glasse said. "It always has been." She pointed toward the undead soldiers who shambled forward on burning legs. "Now concentrate. Together."

Ray and Terra looked at one another, fear and confusion plain across their pale faces, even in the stuttering mix of camera light, static, and flames. They turned back toward the portal.

"We're running out of time here," Haaster said. He kept pace with the backstepping line of riflemen. The camera operator kept his attention on the portal, which continued to grow at a dreadful pace.

"Do it," Glasse said, her voice low. "Close it before it becomes too large."

Haaster raised his rifle, leading his soldiers in another round of fire. Shreds of flesh and bursts of liquid gore erupted out of the dead-made-living. They stuttered and shook with the impact of the bullets entering, traveling through, and leaving their ruined bodies. They paused, as if caught in a sudden, painful intrusive thought, then continued their dreadful advance.

Terra took Ray's hand in her own. When their skin connected, a static-spark formed, and their minds, in sync, focused on the swirling energy beyond. They closed their eyes. Glasse didn't have to provide instruction. They operated on instinct. They concentrated on the portal. On the *idea* of the portal. Of the portal in the abstract, a thing apart from them in the physical sense, and yet deeply connected. They focused on severing that connection.

They floated outside of their own bodies, luminous forms of light and shimmering consciousness moored to the flesh by fragile strands of energy. The portal's fibrous anchors held fast to their astral aspects, to the roiling cores of pain within. They found those fibers of energy channeled toward the portal, flowing from within themselves, from within the *idea* of themselves. Seeing the malleable nature of that idea, of the world itself and their place within its psychospheric superstructure, they willed those connective lines to fray, to burst, to cut loose and wave about in the ether.

The portal disgorged a belch of energy visible to Terra and Ray on the spirit-plane, and spilled forth new phantasms. Men, slouching forward under the weight of Kalashnikov rifles and RPGs on their shoulders, heads wrapped in plain scarves and keffiyeh, emerged from the cauldron of manifestations. Fighters from a myriad of conflicts—perhaps Iraq, Afghanistan, Chechnya, Libya, Syria, or Ireland—marched in an uneven line, wavering from one reality to the next.

Soldiers cried out as the shambling, resurrected forms of dead comrades and insurgent fighters alike reached them and began to claw at their body armor or through their uniforms. Their blood was a bright purple crescendo of light and pain.

Ray and Terra manifested their will as a great, spectral bayonet, a symbol of martial prowess, directed at the entryway that disgorged more phantasms. The blade sliced through the portal, releasing an arterial spray of bright blue ectoplasm. The portal began to fade, its static-wash becoming solid, pixelized squares of energy turning to charred matter, finally rendered unto dust.

Elation washed over Ray and Terra, their connection

vibrating with joy at the realization of the power they now held.

The insurgents were the first to go, their spectral bodies and weapons blown away on the mountain wind in a rush of grey ash. The zombified soldiers were next, a blast of static erupting out from them, echoing through bullet holes and screaming jaws and empty eye sockets, returning to the psychic soup from which they first emerged.

Ray and Terra drifted back toward the glimmering nodes of warmth that were their bodies. Glasse and another member of her medical staff held their arms, pressing needles into veins, inky liquid entering their bodies with the aura of blown-out television screens still flickering with power.

Darkness overtook them. In this world, biology had a veto over spirit.

SICK CALL

Ray's mind returned to the world. He couldn't remember where he had been. He didn't know where he was. His first coherent thought upon recognizing his disorientation was to wonder if he had been drinking again.

Water-stained ceiling tiles came into focus. Aspects of his mind began to work in concert, to give him a sense of place, of self, after an indeterminate period of darkness. Perhaps that darkness—easy, all-encompassing, soft—was what death was like. Perhaps, if there was no God, no feast at the Father's House, no resurrection of the dead, then death itself wouldn't be so bad, if it was just Nothing.

But there is resurrection of the dead, he thought.

"I've seen it."

The sound of his own voice was a spike to the center of his forehead, his brain shaking with the reverberations.

The pain passed into the background of his awareness. He pushed himself up into a sitting position. Old metal springs squeaked. Blankets fell from his legs and feet, revealing his body draped in a blue patient's gown. He swung his feet over the side of the bed. Cool floor tiles kissed his toes. The air was cold and the only light came from tall windows arrayed along the vast expanse of a long, high corridor. Grey, flat moonlight provided enough illumination to reveal a good stretch of the open ward, but its limits were held in shadow.

When he stood up, something tried to hold him back. He found tubes taped to the underside of his right forearm, an IV drip held in place. He pulled up the tape and removed the catheter, then tossed the tubing back at the stand holding the half-empty saline bag. The writing on the bag didn't make sense to his eyes. The characters crawled away as he attempted to focus, twisting and contorting into illegible symbols that implied esoteric, occult meanings.

He tied the hospital gown tight around himself and shuffled away from the bed. The moon hung heavy and low, dominating the sky, pressing its face against the limits of the high windows, peeking inside.

Has the moon ever been so large, Ray?

He turned around, quickly.

"What?" he said, his voice louder than he intended, echoing down both ends of the open ward. He immediately regretted the outburst, feeling like prey making an involuntary noise in the presence of a predator.

Shelves stood against the opposite wall, illuminated by slashes of moonlight. They were made out of a firm, white, textured material, a polymer that was rough to the touch. Hexagonal in shape, they formed a honeycomb that stood out in contrast to the dark institutional grey of the wall beyond.

Inside one of these alcoves he found the running shoes, sweater, and sweatpants he had been wearing... wearing, *when,* exactly? A fresh set of clothes sat piled beyond his sweater: a shirt, underwear, and socks, likely pulled from his locker back at the barracks. Who had brought him these clothes? Did they expect him to wake up and need them? If so, where were the doctors, the nurses—hell, a combat medic from Haaster's cadre would have been a welcome sight. There was just... no one. Just Ray, alone in this massive ward, the air cold, the moonlight colder.

After he dressed, he picked a direction and started to walk. He passed bed after empty bed, hidden in shadow between windows or revealed in wide beams of moonlight before them. The blankets were neatly made, the white hexagonal shelves on the opposite wall full of cobwebs and shadows. His footsteps echoed down the length of the ward, reverberating throughout its unseen dimensions.

Ahead, a door appeared, its handle an ornate, black metal slash glistening in the dark. His stomach dropped out, fearing he would find the handle locked, but the heavy wooden door floated open on quiet, well-oiled hinges.

Where the ward had been tall, wide, and open, this hallway's ceiling was low and its walls cramped. He imagined medical staff pressing against the walls as others pushed by patients on gurneys or wheelchairs. The air was heavier here, too—more humid, and slightly warmer, probably due to the lack of ceiling-high windows made of old, thin glass. Moonlight still touched these interiors spaces, however, just at less-regular intervals, spilling in from rooms with open doors.

As the door slouched shut behind him, Ray paused to listen. It was an old infantry trick—remain still to watch, listen, smell, taste the air—get a sense of the rhythm of the place you found yourself in. Noise and sensations of the natural and unnatural.

Wind pressed against the outer wall. Draughts flowed through the interior spaces, cold and persistent. Odd, metal-on-metal sounds reverberated deep within the structure. Brick and mortar held fast against the deep chill flowing in over the mountains. Quiet.

Ray peered inside the rooms with open doors. Tall windows within admitted the leering face of the great moon, closer than ever. Each room was devoid of patients and medical staff, but held old-style military hospital beds in good order and condition. The air was stale here, but with a faint disinfectant aftertaste.

Ray pushed through the door at the end of the hall and entered the next segment, this one turning right at a sharp angle at its far end. The doors were all closed here. One, on the left—the building's outer side—spilled dim yellow light through its cracks.

Ray pressed himself against the left side of the hallway and advanced cautiously. The light shuffled with shadow. Murmuring voices spoke words that were unintelligible through brick and closed door. There was a small, square window set at about eye level, allowing Ray a limited view inside.

Four medical staff dressed in hooded red surgical gowns stood around a bed on which a patient lay motionless. Silver scalpels and forceps glimmered in the sharp pillar of light cast from overhead. Blinking machines and beeping monitors stood in array around the surgeons, providing information in digital waves and synthetic sounds as they applied their ministrations.

They spoke to one another through crimson facemasks. All four of the hooded figures looked up at another presence in the room. It stood in the far corner, nearest the bed, its back to the window. Ray's mind failed to properly categorize its shape and contours. First, he believed it to be a strange collection of moveable arms for another light source. He jettisoned that explanation, settling instead on an impression of the bent pipes of a tall heat register. When that didn't stick, the collection of bent lines and odd angles *moved*, and he began to see the thing for what it truly was.

The eyes first. Large and bulbous, like baseballs affixed to a triangular head, itself held upright by a narrow pole of a neck. Thin shoulders hunched together over a chitinous shell of a torso, full of shadow and glistening arrays of color that competed in extension and recession, shadow and pale moonlight. Arms, thin and long, bisected at the elbows, leading to bump-covered claws held close to the creature's face, like a boxer with his guard up.

The surgical staff often paused to look up at this creature, which stood and moved and spoke back with the uncanny valley cadence of an animatronic creature from a 1980s dark fantasy film. It gave them instructions. They asked it questions. It gave them answers. One of the surgeons held up a bowl of some kind—a familiar shape, laden with a slick of blood. The top of a skull, cleanly cut.

The creature gestured toward the patient. The surgeon nodded and bent down, out of sight, to return the skull cap to its owner.

The *whirr* and whine of some bowel-rumbling machine subsumed all other noise. Ray stole away back down the hall, trying the nearest door and finding it locked, then the next, and the next, until he was back at the entrance to the corridor. He slipped into the adjacent hall and slowly angled the door shut behind him. He peered over the lip of the small, circular window to ensure the others didn't follow.

The figures in red robes emerged first, pushing carts of monitors and equipment, bloody instruments of their work arranged on trays and in bowls of cleaning solution. They pushed their rattling tools to the far end of the hallway and disappeared around the corner. The creature shambled out next, its movements jarring and unnatural, its long, thin legs working like pistons to propel it forward at an odd, unsteady gait. It paused, then turned back toward Ray, its angular face and bulbous eyes floating in the dark, twin antennae protruding from its forehead, probing the air.

Ray gasped and pulled away from the window, his

own beating heart threatening to give away his position, overpowering the sounds of the environment, deafening him. Liquid streamed down his face. His fingers found it on his forehead, dripping down from the thin scar line wrapped around the upper portion of his skull.

The *click-click-click* of inhuman feet on hospital floor tile receded into the distance. Ray counted to ten, and, when no other horrors presented themselves, he opened the door and crept forward. The soft footfalls of his sneakers on tile threatened to draw the surgical team and their insectile handler back to him. He reached the room they had just left, finding the door shut but unlocked, the lights off, the dreadful moon the only source of illumination. He stepped inside.

Terra lay on the bed, her loose-fitting hospital gown spattered with small droplets of blood, her face ghastly white. She breathed in a steady, peaceful rhythm. Her lips and eyes twitched.

As she laid in repose, something like a Gothic heroine fallen fast asleep, Ray found her beautiful. He always had, truth be told, but he had only seen her in the context of the trauma of the past few weeks—the bizarre counseling sessions, the tests, the strange videos, the secrets of the camp. Here, she was just Terra. Not Terra the traumatized veteran, Terra the drug user, Terra the alcoholic, Terra the down-on-her-luck burnout. Just herself, asleep and without pretense. Ray wasn't sure he believed in the soul, but there, in that cold room in a haunted hospital, he saw hers, as much as one could this side of the veil.

She began to stir, her breathing shifting into a murmur of indistinct words. He leaned over her, one hand on the bed's railing, another brushing across her forehead and the scar that mirrored his own.

"Terra," he said. "Wake up. We gotta go." He shook

her shoulder but kept his voice quiet. Instinct told him that those surgeons and the bizarre creature were long gone, but he didn't want to risk lingering in this cursed place.

Her eyes fluttered open, then shifted, slowly, to focus on Ray. She propped herself up on the bed on her elbows with a grunt, then stared at him with one eye open, one closed.

"Am I late for formation?"

"No more formations," Ray said, placing a hand on her arm. "We need to pop smoke. Can you walk?"

"I feel like the floor of a taxi cab," she said. She blinked hard, then looked around the room, her gaze settling on the great moon pouring light through the room's tall window. "That doesn't look right. Does that look right to you?"

"Terra, listen to me," Ray said. "We have to leave. For good." He walked over to the hexagonal shelves set on the far side of the room to retrieve her clothes and shoes. "Where is your cell phone? The barracks?"

Ray paused, her sweater and shoes in hand. One of her shoes felt heavier than the other. The cell phone in question slid down from the toe to the heel, revealing itself.

"Oh," he said. He grabbed the burner and held it up for her to see. "They didn't confiscate it."

"Who's 'they?'" she asked.

"It's still got power, but no signal," Ray said, watching the screen glow to life.

"It gets signal on the north side of camp," she said, her voice barely more than a whisper.

"We can call for help."

"Maybe. Doesn't mean anyone will answer."

"Are you willing to try?"

"If we can get out of here, you need to be prepared

to go someplace where we can actually get lost. Like, for good. Are you ready for that?"

Ray considered the question.

"I've been lost for a long time. I'll go wherever, as long as it's away from here."

"I'll hold you to that," Terra said. "How's your Spanish?"

"I can learn."

"You're going to have to."

A SIGNAL IN THE DARK

They moved through endless hallways of the great hospital until they found a stairwell lit by faint, blue emergency lighting. It led them down flight after flight of stairs, floor after abandoned floor, slowly providing them a sense of scale of the hospital-labyrinth.

They reached a heavy, brown wooden door with a wide "1" painted across its surface at eye level. Ray pulled the door open. A gust of cool air rushed into the stairwell to greet them. They paused at the precipice, still and silent, listening for sounds of pursuit. There was only the dull hum of the stairwell's blue lighting, the distant metal-on-metal hymn of the ventilation system, and the whispered groans of old brick standing tall against icy winds from beyond.

They emerged into a hallway connecting to the atrium. Dreadful moonlight filtered through frosted-over skylights. They paused at the edge of the open lobby, taking in the reception desk, the waiting areas, the abandoned chairs and coffee tables set at odd angles of disuse.

"No one's home," Ray said. Terra made for the glass doors at the mouth of the hospital.

They emerged into the dead, cold air of night to find a wide-open courtyard, flanked by the hospital's multistory wings of brown stone and grey mortar. An old, crumbling road ran in a roundabout oval up to the entrance. The moon was larger and closer than it had ever been. The night sky was awash with lights and stars unfamiliar to them both, a twisted funhouse mirror of galactic trails and menacing stars, glimmering in unnerving frequency and color. Ray averted his eyes, feeling a headache spin up from where his skull met his spine. The stars remained as burning afterglows.

"I think we're still in Camp Winter Falcon," Terra said, breathing in the cold air. "We must be on the southern edge."

"It's possible," Ray said.

"It's also possible they conjured this out of thin air," Terra said. "Why not?"

Ray chewed on that for a moment. He turned around and stepped back, taking in the full grandeur of the leviathan hospital.

"The mountains are behind the hospital, so that means north is that way." He pointed into the dark. "That's the direction we move."

The night grew colder and the moon never pulled back. Ray tried not to look at the sky. They kept the mountains to their left. Lights from distant buildings appeared in the east.

"If your friend shows up, where are we gonna go?" Ray asked, trying to keep his mind off the cold.

"I have family in Mexicali," Terra said. "There are ways over the mountains to get there. We'll have to get some gear, but I don't think the trip will be much trouble for us. It's coming in stateside that gets you in trouble, not trying to go south."

"So that's it, then," Ray said. "Start new lives in Mexico?"

"Plenty of work for former soldiers in certain parts south of the border," Terra said. "Especially if you're American military with combat experience."

"I was hoping not to have to carry a gun again."

"I was hoping for a lot of things," Terra said. "See how far that got me."

"Sorry," Ray said.

"Not your fault."

"No, I mean, for both of us." Ray said.

Terra shrugged.

"They're not kidding about 'you're government property,' you know," she said. "When you enlist, I mean."

"Yeah."

"I set things up so I could call Jordan if I needed out."

"Why did you do that?"

"Just had a feeling," she said. "No signal yet." She stared into the glowing screen of her burner phone. Let's keep moving."

They walked on.

Fog rose from the earth, low and heavy around their ankles. Uneven ground challenged their progress until they reached the ruined pavement of the camp's wide and forgotten streets threading past abandoned barracks, storage warehouses, and barren training fields. Far behind them, the hospital remained dark. It was soon hidden behind the mountains.

The cold was cruel and cut deep, keeping their sweat at bay even as they breathed out great plumes of hot air, their lungs and legs aching with each step forward. Headaches throbbed along with their heartbeats. A soldier's most important skill is their ability to press on through pain, to locate and reach their objective against all odds and obstacles. Even if it costs them everything.

They eventually reached a set of three rectangular buildings set in a "T" formation. They followed the long side of the first building to its terminus in an open space. The air was heavy with the smell of ash and charred wood.

Terra pointed at the black-seared fire pit in recognition. Ray shivered, but not from the cold.

Soon they passed over more familiar streets, easily avoiding the pools of light cast by those few lights kept on. Then it was down darker streets, past the chapel, past the various buildings that were home to staff offices, meeting areas, and classrooms that had been the program's home these past weeks. The archives and antenna array buildings were hidden by distance, darkness, and fog, and not even the full, terrible moon above revealed them.

Their legs were tired and their throats were dry when they reached the northern edge of the camp. The chain link fence on the east and north sides met at a dark corner in the shadow of an abandoned watch tower platform. The smell of rotting wood and generations of burned-out cigarette butts clung to the air. The fence itself held countless shredded plastic bags, flapping in the icy wind like ghosts trapped in the material plane. Rust-covered razor wire adorned the top of the six-foot-high fence, some of its having come loose from its bindings to form lazy, drooping lengths that rattled and shook with each gust of wind.

Terra held up her cell phone, the screen casting a haunting, blue glow along her face. Ray stood next to her, eager to see if the device would have any signal.

"Two bars," Terra said. "Not much. But it'll do."

"How long will it take him—or her—to get here?" Ray asked.

"Don't get jealous," she said, managing a smile for the first time in what felt like ages. She pointed beyond the fence line. "There. A road. I think it connects to one of the county roads beyond. Jordan's a low-life weed dealer, sure, but he's smart, and if I need help, he'll come."

"Hey," Ray said, putting a hand on Terra's arm. She looked up at him, her face veiled in shadow and cell phone light from below, and yet beautiful to him all the same, even and especially now, under these circumstances.

"I'm not jealous," Ray said. "But if circumstances were different, maybe..."

Terra put her right hand along his cheek and bent her head to the side, her eyes on his, wide and wet.

"But they're not," she said.

"No. No, they're not."

She gave him a sad smile and withdrew her hand. She focused on the phone, found a number, and hit SEND.

The shrill, distortion-laden buzz of a phone ringing so close and so loud made Ray jump. He turned to look back at the camp—most of it dark, barely visible in the fog and grey light of the moon, with some distant shimmering lights indicating human presence—worried the sound would bring a patrol rushing toward him. A patrol of *what*, he wasn't sure any more.

The shrill ringing continued as a series of slurred, degenerated synthetic sounds. Terra's phone held on to the signal, one bar, two, then one again.

"Come on, pick up, pick *up*," she said.

Just as hope began to fade, there was a slow, monotonous clicking sound, and the ringing ceased.

"*HELLO*," a voice said, distorted and distant.

"Jordan? It's Terra."

"*Mmmhmm*," the voice said.

"I was right. The dreams were right. It's bad here. I gotta get out."

"*OUT*," was the response, distorted and jarring. Terra's own voice, reflected back at her.

Terra checked the phone's squat screen to confirm she had the right number.

"Jordan, if you can hear me, I need you to head south. There's a road that connects to one of the county roads west of Colorado Springs. If you swing into the mountains toward Manitou Springs, you should be able to—"

"*THERE'S NO GETTING OUT, TERRA MORALES.*" The voice was laden with reverb and alternating pitch, like a child playing with knobs on a sound engineer's mixing board.

"Jordan?"

"*YOU BELONG TO THE PROGRAM, TERRA MORALES.*" Ray's voice, coming through the phone, filtered through several layers of electronic disturbance.

"*YOU ARE PART OF THE PROJECT, RAYMOND PARNELL.*" Terra's voice, now, an octave too low, but unmistakably hers.

"Jordan? If you can hear me—"

"*WE WILL BRING JORDAN HERE, TOO, IF YOU LIKE,*" the voice said, now both of their voices, speaking in unison, the effect disorienting, drawing out the pain in their skulls. Ray reached for his forehead, which dribbled blood. *"WILL THAT MAKE YOU HAPPY? WILL THAT MAKE YOU MORE COMPLIANT?"*

Terra pressed the END button. The screen didn't change. The call continued.

"KNOWN DRUG USERS WHO WITNESS UFOLOGICAL PHENOMENA ARE EASILY DISMISSED AS UNRELIABLE, UNSERIOUS PEOPLE. BUT IT IS OFTEN THE USE OF PSYCHOTROPICS AND HALLUCINOGENS THAT ENABLES CONTACT. YOUR CHANNELS ARE OPEN. WE CAN INITIATE. REMODULATE. CAN MODIFY THE HUMAN BRAIN FOR OUR OWN PURPOSES BY CONSENT OR BY FORCE. WILLING SUBJECTS MAKE FOR MORE—"

Terra slid the back panel of the phone off, then pulled out the battery. The screen went black as she tossed the power source to the earth below, then chucked the phone at the fence. Tears streamed down her face, her breathing ragged. Ray stood motionless, not comprehending, not wanting to.

"I thought I might find you two here," said a woman's voice from above. A light clicked on beneath the overhead cover of the guard shack tower platform. Stacey's face was illuminated from below as she held her headlamp. "We need to talk, falcons."

THROW WIDE THE GATES

Stacey clicked off her headlamp before starting down the old ladder.

"What's going on?" Terra asked. "Why are you here?"

"Lot of *whys* and *whats* here at Camp Winter Falcon," Stacey said, reaching the ground and approaching them. "Would any answers satisfy you at this point?"

"How did you know we would be here?" Ray asked.

The woman was a shade before them, her face pale and stark in the moonlight. She raised a hand to her forehead and extended her index finger to point at its center.

"A little concentration," she said. "Don't you see where this mission will lead us? I'm beginning to see the ending, the new beginning. You don't have to be psychic to figure it all out, but it helps."

Terra closed the distance between them and put her hands on her friend's shoulders.

"We need to *leave*," Terra said. "I don't care about VA benefits or a general discharge on my DD214 or any of that. This is fucked. I don't want any part of it."

Stacey tapped her forehead again.

"That's not even remotely true," she said. "Being here excites you. Being a *part of something* excites you. Something bigger than yourself. Like the military. You were always a rebel, Terra, until you weren't. Until you found someplace that might be a home. Where you could belong. You don't have to look for that place any more. Camp Winter Falcon found *you*."

Stacey reached for Terra's shoulders, returning the embrace.

"You belong here. With me. With him. With all of Class Zero-Zero-One. And all those who will come after."

"No."

"Veterans of wars lost, our friends and comrades killed and wounded and damaged, our own minds and bodies riddled with anxiety and guilt for what we did to the Iraqis or the Afghans. How many civilians died in your unit's area of operations, because you wanted to *belong?*"

"Don't talk like this, Stacey. Please."

"You've got nowhere else to go," Stacey said, her voice softening. "But you have so much more to see, here."

Terra released her grip on Stacey's shoulders, then stepped back.

"I'm sorry, Stacey. But I can't." She glanced back at Ray. "We can't."

Stacey nodded.

"It's strange how it works. You've had the benefit of a strong resonance partner. You've received their surgical touch. You're just behind on the conscious-cognitive acceptance of the processes occurring within and beyond and intersecting through your own mind. I get it."

Terra backed away, slowly. Ray did, too, keeping his eyes on Stacey. A light emerged above her eyes. Deep blues and greens spilled forth from a localized portal of blinding radiation manifesting at the center of her forehead.

"*YOU ARE CLOSER THAN YOU HAVE EVER BEEN,*" something said through Stacey, its voice splitting the air and discharging static. "*YOU NEED ONLY OPEN YOUR THIRD EYE.*"

The light spilled across them in staccato bursts of radioactive illumination, giving their sudden flight a choppy, film-strip rhythm of disorientation, of multicolored chaos, of Technicolor terror. The voice of an alien intelligence bounced between the walls of their fracturing minds. Their hearts pumped and their blood boiled their brains. They made for the heart of the camp. They tumbled toward cataclysm.

The light faded behind them. New lights emerged ahead. It didn't matter which direction they took, which turn at each random, numbered building they made. They ran toward the chapel, or the camp brought it to them. The spirits watched from the fog, eager eyes on the restless living, both damned.

Slats of glimmering blue and green light spilled from the chapel windows. A chorus of voices rose and fell in synthetic waves, buoyed by electronic wash. Almost-words, harmonic and hypnotizing. A marching cadence, drawn out into a religious hymn. A song of homecoming.

Thirst wracked their throats. Cold air savaged their lungs. Exhaustion was a fire in their legs. Their minds threatened to split as blood trickled down from scars along their foreheads.

The doors to the chapel swung open. Featureless shadows shambled forth from a column of blinding light and smoke. The hymn grew loud and vast, covering the whole camp, the entire world. The wind carried the wet-paper smell of the tunnels and caverns below Camp Winter Falcon. All things hidden were made known.

Ray and Terra fled from the grim procession, hands clinging desperately to one another. The singing voices behind them were ecstatic with religious joy. Rapture was at hand.

Beyond an empty clearing, a familiar structure stood alone. They reached it in no time at all, not that time had any authority here.

"Tool shed," Terra said, gasping for air. Fate led

them toward it, a circle bound for completion.

The combination lock sat securely in the metal latch. The latch came off with three blows from a rock held in Terra's shaking hands, spurred on to effective violence by adrenaline. Inside was dark. The air smelled of death and gasoline. The chainsaw on the far wall was barely visible in outline.

"You ever use one of those before?" Terra asked, nodding at the saw. A glimmer of metal caught her eye, and she accepted an axe into her shaking hands.

Ray took the chainsaw from the brackets holding it aloft. He brought it back out to baptize it in the moonlight. Choke, ON/OFF switch, pull cord, blade. Terra crept up to the open doors, the axe head leaning against her right shoulder. She gripped the handle like a hitter coming to bat for the first time.

FINAL FORMATION

Class 001 marched in step to a point about a dozen meters from the open doors of the tool shed. Sergeant Major Haaster left them at parade-rest, hands held behind their backs, legs set apart, standing below the leering moon.

Dr. Glasse came up from behind them, a clipboard in one hand. She met Haaster at the head of the formation. The NCO and the doctor exchanged hushed whispers. Haaster shook his head. Glasse *insisted* something. He nodded, reluctantly, his support secured.

"Good news!" Glasse said, her voice projecting out and echoing back from the scattered buildings nearby. "We are well ahead of schedule. I do wish you had taken the time to rest after your operations. It took a lot of time and investment to make that facility suitable for such complex surgical procedures."

No response came from the shed. Shadows lingered beyond the precipice of the doors, which stood parted a few inches, revealing only darkness within. When Ray and Terra did not respond or appear, Glasse continued.

"The others are in an advanced state of integration, of awakening," she said, pointing back to the rest of Class 001, who stood silent and still in their disciplined formation. Light erupted from shimmering ovals of static, splitting through the flesh of their foreheads, coating the area in a soft, purple glow.

"But you shouldn't feel left behind," Glasse said. "Not at all! Your little sojourn into the tunnels triggered an advanced mutation. I am not sure what you saw down there. I am not allowed past the elevator, you see. You will have to tell me what it is like to be in the presence of a living god."

As Glasse spoke, others approached the clearing.

Shapes like ruined human bodies. Twisted limbs and malformed heads, bent low in animal crouches or raised to impossible heights. Coming forward for altar call, emerging from fog that emitted bursts of visible spectrum radiation, pillars of nauseating light. Planar transference, spirit-become-flesh. Communion at hand.

"Are you worried because you don't have your eyes, yet?" Glasse tapped her forehead for emphasis. "You shouldn't be. You're not behind the curriculum. Not at all! Whereas the others met our expectations in achieving personal resonance cascade thresholds, you have exceeded them, especially when working as a pair. Just imagine if you had thought to bring Mike with you on your little spelunking adventure. He and Stacey would be in the same class as you two! Although her progress continues apace, even with her partner missing." Glasse turned back to offer a smile at Stacey, who stood at parade-rest in the front row of the formation, face flat, forehead glowing, eyes rolled back to reveal hideous whites.

"You should know that I had no idea that your trauma-response could open a portal of that size and power," Glasse said. "It had a self-sustaining psychokinetic upcycle. I have only ever seen that on a recording. A video, actually. Shot in a temple deep below the sands of Iraq. The team had to use the skull of a dead saint to trigger that resonance. It cost us the lives of several of the Special Forces soldiers who—"

Haaster interrupted her with a whisper, pointing beyond the shed, at the glowing forms massing and emerging from the fog on all sides. Glasse took notice of the perimeter of inhuman horrors forming around them and nodded.

"We don't have much time, but it is important that

you know the context. It is important that you know how *special* you are, to this program, to me, to your country. Your power is still gestating. You are our honor graduates for this class of recruits, no question about it. We did not expect resonances at your levels until at least a year from now, after several cycles of the program. You have seen so much more, and will benefit from the surgical enhancements generously provided by our co-principal investigators."

Glasse moved her index finger to run along the rim of her head for emphasis.

Haaster began shouting out orders to the rest of the class. They responded quickly, snapping to attention and stepping off with precision. They sprinted forward to join Haaster and Glasse, forming a protective circle around them, facing outward, as the mass of strange bodies and shifting fog closed in around them. The light spilling out from their foreheads began to shimmer violently, stoked by threat.

"Let us head back to the altar, where we can initiate the final resonance cascade and complete this evolution," Glasse said, urgency underpinning her words. She glanced at the shambling bodies and shadows. "We must act quickly to close the doors, to secure what we've struck open by force of your minds. We have a foothold in their world, and they in ours. We must secure our objective. Only you can achieve that."

"And then what?" Ray shouted through the parted shed doors. "We just go home? You were supposed to help us, not turn us into—into *that*." He pointed at his fellow patients, who stood leaking starlight from their foreheads, facing the shambling approach of a wave of horrors emerging from unreality.

Glasse smiled.

"No, you're not going home," Glasse said. "You

cannot now, nor could you before. We have walked down this road together, Ray. Even before we met, we had a kinship. We went *over*. We saw evil and did evil in the name of our country and its secret masters. Now, together, we have a new mission. We are knocking on the doors of haunted houses and pulling them wide open, daring the ghosts to come out and say 'hello.'"

She raised an arm to the creatures advancing upon them, a stage-play gesture, full of drama, heralding revelation. "They answered. They answered because *you* called. You and Terra and the other patients here. You called them, and now no one else can close those doors again."

"If you're holding weapons," Haaster shouted, "they won't do much good."

"They are going to help us," Glasse said, as if to Haaster, but spoken loud enough for Terra and Ray's benefit. "They are soldiers first and foremost. They are loyal to their comrades."

Terra stepped forward to shout through the parted doors.

"You're not giving us much of a choice!"

"If we die here now, do you think this all ends?" Glasse said. "This research predates my time with Malthus and the Department of Defense. My work is part of some much larger, clockwork mechanism within and beyond the government, something older than our wars in the Middle East or our corporate partnerships. This is not merely a research program—it is a process, one that goes back to the founding of our great and terrible nation. I suspect it stretches even further back in time."

She glanced off toward the mountains, where a terrible, purple glow rose and streaked across the twisting, unfamiliar stars.

"How old was that thing in the tunnels? Do you

think time even has meaning for something like that?"

"I don't remember any of it," Ray said.

"No? Then let me help you. Whatever lives here—if it can be said to be alive—it is related, somehow, to what you all have encountered before. The strange, non-human intelligences and entities, the missing time. The abduction experiences. It responds to your—*our*—pain. Imagine if we can make good on the promise of that collaboration—if we can harness those forces. If we could weaponize them. There would be no need for large occupations. No IEDs, no drone strikes, no friends and comrades getting killed or wounded. Just *power*. Final victory. Something you did not get to experience in Iraq or Afghanistan."

"Being in this fucked-up country damaged me," Ray said. "Being born with some mental illness or whatever, *that* damaged me. I was screwed from the start. It's got nothing to do with aliens or ghosts or whatever the hell all this is!"

"You think those things aren't connected?" Glasse said. "You think those threads of pain and disease and evolutionary mistakes and ideological poison you have been fed all your life are not controlled by the same forces?"

"I don't want to fight any more wars," Ray said, his voice shaking.

"Then help us end them all," Glasse said. She turned and nodded at one of the patients, who stepped forward carrying a wooden box. *His* wooden box, the box from his mind, where he stored the memories too painful to face, where he kept his pain and insecurities locked away.

"The whole world is a crypt of blood," Glasse said, lifting the lid. "And we are its keepers." She withdrew a pair of oval wafers, then held them aloft as an offering to the streaking lines of purple light and cosmic interference spreading across the sky. "Tragedy in Babylon."

"Tragedy in Babylon," Haaster said, echoing the prayer.

The procession of the dead and the inhuman closed in around them from all sides, a wall of desiccated faces and glowing eyes, of short, squat horrors gesticulating in anticipation, of horned beasts loping forth, warped skin and hardened scales. Mouths snapping and teeth sharp. Grey and blue entities with flat faces and wide, black eyes, lingering behind ranks of twisted predators.

The patients took a coordinated step forward, expanding their perimeter, light bursting from their foreheads in flat, brilliant beams that began to saw along the edges of the advancing horde.

ENDEX

Glasse took several steps toward the shed, the wafers offered for them in her upturned palm. "Take communion. Complete the third and final resonance ritual."

Terra kicked the shed doors open, running ahead of Ray without warning, axe raised high.

Glasse's face went slack with surprise. The wafers slipped from her palm and landed in the dirt. Terra buried the axe in the doctor's forehead, collapsing the frontispiece of her skull and ruining her pretty face and the well-educated brain behind it.

"No!" Haaster shouted, rushing Terra. She struggled to free the axe from Glasse's collapsed skull, blood arcing up in thick geysers, staining them both in bursts of dark crimson.

Ray found the chainsaw alive in his hands. The trigger eagerly received the pressure from his right finger. His legs carried him over haunted earth. The blade accepted the flesh and bone of Haaster's hip and left leg. A not insignificant portion of his thigh and outer femur became a heavy flow of bloody slurry, pulled along metal teeth and sprayed out in a wide, red spray.

Terra, in command of the axe once more, ended the senior NCO's screaming with a chop to the throat, splitting the flesh neatly and unleashing a flood of red into his parted esophagus. His head snapped back but didn't quite part from his neck. Blood cascaded down into his stomach and lungs as he collapsed to the dry earth, which accepted his ichor like desert soil in a light rain. Terra swung again and again, and Ray—feeling sick but finding his own instincts overpowering him— passed the bottom edge of the chainsaw blade along the

NCO's torso, revealing a roil of ruined intestines and masticating his organs.

The patients stood in their circle formation, light lancing out in wild, blinding arcs from their third eyes, taking no notice of the slaughter behind them. The advancing line of ghosts and goblins did, however, letting out ribald cheers and the screeching of excited carrion birds. Many-eyed heads twisted in rapture. Claws snapped and twisted mouths hissed and cooed in pleasure. Blood and gore and fun for everyone. The night was young and eager.

Ray flipped the switch to OFF on the chainsaw, letting the blade spin to a halt after its grisly work. He tasted blood and their hearts pounded heat through their bodies. Their nervous systems were alive with a pale, erotic light, a resonance with death and the arousing knowledge that they were responsible for it. Blood poured from the center of their foreheads where the skin began to fray and split.

"Glasse was right," Terra said, letting the axe fall to the earth, its blade settling in the conjoined pool of blood forming between Glasse and Haaster. "There's no going home."

"There never was," Ray said, dropping the chainsaw.

Streaks of purple and green light spread like a spider's web over the cosmos, originating from the mountains along the camp's western edge—from one mountain in particular. One with a tunnel, and an elevator, and a labyrinth of concrete and runes carved in obsidian. Horrors beneath, where something lived in death and reached out to corrupt the sky.

They felt its call, deep within their pounding hearts, behind their eyes, in the center of their brains, veiled behind parting skin and quivering skull plate. They felt its thoughts, clumsy and groping. It found Ray's pliant and fraying mind and deposited the seed of an idea there.

Ray bent down and picked up his memory box. Now made of old, polished wood, wrapped in veiny deposits of pale, quivering flesh. Blood smeared its surface. Something rattled inside. He held it tight.

The line of horrors advanced. Horns and half-faces and many-faces and eyes spread across backs and lips leering and teeth chattering and fur stained with tar and tails snapping like whips and hooves splitting into digits in mockery of human hands and the howls of the hungry and the damned. A wall of spirit-flesh, of the dead, of something else entirely. Golgotha rose and fell before them, its advance frustrated by the wall of mind-light projected from their fellow patients, the names and faces of which were familiar to Ray and Terra, but the distinctions meaningless now in their collective effort to hold back the tide of the abyss. Still, they held, their power released at full-tilt, forming a final protective line that would have pleased even their drill instructors.

Ruined, skeletal hands reached for glowing foreheads and were pushed back, but only for a moment. Great, prehensile limbs lined with scattered teeth and razor edges swiped forward, missing human arms and legs by inches, but growing closer, growing bolder, as the psychic shield degraded and the pressures flowing through the wide-open gateway behind the advancing tide became too great to contain. The *pop-pop-pop* of 5.56mm rounds echoed somewhere nearby, Haaster's remaining security force finally roused from their other duties to fight and die like warriors.

Terra, in her despair, began to summon the reserve of fear that sloshed back and forth within her core like too much wine. There was an outlet for that energy.

She felt it in her heart. A meaningless, futile gesture at comradery gestated within. The glowing, shining core of herself forged in her early years as an enlisted soldier, when she combined the best, most selfless aspects of herself with the good—what little of it there was—aspects of her military training. Here, finally, at the end of all things—maybe even the end of the world—was an opportunity to stand with her fellow soldiers, to be a member of Class 001 after all.

"We should help them," she said.

"That would mean—"

"I know."

They were interrupted by a sudden burst of light and a roar of a great beast, roused from its slumber to do violence against the tumbling and sprawling artifice of terrors surrounding them. Bodies unrecognizably inhuman went sprawling, limbs and bones cracked and broke, eyes and brains splattered, becoming ash, fog and smoke, pulled apart and ground beneath the sturdy tires of a VA bus, now leveraged against their ranks as a great battering ram.

The bus slid to a halt before them, neatly separating the advancing ranks of monsters from the patients making their last stand, now granted a brief reprieve.

The doors slid open with a hiss of hydraulics and a groan of metal. Mike Dodonna sat in the driver's seat, leaning to shout out the open doors.

"Get a move on, troops! We're getting the hell out of here!"

The adrenaline charge of the past few hours threatened to wear off, to leave Terra and Ray shaking and weak. Each step forward was a triumph of grit over exhaustion, over the pounding pain in their heads, over the groping intelligence that settled over their minds that first threatened—then begged—them to stay, to commune.

Mike leaned down the bus's shallow stairwell and pulled Ray in first, then helped Terra scramble inside. Mike rushed back to the driver's seat while Terra hesitated, standing on the first step, hand on the railing to keep her balance. Romantic notions of comradery and Valhalla snapped in two, cleanly broken by the reality of the tactical situation. The others were lost, and no amount of bravery on her part would save them.

The defensive line broke. Faces, once familiar, were absorbed by the light cascading from their foreheads. Adams stepped forward, either through bravery or compulsion, to hold back the tide of swirling, inhuman monsters and mist. His face disintegrated into a shower of white-hot purple light, until only the orifices of his skull were recognizable in shape and form. Hands and claws and roiling fog cut and slashed and absorbed him, his blood a geyser of blue energy, his flesh emaciated by a flash of teeth and horns dripping with ichor.

Calhurst and Halloway, tall and imposing soldiers each, found their size of no use in a battle played out on the psychospheric plane. Their skulls collapsed within the claws of a shrieking, pterodactyl-like creature that swooped in low out of the darkness, absorbing the shimmering light of the moon in a flapping cacophony.

Garcia and Robertson erupted into pillars of light, pushing their minds and newfound abilities to the limit to hold back the onslaught of degenerative reality, their screams echoing across the open field and through the minds of those still alive to witness their localized cross-rip event. Ghouls wearing the shredded uniforms of American soldiers—and some wearing the mismatched civilian and military attire of insurgents— rushed forward at the last second, only to be absorbed in searing fountains of psychokinetic energy.

Stacey Bozell—Mike's partner and fast friends with Terra and Ray—stood at the center of that rapidly collapsing formation. She offered a quick glance back to the bus, her face blank, and yet her shimmering eyes somehow communicating a longing for a different outcome, another way forward, a few choices made differently. A great, towering creature of stone flesh and obsidian eyes pushed through the shimmering shield of her psychic defenses to lay its three-fingered hands on her shoulders and waist. It tore her clean in half.

Mike slammed the door shut, sealing Terra inside. He hit the gas and the wheels spun up mud, the ass end of the bus swinging like a pendulum on a doomsday clock. Time was running out.

This is how the world ends, Terra thought.

The bus caught traction and lurched forward. Mike gunned it and sent the bus straight through the first rank of leering mouths and snapping teeth and undead soldiery, the bus's front end smashing through semi-transparent physical forms and liquifying them, the wheels churning over brittle bones and collapsing skulls with non-Euclidean contours into iridescent dust and radioactive paste.

The murk obscured Mike's view through the windshield. The glowing cosmos overhead reflected on the glass. A razor-thin line of flesh parted along his forehead, permitting a faint glow of light to emerge. His hands spun the wheel. The bus shuddered and groaned, threatening to tumble over itself, until the tires found asphalt and the straight line of a road barely visible in the occlusion of fog and terrors from beyond. The road bent and their path bent with it, until they were past humanoids and beasts of nightmare, careening through humidity and fog but free of obstacles, save for one: the closed gate of Camp Winter Falcon.

The glass of the windshield cracked under the burst of an errant rifle shot. Terra crouched in the bus's stairwell. Ray balled up on a seat, clinging to that small wooden box. Mike lowered his head but kept the wheel straight, his foot pressing the gas to the floor.

The bus blew through the closed gate, smashing one of its headlights, sending the crisscrossed chain link fence and supports up and over the windshield, where it held on to the edge of the roof for a few desperate moments, then tumbled back over the end of the bus.

The light in the rearview mirrors was blinding. A flurry of competing psychedelic colors emerged from the pulsating fog, like a cosmic star-rise in the deepest reaches of space.

The distance grew between them and Camp Winter Falcon. The sky lost its strange and hideous illumination, even as the stars remained cold and alien.

HERALDS OF THE NEW AGE

Ray fell. Air and wind ripped past his ears as he tumbled into the dark. A point of light appeared, spinning around him, adding to his disorientation. Then came another, and another, their light pouring down upon him in great, brilliant rays. More lights emerged from the dark, like spotlights sweeping over a field in search of deer. Those lights found him, of course. They always did.

He sat upright in the bus's creaking, misshapen seat, groping around in the dim gloom. His throat was scratchy and dry. The pounding in his head subsided, but his eyes were bleary and his whole body ached. He hadn't felt this exhausted since Afghanistan.

Outside, the world was dark. The moon had returned to a sane and sensible size and position. The mountains were still tall and sharp in the far distance, but the snow-kissed landscape around them spoke in small rises of hill and plain, errant trees and low-growing scrub. High desert under strange stars.

Terra lay curled up in on herself, a fetal sleeper. Her feet hung off the edge of the seat, sneakers over the aisle.

At the front of the bus, Mike stared through the spiderwebbed windshield at a road illuminated by a shuddering, uneven glow from a single headlight. The bus was wounded, but the parts that moved still moved, and it would ferry them on to wherever it was they were meant to go. Mexicali, maybe, like Terra had suggested, if they could find an open stretch of borderland and survive the crossing. Maybe they could start new lives, or try to pick up the pieces of their old ones, if that was possible. Maybe they were going nowhere at all.

Ray's hand buzzed with a dull arthritic ache. That

hand gripped the small wooden box tight—the box from his mind, from his subconscious, somehow made physical. Another mystery presented to him by Camp Winter Falcon, another answer taken to the grave by Glasse and Haaster.

They pushed us to it, Ray thought to himself. It felt like a lie. It came too easy.

The box vibrated, a feeling at odds with the rhythmic motion of the bus's wheels on empty desert highway. Blood-pumping tissues spread across the box's surface, cold and unpleasant, leaving a phantom wetness on his fingers. He considered cracking a window and throwing the box out into the wasteland. He considered screaming until his throat went raw. He considered a lot of things.

"Thank you," he said.

"Huh?" Mike glanced back. He sat up straight. "You two okay?" Ray considered this for a moment.

"No."

"Me neither," Mike said. "I saw—I saw a lot of things I can't explain."

"You saved us."

"I will never leave a fallen comrade," Mike said, reciting a line from a creed that felt hollow and cold. "I'm glad you two made it out."

"I'm glad you got us out."

Mike looked at Ray through the mirror set above the windshield. His face was pale and gaunt, his eyes tired. Ray had seen that look before. He had seen it in his own mirror countless times.

Ray opened the box.

It smelled of wood polish and gunpowder. Of sand-storms and blood under a desert sun. Sweat and loneliness; long weekends spent at the drill hall; summers at Fort Carson and of mobilization training at some backwater post of despair in the deep South. Mold-encrusted barracks; pop-up tents set up near sewage runoffs. It smelled like downrange, with the smoke of plastic and batteries rolling off the nearby burn pits. It smelled like war and the closed loop of his own potential, of lives he would never live.

A tape lay inside, a white label spread across its surface. "PARNELL, RAYMOND. TAPE 322" in neat handwriting. Dr. Glasse's, maybe.

A buzz of static erupted from somewhere behind him.

A television sat on a metal stand at the far end of the bus. A compact video cassette player was on the shelf below. Its top-side receiver popped open, eager for the tape. A digital readout blinked the time:

3:22 A.M.

He knew what he had to do. If he hadn't wanted to do this, to see, to know, he never would have opened the box in the first place.

He was in front of the TV set, staring into a field of grey static. He slipped the tape into the receiver and pressed the device closed. The PLAY button was marked by a rightward-facing green delta. The device whirred in pleasure and the screen hummed and snapped, hiding its static field behind a wall of shimmering black and tracking lines. It revealed its secrets.

A shallow, unfinished basement with a low-hanging ceiling. Shadows pressing in from all sides, the concrete bricks of the far wall and the laundry machines before them barely discernible in the dark. Ray entered from stage left, carrying a chair. He deposited it dead-center, then sat down facing the camera. The gun was a gift from his father. A .45 caliber pistol. *More stopping power*, dad had said. Ray opened his mouth, inserted the barrel, and took his word for it.

On the bus, Ray flinched at the gunshot. He tried to turn away from the eruption of scalp and brain and skull, but found he couldn't. Or wouldn't.

The tape rewound. His disordered brains returned to their fleshly prison. The gun left the grip of his teeth. The screen said *"PLAY"* in clumsy digital typeface in the upper left-hand corner.

The ceiling retracted, gaining elevation by unseen stage mechanisms. The gun was gone, now, but the Ray on-screen didn't seem to mind. He had other ideas.

He carefully climbed up the chair, then stood facing the camera, his eyes never breaking contact with himself. A rope dropped down from above, courtesy the crew of this awful little stage play. He guided the thick cord around his neck, then gave a pair of quick tugs as signal. The rope's line went taut.

Ray smiled. He kicked the chair out from under himself. The rope held him, swinging back and forth at varying angles like a defective pendulum. His face went puffy and white and his eyes darkened and flooded with regret. Nasty way to go, and not very efficient, he realized, too late.

Eventually, the struggling ceased. A dark spot appeared along the inner pant legs of his Army PT sweats. The rope groaned and swung in slow, diminishing circles.

The tape rewound. The chair returned to its place. The rope snaked back up through the top of the screen. The ceiling lowered back into position.

PLAY.

No gun, no rope, no chair. Just a bottle of cheap beer in his hand, vomit stains down the front of his sweater like a priest's vestment. Others appeared, stepping forward into view, backs to the camera. Others he could name, if he really wanted to. Names that meant something to him. People who mattered.

The volume was too low to hear the exchanges, but he knew what was said all the same. He only had to watch himself argue, and shout, and throw his beer bottle across the goddamn room. He only had to witness the dull glare of *angry fucking drunk* in his own eyes, accusing and menacing, finding each person in turn, sending them back behind the camera with each withering glare, chasing them out of his life for good.

REWIND.

The walls of the basement fell away. New walls were carried forward by swift ghosts. Ray, in a cramped apartment, a handle of vodka on his night stand, a bottle of pills rapidly emptying down his throat.

Ray, at a bar, tossing his last five-dollar bill for a shot before starting a fight with a stranger. Or a friend.

Ray, in the desert, smoking a cigarette outside as the rockets landed somewhere nearby, harmless, but breathing the smoke from the burn pits, too, which wasn't so harmless. The war would catch up with him eventually, one way or another.

Ray, tearing apart the home of a family, looking for AK-47s and rocket propelled grenades and finding none, but leaving the home trashed all the same, the women and children pressed away from him in terror.

Ray, face blank, skin pale, a shower's steady stream striking the back of his head without provoking a reaction or a blink, but washing away blood down a drain.

Ray, in his childhood bedroom, peering through parted curtains at light spilling out of his nightmares, at eyes and a face that were not human, but that called to him, that warned him, that said if he kept looking, it would be with him forever. There would be no turning back.

Stars turned dark and collapsed in on themselves. The rotting flesh of a billion human beings was carried off by insects and carrion birds with a cold, eager efficiency. Light and heat floated through frozen time to a place beyond terror. Ray sat on a chair in a basement and put a gun in his mouth. The trigger pull got easier each time. Over and over again.

EJECT.

The deck whined and groaned, but gave up the tape. Ray considered throwing it out of the window, finally. The bus's shuddering deceleration distracted him. He turned to see Mike slumped over in the driver's seat, leaning forward, struggling to guide the vehicle to the shoulder safely.

Terra sat up, clutching her forehead. Ray walked up the aisle and held on to her seat as the bus came to an exhausted halt.

"You okay?" he said, his voice dry and cracked.

"My forehead hurts like hell," she said, turning her face toward his. He stepped back in shock, eyes blinking rapidly at the after-image of her third eye.

"Ray," she said, voice flat. Any sense of urgency was long gone.

At the front of the bus, Mike slumped over the steering wheel. The engine idled.

"How much gas we got in the tank, Captain?" Ray asked, just to have something to say, an excuse to get away from Terra.

Mike lifted his head from the steering wheel. Blood poured down his face, leaving a trail on the wheel and dash, liquid splattering against the floor. Ray turned away before the light overwhelmed him, reaching for the manual door control handle. Its metal and polished wood was cool to the touch. The mechanism made an unpleasant squealing sound as the doors folded open. He stepped down the stairwell and out into the night. Clouds moved in from the west, bringing with them a veil of snow. The lights emerging from Terra and Mike grew brighter.

The high desert was a vast expanse of low brush and gnarled trees twisted by years of drought and unrelenting sun at elevation. The mountains cut a sharp profile across the landscape in the distance, meeting the sky on their own, ancient terms. A sky that was dreadfully wrong.

Purple and green light bled upwards to the north, seeping out of a wound deep within the corrupted earth. Ray turned away from that dreadful beacon and walked ahead of the bus, keeping parallel to the highway. Telephone poles stood at odd angles at uneven intervals, like a line of soldiers conducting a road march. The snow began to accumulate and swallowed up the sounds of his footsteps. He felt eyes staring at him from behind. If he turned back, he would have seen Mike and Terra watching—seeing him better than they had ever seen anything before.

Instead, his legs burned. Two and a half weeks of morning PT had not been enough to train him for the exhaustive marathon of the past day or two.

A Joshua tree grew out of the earth ahead of him, its branches nearly vertical, spreading out like veins before the rush of alien stars and streaks of cosmic light overhead. A great shadow perched within its twisted boughs, wings like an empty night sky, eyes flickering with the fires of apocalypse. Its face was familiar. He had seen it at Camp Winter Falcon. He had seen it in his dreams. He had seen it outside of his bedroom window, floating in the dark, warning him of the wonders and terrors that would haunt him his entire life.

Ray reached the base of the tree, stepping over roots that writhed in place, upturning and re-settling sand. The tree loomed higher and taller and wider, a fractal expansion that occluded the sky. The familiar looked down upon him, something like pity in its eyes, something like excited anticipation in the quivering of the limb it extended to offer an open palm. Its black, branch-like fingers opened and revealed the communion wafer.

"Pain was the important part," Ray said, receiving the gift. The familiar withdrew its arm. Its eyes trembled with tears. Its head became a crown of fire.

Ray raised the wafer to his parted lips. Flesh began to pull and snap along his forehead, allowing a faint, blue-green glow to reach out from within his brain, from the deepest recesses of flesh and blood and incomprehensible energies that made up his *mind*, that earthly seat of the soul. The wafer tasted of ash. Burning wicks and wet paper-smell on the air. Whispered prayers from behind him. A steady gaze from above.

Ray took communion and waited.

The tree cracked and groaned under the sorrowful pressures of the world. The mountains produced a low rushing sound. Purple light sputtered out, far to the north.

The power generated by his pain—his isolation, his alienation, his self-hatred—sizzled and strained against the narrow confines of his mind. Those forces pushed and flowed and smashed against their constraints until they found the weakness in the armor.

Ray's third eye burst open, finally and fully, blood spilling from splitting flesh and cracking skull. The world revealed itself as a brilliant cascade of impossible colors and rays of delirious energy, limitless subatomic and gravimetric interactions that overwhelmed every fiber of his perception, their signals reaching through the makeshift hologram of *present* and *self-in-context* to shatter his mind and reform it anew. Ray knew and felt his place and purpose within the world, within that rush of radiation and ley line energies, within the endless combinations of particle-level permutations. All matter and energy were a vast, interconnected web of terrible beauty.

He saw what the future held for him and for those like him, in service not to his country, but to a force greater and far older than the mundane bloodlust of the American Empire. A force that was alive and alien to this planet well before mankind transcended its multi-species prehuman origins. One that grinned and hungered for consciousness to mold and direct, even before the foundational, errant proto-proteins assembled in alchemical pools among the vast, dead wastes of a young world, awaiting the lingering gaze and lifegiving touch of God.

Reality and all its potentialities vibrated beneath his feet, pulsing in rhythm to the blood flowing through his body, glowing an ethereal blue beneath pliable skin.

A new, final age of woe and madness lay ahead. Ray would be its herald—one, out of many, one of many. Mike and Terra and the others to come—soldiers all for the war ahead.

They could be part of something bigger than themselves. Something truly wondrous. Something truly terrible.

The night's terrors were theirs now.

MF 22

ACKNOWLEDGMENTS AND NOTES

Thanks, as always, goes to my wife Jess for providing the time, space, and support necessary to write this novel. She served as my first beta reader and gave me notes and suggestions that improved the draft I managed to produce in short writing sessions before work and on the weekends.

Sean M. Thompson provided critical edits which helped temper this manuscript into the novel it was meant to become. Tom Breen provided his perspective on an early draft that gave me the confidence that I was on-target with a project unlike any I had attempted before. Blake Austin provided excellent artwork for the cover. Mat Fitzsimmons contributed an inspired section break icon. Christopher Slatsky provided a wonderful promotional quote after reading the manuscript. Thank you also to Orrin Grey for the frequent and very vocal support of my recent work, and for giving me permission to use one such endorsement here.

This novel is told primarily from the perspective of American veterans because I am one, but the true victims of our wars are the civilians we harmed—and continue to harm through sanctions and meddling—and the generations who will live with birth defects, environmental contamination, poverty, and violence. Please consider supporting anti-war and anti-militarization groups like Veterans for Peace, of which I am a proud member. Please also support robust domestic efforts to rehabilitate and care for our veterans—and not to shift that responsibility of care to a profit-driven model.

The themes of alienation, substance abuse, and mental health crisis are drawn from my own experiences and from those with whom I've discussed these topics, veteran and non-veteran alike. If the struggles of these characters are familiar, I encourage you to seek out professional mental health services, and, at the very least, talk to a trusted friend or family member about your pain. There's no good reason to suffer alone.

ABOUT THE AUTHOR

Jonathan Raab is the author of *The Secret Goatman Spookshow and Other Psychological Warfare Operations, The Crypt of Blood: A Halloween TV Special, Camp Ghoul Mountain Part VI: The Official Novelization,* and more. His short fiction has appeared in numerous magazines and anthologies, including *The Best Horror of the Year Volume Fourteen.* He is also the editor of several books from Muzzleland Press including *Behold the Undead of Dracula: Lurid Tales of Cinematic Gothic Horror* and *Terror in 16-bits.* He lives among the Gothic landscapes of upstate New York with his wife, son, and a dog named Egon. He was a soldier a long time ago.

COMING SOON

PROJECT VAMPIRE KILLER

a Gothic horror novel about bloodsucking freaks,
systems of control, and the movies